Evelyn Weaver is a Later Life Diva

K.L. CREAR

CREAR PUBLISHING

Contents

Dedication   VI

Epigraph   VII

1. Chapter 1   1

2. Chapter 2   8

3. Chapter 3   17

4. Chapter 4   30

5. Chapter 5   40

6. Chapter 6   52

7. Chapter 7   65

8. Chapter 8   77

9. Chapter 9   83

10. Chapter 10   92

11.	Chapter 11	99
12.	Chapter 12	105
13.	Chapter 13	112
14.	Chapter 14	116
15.	Chapter 15	123
16.	Chapter 16	131
17.	Chapter 17	142
18.	Chapter 18	145
19.	Chapter 19	154
20.	Chapter 20	160
21.	Chapter 21	168
22.	Chapter 22	175
23.	Chapter 23	182
24.	Chapter 24	189
25.	Chapter 25	191
26.	Chapter 26	193
27.	Chapter 27	201
28.	Chapter 28	207
29.	Chapter 29	216
30.	Chapter 30	224

31. Chapter 32   233

32. Chapter 33   243

33. Chapter 34   250

34. Chapter 35   255

35. Chapter 36   260

36. Chapter 37   268

About the author   274

Also by K.L. Crear   276

To my mum, the most sensational septuagenarian I know.
Love you x

"Do not go gentle into that good night,
Old age should burn and rave at close of day;
Rage, rage against the dying of the light."
                    DYLAN THOMAS

Chapter 1

♥ · ♥ · ♥ · ♥ · ♥

The post was late – yet again. I heard it hit the mat with a resounding thump that made me jump slightly and hug myself tightly inside my flowery dressing gown.

I shuffled down the hall in my big pink fluffy slippers, the ones Lottie had bought me for Christmas. Even though now in her forties, my daughter seemed to favour a rather childish style in sleepwear; and for some unknown reason, she seemed to think I should follow suit. I would toe the line insofar as the florid slippers were concerned, but I would not be coaxed into unicorn pyjamas or those quite frankly hideous onesies any time soon. It was bad enough that the gaudy footwear made my feet look like they were stuffed inside fairground candy floss, but as they were a present, and I loved my daughter dearly, I felt obliged to wear them.

I bent down to retrieve the small pile of envelopes, but immediately I could see there was nothing exciting: just a few thin white envelopes that appeared quite official, so likely from my bank or some such; and one of those flimsy brown ones with the NHS franking at the top. I knew with a sinking feeling that this one was from the hospital. No doubt something else inside my ageing body creaking and dropping to bits and requiring immediate attention.

Or maybe I was due my two-yearly bowel screening, and my poo needed to be sent off again for inspection. I shuddered at the thought of one of my bowel movements winging its way via Royal Mail to be examined by some poor medic in a lab somewhere. Fancy poking through strangers' number twos for a living. I really hoped they got paid handsomely, they certainly deserved it.

There was simply no glamour in getting older. Ageing most definitely wasn't for sissies. Once upon a time I used to send love letters to dashing beaux through the postal system; now, alas, I sent slivers of faecal matter.

My back twinged slightly as I stood up again. Maybe it was time to invest in one of those wire mail catchy thingies that attached to your letterbox. Or maybe an old lady grabby stick that could also pick up rubbish and stray condoms in the park. I felt sure I'd just seen a smart-looking one on sale in one of those catalogues I kept receiving through the post.

It seemed that as soon as I had turned fifty, not only did my youthful glow become beiger, but my junk mail did also. No longer would I receive information about chic events or glamorous outfits; oh no, suddenly I was being plied with age-appropriate elasticated skirts and comfortable wide-fitting orthopaedic sandals in muted shades of brown. I blamed the algorithms I was always hearing talked about on Radio 4.

That in itself had been bad enough, but now I was in my late 60s it seemed that every man and his dog wanted to push funeral plans, stair lifts and mobility scooters on me. It really was all quite depressing.

As I ambled back towards the kitchen and my half-eaten toast and cup of tea, I noted a little chink of pale pink poking out below the assorted brown and white stationery.

Once I was sitting comfortably at the sturdy oak table with its bright sunflower wipeable tablecloth, I pushed my reading glasses back firmly on my nose and gave the mail my full attention.

The letter from the hospital was just for a general MOT appointment: check my oil, that sort of thing. And the rest of the innocuous envelopes produced nothing of much interest. There was of course the standard pamphlet extolling the virtues of magnetic bracelets and long-handled toenail scissors, but I pushed that aside with barely a glance. The bright pink envelope had my full attention.

I knew the swirly handwriting filling the front of the square envelope only too well. This, without a shadow of a doubt, was a letter from my sister Isadora. I didn't know whether to feel excited or trepidatious. My sister, at the ripe old age of 61, was eight years my junior. We were the only two siblings in our family, so she had been, and would always be, the baby. I think she took that sentiment fully to heart, since I'd say that she had never really grown up.

Although now in the autumn of her life, this didn't stop her behaving like a truculent teenager at times, and rather unfortunately having a penchant to dress like one too. I was forever wagging my finger at her choice of clothing. It wasn't "cute", as she liked to believe – unless of course you found Bette Davis's style in *Whatever Happened to Baby Jane* as appealing as a basketful of fluffy kittens.

She had been widowed for seven years now, since her husband of over thirty years had passed away suddenly from a brain aneurysm at just 54 years of age. Oscar had adored his wife and always planted her on a princess pedestal, from which he never let her topple. Despite the thirty years of wedded bliss, he had always looked at his wife with the gaze of someone who couldn't quite believe his luck.

They had been true soulmates. For a couple of years after his absence, Dora had been completely lost: a sad carbon copy of the vibrant creature she had previously been, shambling through life with little purpose, under a thick cloud of despair that had completely engulfed her. But eventually those clouds had lifted, heralding a new dawn – or rather a new Dora. Accepting her widowhood, Dora had a completely different mindset. Oscar and she had never had any children, and upon losing her beloved spouse she decided to live life exactly how she wanted to and on her terms. She would enjoy life unapologetically and at full throttle. She really couldn't give a flying toss about anyone's opinions of her, it really was none of her business.

She had already lost the most important thing in her life, her darling Ossie, so there was nothing else to lose that would come even close to that. He was gone but she was very much still here, and until they embraced again in heaven, she was going to kick up her heels and grab life by the dangly bits and give it a damn good shake, no matter how bonkers that made her appear to everybody else. She often liked to quote Dylan Thomas: there was no way she was "going gently into that good night". Nope, she was going to rage, party and embarrass the living daylights out of her nearest and dearest and anyone else who happened to be in the vicinity.

This meant she had enjoyed the company of various gentlemen over the years; however, being sceptical of long relationships, she preferred to make a guest appearance in men's lives and bow out after a few dates, thus denying any of them the chance to deposit their slippers under her double divan. I once overheard her referred to as a "seducer of the elderly" who had more strays in her bed than the local dogs' home. I was utterly appalled on her behalf, but Dora found it hilarious. In her mind she was the fabulous femme fatale of her neighbourhood, which to her was as good as celebrity status. And actually, the sleepy cul-de-sac where she lived was so prim and proper that even if she decided to air all her dirty linen in public, her neighbours would probably decide it still needed another good rinse a week later. Dora really was a square peg in a round hole as far as they were concerned.

I suppose I shouldn't be so critical of her. I knew how devastating it was to lose a spouse at a relatively young age. My own darling husband Andrew had died just over five years ago, and the hurt of his loss could still take my breath away at times. But I took comfort in keeping a stiff upper lip and a sense of good British refinement about myself. I, unlike my sister, would not be heading to Benidorm any time soon.

But all things said, I really did love my sister. She truly was a good old stick. Even if she was forever telling me I had one planted firmly up my arse.

I brushed the breakfast crumbs from my dressing gown. I had only managed one slice of toast this morning, though spread with thick-cut orange marmalade. It seemed the older I got, the less of an appetite I had. Well, at least for food; strangely enough, other appetites hadn't waned in the slightest, more was the pity.

With a sigh I started to read, struggling to decipher occasional unfathomable words. Like everything else to do with my sibling, even her handwriting was flamboyant. But as my eyes scanned her erratic writing, I felt my heart sink faster than a broken biscuit in a mug of cocoa.

"Dear Evie,

Hello, my dear heart, I hope you are doing well. I myself am fabulous (as per usual), but at times must admit to feeling a tad disillusioned with this little journey we are on called life.

I asked myself what would cheer me up, and the answer came to me in a flash. Why, go and visit Yorkshire and see my wonderful big sister!

It seemed such a splendid idea. Anyway, I'm booked on the 08:54am train on Friday 12th, but no return ticket as I thought I could stay with you for a while; well, until you start annoying the life out of me, ha ha.

Won't it be lovely? We can do so many fun things together, like when we were little.

Ciao for now, and I'll see you soon.

Lots of Love,

Dora xxx

P.S. The red stain isn't blood; it's just a bit of sloe gin I sloshed on the page by accident while I was writing. It might taste all innocent and fruity, but it really is stronger than you think!"

I put the letter down on the table and removed my glasses to rub my eyes wearily. It was only just after 10 a.m., but suddenly I felt exhausted by the day, as if I had run a marathon or at least taken a brisk walk around the garden.

I worried I had the stirrings of a migraine beginning and rubbed my temples gingerly.

Isadora was arriving on Friday for goodness knows how long. Only two days away.

Chapter 2

L eeds train station was surprisingly hectic for a Friday morning in March, maybe because of the impending weekend. It seemed that all manner of humanity was either boarding or alighting from the various trains that morning. Businessmen appeared stressed in their sharp tailoring and shiny shoes, barking into their mobile phones as they ran along the platforms, desperate not to miss their connecting trains. Meanwhile harassed families tried to organise their children with all the appearance of herding cats.

There was also a large group of scantily clad young women who appeared to be already the worse for a small sherry or three. They wore shiny pink banners with gold writing announcing it was *"Shannon's hen party. Lock up your sons/husbands/grandfathers."* One of them, a heavily tattooed woman in the shortest shorts I had ever seen outside Wimbledon, was cradling what appeared to be an inflatable pink phallus, exactly the same shade as my slippers at home. This appendage had a photocopied image attached to it of a young male who I could only assume must be the lucky groom. I wondered to myself if the image was Photoshopped in some way, as the unfortunate fella seemed to have a nose so large he could have smelled a Sunday roast on Tuesday. I could hear the clank of various bottles of alcohol packed into oversized tote bags displaying the same message as the banners.

I shook my head: they certainly looked like trouble to me. But nevertheless a small tug of wistful regret told me I would not be enjoying a weekend like that again. Not that I often had, even when younger. Maybe on reflection I should have; but no, all that gaudy showmanship really wasn't my thing. So why then did I feel the stirrings of regret for what might have been?

Now, sadly, the most fun I seemed to have was treating myself to a small dry sherry whilst watching *Tipping Point* on the telly, taking tiny sips as I waited for my Marks & Spencer beef hotpot for one to cook. I'd carefully keep one eye on the tumbling coins on the screen while one ear was cocked towards my galley kitchen, waiting for the ping from the microwave to tell me my gastronomic delight was piping hot and ready to scald the roof of my mouth.

I didn't really approve of convenience foods: wasn't it better to cook from scratch? My mother always said that "good food wasn't fast, and fast food wasn't good"; but most nights I just didn't have the heart to start chopping veg and marinating meat when it was just for little old me. It didn't seem worth the effort.

Suddenly, a high-pitched whistle echoed through the station, making me wince. The reverberations on the brickwork suggested it might come from a yodelling Alpine shepherd. My head swivelled toward the source of the din. There was only one person I knew who could whistle like that.

And then I saw her, two fingers still in her mouth post whistle, and dragging a multicoloured suitcase in her wake that was large enough for a family of four on holiday on the Costa Brava. I winced again: the baggage was so battered it looked as if it had been commandeered by forensics, possibly with a corpse rotting inside it. It was also clanking, as if she'd got a whole Duty Free zipped in there too, for good measure.

There she was. There was Dora.

"Evie, my darling, how lovely to see you! Please give your little sister a hug."

She let go of her case and rushed towards me, her striped kaftan billowing out around her like a spinnaker in a gale. Despite her generous proportions, my sister liked to dress in a bright and eye-catching way – never one to settle for "flattering black". No, Dora liked to have at least ten vibrant shades fighting for attention in any given outfit, plus enough costume jewellery to sound like the percussion section of an orchestra tuning up whenever she moved. She said she loved people smiling when they saw her coming. I wasn't convinced that some weren't in fact grimacing.

She engulfed me in the tightest of hugs, and kissed me warmly on both cheeks. It was impossible to ignore the fragrance of alcohol on her breath. Her bright scarlet lipstick was no doubt now high on both my cheekbones, making me look as if I'd had a hard slap around the chops.

Along with the pungent smell of booze, her excessive Estée Lauder Youth Dew hung in the air. It was the scent she had always worn, just as our mother had. It suddenly reminded me of a time many decades before when we had again embraced at a train station. Our dear mother had been with us on that occasion. I had been leaving my native Bristol to relocate to Leeds for Andrew's work: excited and apprehensive in equal measure about starting a new life in an unfamiliar city and leaving all my family and friends far behind.

We had been so young and vibrant and full of hope for the future back then. It was strange how evocative certain smells could be; they could instantly transport you to a single moment in time, like it was yesterday. Odd really, as these days my mind seemed about as sharp as the butter knife I spread my marmalade with every morning.

I was constantly walking into rooms forgetting why I had gone there in the first place. Only yesterday, I had found my purse sitting in the fridge on top of a half-opened pack of streaky bacon, while a pound block of mature cheddar was tucked neatly inside my handbag. I wasn't going to worry about that too much though, as in my defence the purse and the cheese were roughly the same size, and both a vibrant shade of yellow. So I was confident it wasn't the dreaded Alzheimer's taking hold; well, at least not yet, I hoped.

I promptly stepped back from my sister and rubbed swiftly at both cheeks to remove the lipstick stains I suspected were there; most probably I appeared like a deranged porcelain doll.

"Have you been drinking, Dora?" I knew my voice had an accusatory tone, but after all it wasn't even midday.

She smiled at me with a definite twinkle in her bright green eyes.

"Quite possibly, my dear, quite possibly. Anyway, stop being a judgmental Mother Superior. Take your wimple off and give your little sister another big hug; it's been a long time."

As instructed, I hugged her again. I was pleased to see her, really I was. I just wasn't what you would consider a natural hugger, never had been, and although Dora seemed perfectly relaxed in our embrace, I felt as if my body was stiff and rather unyielding.

I was at least thankful to see she wasn't lugging along a pet carrier. Phew! That meant she hadn't brought her mangy old cat Feline Dion with her. Never mind "My Heart Will Go On"; it was more likely my heart would stop dead with that tortoiseshell terror around.

Dora always said I exaggerated my fear of her beloved pet. However, I was convinced the furry assassin was forever plotting my demise. She would lurk on Dora's swirly patterned stair carpet just waiting to trip me up with a well-timed paw. Or if that didn't work, the malevolent mouser would launch itself at my paperback Daphne du Maurier whilst I was relaxing before dinner, obviously hoping for an afternoon aneurysm brought on by shock.

I was just relieved that she must have left the miserable old moggy behind with her long-suffering next-door neighbour, Keith. He was a mild-mannered retired accountant who had lived in the semi-detached property next door to my sister for decades, and yet still seemed just about able to tolerate her. His wife had passed away a few years before, and he would pop in on my sister occasionally for a sloe gin and an even slower game of Scrabble. I often wondered if they were more than just neighbours and enjoyed a frisson over a triple word score, but I had never asked; matters of anything carnal always made me feel uncomfortable.

I had met Keith a few times, and he seemed a thoroughly good egg. Possibly under duress, he had agreed to take in Feline the tortoiseshell tyrant when Dora went away for a few days. He really was a terribly sweet man, and so tolerant to put up with that moulting furball all over his Barker and Stonehouse three-piece suite.

Celine Dion was my sister's all-time favourite singer, and Feline could also hit the high notes, mostly at 3 a.m. when the neighbourhood was quietly slumbering. The petulant pussycat also had claws like Edward Scissorhands, and wasn't afraid to use them, especially on a decent pair of 20 denier Marks and Spencer tights.

Yes, I was thoroughly relieved my sister had not brought her pet along to share her holiday. I did not miss seeing that antagonised alley cat scowling out at me from within the prison-like confines of her pet carrier. My heart would survive quite happily, thank you very much.

I felt our hug had lasted sufficiently, so stepped away from my sister's embrace and forced the brightest smile I could muster.

"So tell me, was your journey good?"

She threw her head back and let out a bellowing laugh, her curly shoulder-length salt and pepper hair merrily bouncing like wiry cork springs as she did.

"I should say so. It was an absolute scream. I got speaking to the most fabulous group of young women. They're celebrating Shannon's hen do, and they've adopted me as Mother Hen, would you believe?"

I believed it. My sister was the sort of person who could make friends in an empty room; or sometimes clear one too, depending on her rude jokes and even ruder flatulence.

"Anyway, they were such lovely young ladies, and the conversation was simply fascinating."

She gave me a conspiratorial wink. "What those girls don't know about blow jobs you could fit on the back of a stamp. And from what Shannon was saying, that's about the size of her fiancé's equipment, if you know what I mean? Mind you, a stamp probably gets licked a fair sight more."

She threw her head back again and honked with laughter, completely oblivious to the startled looks she was receiving from others. They probably worried that a herd of geese had been let loose on platform 9.

I smiled thinly at my sister and reached over to grab the handle of her humongous suitcase. I couldn't help noticing that it hadn't been packed particularly well: there appeared to be a bra strap trailing out of the end of the zip. I imagined my sister had left her packing to the very last minute, as was the norm with her; no doubt she'd hurriedly dumped everything bar the kitchen sink into it, before straddling it in an attempt to get the zip to close.

"Come on, Dora, there's not much time left on the parking; we really need to get a move on."

She nodded briefly before carrying on her chatter. She was virtually jogging next to me to keep up with my spritely pace, her resin jewellery sounding like a Caribbean band in full swing.

"Honestly, Evie, these girls are so lucky to be living in these times, you know; far from the drab old days we experienced growing up. Bethany was telling me all about the booty calls she has with various young men. She has them arranged in size order on her phone, so she knows exactly what to expect when she rings their bell."

She gave me a suggestive little wink. "She doesn't want to get short-changed, if you catch my drift."

Her drift had shot past me at warp speed.

"Beauty call – what on earth is that when it's at home? An appointment for her nails with a male beautician?"

My sister was laughing again. Her face was crimson, and she appeared to be having difficulty breathing. I honestly couldn't see what was so funny.

"No not beauty... booty...oh, never mind."

She stopped for a second to catch her breath, sounding like a sixty-a-day smoker; which was strange, as she'd never been one for the evil weed in her life. Well, as far as I knew. Probably this was the only vice she had so far managed to avoid.

"Probably I shouldn't have drunk all that prosecco and eaten quite so many salted peanuts, but it would have been rude to say no after the girls had so kindly invited me into their group."

She let out a little gassy burp. "Ooh, that's better. It's just like I said to my doctor about my constipation: always better out than in."

I shushed her loudly, glancing around the busy station, embarrassed by her behaviour. However, nobody appeared to be giving us a second glance; far too caught up in their own lives to care a jot about two ladies getting on in years while dragging a suitcase as big as a minivan along the concourse.

"Sorry, sis, I forget that when I'm half-cut my decibel level goes up a notch or three."

"So, you are drunk then?"

"No, I wouldn't say drunk; well, maybe just drunk enough. Anyway, I'll be quiet now; don't want to show you up."

She made a zipping gesture along her mouth to demonstrate her intention to stay silent from now on. It lasted exactly five seconds before she started chattering again.

"But who knew you could get all those different cocktails in cans now? It really is an exciting new world. Fancy being able to buy a tin of Sex on the Beach from Sainsbury's. We'd never have been able to get away with that in our day. Imagine us going into Lipton's grocers when we were girls and asking for that. Mother would have washed our mouths out with soap and water. The closest we ever got was a tin of warm shandy and a firm handshake on Blackpool beach."

She roared with laughter once again.

I was glad when I finally spotted my little blue Vauxhall in the distance. I pulled the key fob from my handbag and unlocked it remotely with a weary sigh.

I didn't know how long my sister was going to stay, but I already knew it would feel far longer.

Chapter 3

T wo days had passed since I had picked my sister up from Leeds train station. Only two days, but it already felt like eternity.

I had been biting my lip so much to stop myself snapping at sister dearest that it was a wonder I hadn't drawn blood. We were just so different. Nobody would ever peg us for siblings in a million years. I was down to earth and dependable; and Dora ... well, Dora was a disaster of epic proportions.

My house was my pristine little palace. I was a devoted advocate of an organised way of living. It just made sense in a world of mishaps and mayhem to have order within your own personal universe.

However, my normally neat as a pin home looked as if a minor earthquake had shaken it to its foundations. There were clothes and assorted pieces of costume jewellery in every colour imaginable scattered around every inch of the property. Even the bathroom, which was barely big enough to swing a cat (oooh, how I would have loved to swing Feline Dion around there by her scrawny neck), and had just enough space for the toilet, tub and vanity unit, now had a messy tangle of tights hanging from the shower fitting in the dreary shade of creamed cappuccino – no different in tone than the American tan tights our mother used to buy for us from Woolworths all those decades ago.

I could feel my features settle into a stony scowl as I caught sight of my beautiful bronze silk damask cushions in a heap on the lounge carpet. They should have been where they belonged, at perfect right angles on my beige leather couch; but alas, now they sat in a mound like chubby piles of cow dung with my sister reclining on them, humming like an old fridge freezer. And rather like with said fridge freezer, I had to quell my impulse to give her a swift kick.

Instead, I glared down at her from my position of height.

"Dora, what on earth are you doing now?"

She opened one eye and stared up at me for a few seconds as if she couldn't quite place where she was and who was addressing her. Then suddenly a warm smile cracked her heavily made-up face.

She hadn't left the house for the last couple of days, but always insisted on wearing a full face of make-up. Lipstick, powder and paint were a must in my sister's book, and enough scent to send my allergies into overdrive. She insisted that you never could tell when a handsome stranger might turn up on your doorstep, even if it was only the myopic chap from the local chemist's delivering my prescription for anal suppositories.

"Oh hello, my dear, I'm just meditating, stripping myself of life's perceptions and allowing myself to be completely free. The enormity of earth's gravitational pull is soothing my very soul."

It sounded like codswallop to me. More likely she was taking a quick nap after the couple of glasses of wine she'd consumed over our ham and cheese toasties at lunch.

I knew I was rolling my eyes again. Soothe her soul? The amount of camomile tea she'd been guzzling of late, leaving the little stringy bags everywhere but in the bin, should have ensured she was more zen than the Dalai Lama, or a sloth dangling from a tree in the rainforest by its toes.

I flopped on the sofa sans cushion behind my back to ease my sciatica and huffed silently to myself. I had been hoping to catch up on last night's *Coronation Street*. I had missed it, and it was at quite a cliffhanger moment, storywise, involving Rita at The Kabin and some argy-bargy around mint imperials and theft thereof. A new family had moved into the street, and the youngest of the offspring was a feral wee whippersnapper. In truth it was getting extremely riveting, and I felt sure the spotty scoundrel's dénouement would be coming up in part one of my missed episode.

However, Dora had other ideas and insisted we should give my wardrobe a quick going over; or a "reinvigorating revamp", as she called it, so my relaxing afternoon of soap opera viewing was no longer on the cards. She was also insisting we get out of the house that evening to the local pub for a sandwich and a swift one, as she was going, in her words, "batshit bonkers" being cooped up in my home, where "all things beige came to curl up and die".

She clambered up from her position on the floor, looking like an upturned woodlouse as she struggled; clearly getting to her feet took considerable effort as it was accompanied by much moaning and groaning. My precious cushions were now abandoned in a dishevelled heap, the silky fabric thoroughly squished and bearing what was clearly an imprint of my sister's sizeable posterior.

Well, the quick wardrobe once-over turned out to be three excruciatingly long hours of my life that I'd never get back. My sister was aghast to discover my universally muted tones of clothing, as well as my understated gold jewellery with nothing tribal or plastic and no discernible taste.

There were distraught cries of "Your clothes have less personality than a Tory MP with a migraine" and "Who knew there could be so many shades of dishwasher dull". She even asked me if my wardrobe was a portal back to the 1950s, and seemed quite surprised that Mr Tumnus or a procession of Daleks hadn't come waltzing out of it.

She pulled item after item out of my mahogany wardrobe to fling on my single divan bed, upon which I quietly picked them up and replaced them without her even noticing. She really was away with the fairies most of the time.

I only managed to stop her frantic fashion endeavours by promising we could go shopping in a few days' time, when I might treat myself to something a little "jollier", as she put it: something not in my favoured shades of taupe, nude or black, anyway.

She looked at me warily, her green eyes narrowing a little. "I hope you're not just humouring me, sis; I really want to see you in something that doesn't look like you're off to a funeral. You really have a cracking figure, but everything you drape around it is so sackcloth and ashes; you should be flaunting your *sexier clothed ass*."

I fixed her with my most withering glare. My days of "sexy" were well and truly gone. In fact, I don't know if

I had ever given off a vibe of sexy at any stage of my life. I was confident my style had always been more timeless chic than foxy chick. Surely understated was best, anyway.

I was only granted permission to return to my TV programme and relax on the sofa when I had agreed to wear the most "festive" outfit I possessed: a green knee-length wrap dress that I personally thought made me look more washed out than last week's dishcloth; but Dora insisted it was quite fetching against my shoulder-length auburn hair.

Several hours later, I was sitting in the kitchen dressed appropriately, though not in the green dress. I had put it on, but quickly changed again, feeling it made me look quite bilious with my pale complexion; instead I'd dressed in one of my most favourite outfits. I was patiently waiting for my sister to grace me with her presence, so we could be on our way to the pub. It was already after six and I didn't like to eat too late; it really wreaked havoc with my digestion.

I poured myself a small, rather conservative measure of gin and tonic, with just a whisper of Bombay Sapphire and a hearty slosh of slimline; then found myself tapping my short pearlescent fingernails impatiently on the kitchen table. It was just like being teenagers again. On the rare occasions we socialised together, I was always ready in plenty of time, left waiting for my younger sibling to flounce in way behind schedule, then delight or possibly fright with her latest flamboyant ensemble.

True to form, when Dora eventually descended, I was nearly blinded and in desperate need of sunglasses. Polar opposite to my timeless and elegant garb, she was decked out in what would only suit a bad taste party from the 1980s. The lime green and orange horizontal stripes on her voluminous maxi dress could not be considered flattering under any circumstance, in fact they were positively shudder inducing. The dress was bad enough, but why the neon orange faux fur fluffy cardigan as an accessory?

I thought back to our mother's sage words of advice: one should never wear horizontal stripes if there was more than "an inch to pinch". Quite clearly all and sundry could "manhandle a handful", where my younger sister was concerned. But against her better judgement, or in fact any judgement at all, she was choosing to forget those matriarchal words of wisdom doled out by mother, just as she doled out the steamed fish and cabbage for our diet-friendly dinner. But then again, unlike me, Dora was never one to worry about such trivial matters as calories and clothes sizes; nor was she likely to return to a diet of mushy fish and overcooked cabbage any time soon.

She was forever scoffing indulgently on something sinful, whilst sighing with rapture over how creamy or cheesy it was, or how chocolate was in her opinion better than sex. Her mission in life was never to turn down a slice of cake when offered as, in her words, "it would always be somebody somewhere's birthday". Which gave me great pangs of hunger and envy every time: not sure which I was missing more, the buttery sponge cake or the bedroom shenanigans. I had never really been able to indulge myself the way Dora could, chocolate, sex or otherwise.

Unlike my sister, I believed it more appropriate to take a regimented approach in all things, and most certainly with my diet. It was all about willpower after all, and I had that in abundance. Plus, I was proud I could still fit into a size 12, well, from Marks & Spencer anyway. Some of the other shops I felt were a bit mean on their measurements. But I knew I'd maintained my girlish figure. OK, maybe not exactly girlish, but at least I hadn't abandoned the fitted waistband for the false security of an elasticated waist and acres of Lycra. My sister, however, seemed happy enough to wear *all* the Lycra, and from the look of this current colourful creation, the fabric was stretched within an inch of its life. And although Lycra was very forgiving it still wasn't magic and still governed by the laws of physics.

I smiled at my sister over the table in what I hoped appeared to be approval. I doubted whether it reached my eyes. I really didn't want to be mean, but she looked an absolute fright. It was an eye-catching outfit all right, enough to make one's retinas explode, and if anyone caught my eye in the Swan and Key public house we were destined for later, I sincerely hoped they wouldn't give it back; save me from the horror of the multicoloured monstrosity.

Dora did a 360-degree spin to showcase her dress to me from every conceivable angle. It somehow managed to appear even worse from the back, like a gaudy galleon in full sail.

"Well, what do you think, Evie? Pretty snazzy, eh? And it was reduced in the January sales too; can you believe my luck?"

Reduced? Well, it was certainly reducing me to tears.

I smiled stiffly again, repeating a mantra over and over in my head: "Just nod and agree, just nod and agree, just nod and agree."

True to form, I couldn't help myself though; before I knew what was happening, the words were bubbling up and out of my mouth before I could clamp my hand against it.

"Could you not have picked something a little less gaudy? We're only going to the local pub; it's a week night, after all, and it's going to be quiet. You look like you're decked out for a carnival."

I took a long sip of my gin, perhaps for a bit of Dutch courage, before continuing.

"I mean, exactly how many of the Muppets had to die in the manufacture of that cardigan? The thing's an absolute eyesore."

Dora was clearly stunned, her twirling abandoned; she stared at me with eyes wide in shock. Perhaps I had gone too far? But no, the kitchen clock had barely ticked five seconds in the silence, before my sister was bent double laughing.

"Stop it, Evie." She was wiping her eyes with the sleeve of her cardigan. "You know, at my age, if I want to be egregiously overdressed on a week night, then so be it. Life really is too short to just fade into the background; and if I want to get all gussied up, then I will and there ain't nobody who can stop me."

At this she met my eye, and I knew what she was getting at. I didn't agree. OK, I was conservatively dressed, but I wasn't fading into the wallpaper in my understated outfit, I really wasn't.

Dora's expression brightened again. "You really need to stop cracking the funnies like that though...muppets indeed. I haven't even got my Tena ladies on; I'm wearing my silky smalls in case I strike it lucky with a local lothario down the pub tonight."

Strike it lucky with one of the locals? The Swan and Key public house on week nights was mostly frequented by welly-wearing dog walkers and elderly men cradling half pints of mild. The most outrageous fashion accessory that would be sported in that establishment was likely a jaunty sock poking out of a slip-on tan brogue. Heaven alone knew what they would make of my sister.

Anyway, as far as I knew, there was a meeting of the allotment society tonight, their monthly get-together to discuss all matters horticultural. But whether one of them would break off talking about aphid infestations and communal manure piles to take a crack at my sister was another matter.

She twirled around the kitchen once more, her movements causing a definite crackle of static electricity in the air that seemed to make her corkscrew curls bounce even more manically.

"Anyway, you're a fine one to talk. OK, my dress and cardi may be a wee bit jolly, but I think I look absolutely darling! And anyway, just look at you. Where's the lovely green dress we decided on? You've got every shade of beige going on in that sensible twinset, and never mind the shoes. That shade of brown on a foot should only ever be reserved for when you inadvertently walk through a pile of dog turd. And I know we both favour a flat shoe these days, but you look like you've wedged your trotters into a couple of Cornish pasties."

I was aghast at this. My trouser suit was my absolute favourite: a muted mushroom-toned two-piece that the lady in the upscale boutique in town had confirmed was befitting for an elegant lady of my vintage. And my buttery soft suede moccasins bore no resemblance to flaky pastry that I could see.

Dora reached across the table to the gin bottle and poured herself a measure, an exceedingly generous measure at that. It really was quite the pour: there was barely room for a thimbleful of tonic in her tumbler by the time she'd finished. She took a long gulp of her drink and sighed with obvious satisfaction before addressing me again.

"Honestly, Evie, I wouldn't be seen dead in your clothes."

I snorted rather unattractively at this. "Seen dead in my clothes? You would have to have been dead for at least six months to fit into them." There was silence again as Dora appeared to have been stunned once more into silence. It was a nice change of pace from the constant chatter I had had of late, but I felt a prickle of anxiety course through me. I really hadn't meant to hurt her feelings.

I needn't have worried: my sister as usual took no offence at my cutting words. She just threw her head back once more and roared with laughter.

"Ha ha, Evie, you really are a card; and to be fair you've got it spot on, so I can't argue. I've had a lot of fun cultivating my curves over the years. Not all of us can have a sylphlike figure like you, my dear; some of us prefer cheesecake to crispbreads, and a double portion of anything delicious."

I felt my bottom lip jut out in the manner of a petulant toddler. "Well, I really like my suit; it was a little post-Christmas treat to myself for not going mad on all the mince pies."

"Christmas treat? That outfit is really your idea of a treat? I would rather have eaten a mountain of mince pies and every boiled sprout in Swarcliffe than put those dreary old rags on my body."

She reached over and gave my auburn locks a little ruffle before taking another gulp of her gin.

"But let's forget your clothes for a minute; not everyone can curate a cute outfit as successfully as I can, but you should really let me get to grips with your hair: a bit of a trim, some backcombing and plenty of lacquer, and I could have you looking like something off *Dynasty*.

I moved my head far away from her reach. There was not a chance I was letting my sister anywhere near my barnet. I had been going to Alessandro in the precinct for decades, and I could only imagine his vitriol if I turned up to my appointment in a week's time after Dora had had a go at my graduated long bob with my blunt kitchen scissors.

"No thank you, Dora, I'm perfectly happy with my hair the way it is."

She shrugged her shoulders good-naturedly. "Fair enough, sis. Isn't this nice, though? Us being together like old times, fashion tips and teasing each other; it's a real tonic."

"Well, I'm glad it's a tonic, as there's no gin left. You've finished *another* bottle."

"Have I really? Whoops, sorry about that. I'll pop to the shops tomorrow and restock the supplies. But you do know what I mean, don't you? We've been far too distant of late; I know we're like chalk and cheese and all that, but it's so good to see you. Time passes so quickly, and after all you're the only sister I've got, so I'm stuck with you."

She was right about one thing: time really did pass quickly, and not always comfortably. In fact sometimes it flew by with all the appeal of Ryanair.com. In fact, only a couple of days ago I had been in a department store browsing and noticed a vaguely familiar woman in the distance in the home furnishings department. I raised a hand to wave to the old dear, before realising with a start that I was waving to my reflection in the spotless mirror. I was mortified. When had I become so old? But fair play to the store: they really kept their mirrors fabulously streak-free.

Her eyes filled again, but not from laughter this time. Maybe her cobalt blue mascara had seeped into her eye? She'd certainly got enough of the stuff around them. She furnished me with the brightest smile that simply lit up her face. Even with the florid shade of orange lipstick that matched her cardigan, bleeding slightly into the lines around her mouth, there was no denying she was a fine-looking woman. In fact, for a second, I was vividly reminded of the vibrant girl she had been all those decades ago.

I softened slightly. She was right, we were sisters, and we were both getting older. There was no slowing the hasty hands of time. And I did love her. I really needed not to be such a miserable old moo. Perhaps it hadn't been *all* bad having Dora around the last few days. If I was completely honest with myself, although she was driving me mad, and I couldn't wait for her return journey home, it wasn't the worst thing in the world to have some company again.

In truth I had been a little lonely of late. Sometimes I even kept the radio going on low all night just so there was another voice in the house to break up the silence – a silence that could feel deafening. Just to hear the shipping forecast on Radio 4 made me feel less alone under the dark inky cloak of night.

Of course, I had my daughter Lottie, and we still tried to meet for our weekly catch-up over lunch or coffee and a sliver of cake. But she had a new boyfriend now and was even thinking of moving in with him soon. With this new relationship and her exciting fashion ventures, there simply weren't enough hours in the day to fit in her old mum too. I was pleased for her, of course I was. It was so edifying to see my daughter finally able to pursue her dreams after being with her ex-husband Daniel for all those years. He really had been an overbearing, unkind, selfish, steaming dog dollop of a man. But Leo thankfully was nothing like him: he was simply a lovely gent, and I could find no fault with her new beau. He reminded me a little of one of the dashing leading men from my daughter's favourite old films. So charming and mannerly, almost timeless, as if he had just sauntered off the set of a black and white movie; a modern-day Cary Grant or Laurence Olivier.

Not at all like some of the young men you had the misfortune of seeing around town these days: more ignorant than elegant, more's the pity. And the way they dressed so unstylishly too, as if they'd just stumbled out of bed and fallen into yesterday's clothes, hair a dishevelled mop. And don't get me started on the ones that have half their posterior hanging out of their low-slung jeans. Really, I ask you, what's wrong with a decent tan leather belt or a pair of good old-fashioned braces?

Plus, I can't blooming well understand most of what they're saying. My grandson Jacob just shakes his head affectionately at me and tells me, not unkindly, that I just don't understand the modern style and vernacular. Well, if that's what's considered style and proper conversation these days, you can jolly well keep it.

My sister shut the metal clasp on her sequined clutch with a resounding click, which snapped me right out of my musings. It was a veritable call to action. Her drink was drained, and she was ready to get to the pub quick smart for another.

Chapter 4

• ♥ • ♥ • ♥ • ♥ • ♥ •

The interior of the Swan and Key was pretty much as I had expected: not exactly rammed to the rafters with customers. There was a group towards the far end of the bar where two tables of differing heights had been pushed together to accommodate the Allotment Society folk. They were all deep in conversation: something about overdue Michaelmas allotment rents and aggrieved mutterings about pulling up one's cabbages at threat of lifetime bans drifted towards my ears. Apart from that, there were only a few patrons randomly dotted around, some looking bored, others engrossed in their paperbacks or newspapers, and one man staring miserably into the middle distance. He looked so forlorn I worried he might drown himself in his pint of mild.

It was hard to ignore the aroma of burnt cooking fat, heavy in the air. Although the Swan and Key rather fancied itself as a fine dining establishment, I had never found their food particularly worthy of a Michelin star, and doubted very much whether any celebrity chefs would be beating a path to its door any time soon.

Dora was standing beside me, her arm linked through mine, clearly out of breath, although we had hardly power-walked the five minutes from home; more of a sedate sojourn than a spritely sprint.

"Well, that's my exercise done for the day, I suppose?" she grumbled, wiping the sweat from her brow with a dubious-looking tissue that she had fished out of her coat pocket, maybe there since before lockdown.

"I would hardly class it as a vigorous workout, Dora. We only strolled a couple of minutes from the house."

"Well, it's more than enough huffing and puffing for me, thank you very much. I already pulled a stomach muscle laughing at you earlier, and that constituted more than enough exercise in my book."

She unwound her thick woollen scarf from around her neck to showcase her outfit to the fullest. "It doesn't really live up to the hype though, does it?" she muttered, casting a beady eye around the interior of the mahogany-trimmed bar.

"Hype? What hype?"

"Well, if you're gonna call yourself 'swanky', then you ought to live up to the name; but looking around this joint, you could drop the 's' and it would be far more fitting." She delivered a cheeky wink before making her way towards the bar, her hips jiggling slightly as she went.

I sighed to myself as I followed behind her. She really was the limit. She knew only too well the name was the Swan and Key. Why did my sister always have to be so flippant and make a joke out of everything? She might find it funny, but I did not.

Once arrived at the sticky bar top, she dumped her tatty satchel bag down and looked left and right in an attempt to locate a member of staff. She hauled herself up onto one of the rickety bar stools, muttering expletives under her breath that would have made a sailor blush as she struggled to get comfortable.

"Ooh, where are they? I'm absolutely starving. I could really do with a decent bit of nosebag, plus a good measure of something nice and chilled to wash it down." She positioned two fingers in her mouth and before I could stop her, the piercing whistle was reverberating around the wood-panelled joists of the sedate Edwardian building.

The customers all cranked their heads towards us, like a mob of meerkats. It would have been quite amusing if I didn't feel so utterly mortified. Once they saw it was just the flamboyant old floozy at the bar causing the commotion, they returned to their reading or polishing off packets of pork scratchings in peace. Only one man, a formidable-looking chap with a ginger moustache and a head as bald as a bean, fixed us with a hostile glare. He looked more than a little displeased, almost like he was suffering from a fart intent on coming out sideways.

A young man eventually appeared from the shadows, wiping his hands on a bar towel. He was young and not unlike my grandson; a little reminiscent of Robert Downey Jr in his younger days.

Dora was clearly delighted to see him. "Ahhhh, barkeep, there you are; we've been dying of thirst out here."

The young man, who I imagined was only in his early twenties and dressed in a T-shirt displaying a band I had never heard of and those God-awful low-slung jeans, beamed at my sister, clearly delighted to see her in all her man-made fibre-mix glory. No doubt she brightened up a dreary weekday in this sleepy little idyll in Yorkshire. I wondered what he actually thought of her. I couldn't help thinking, rather uncharitably, that she rather resembled a burst mattress.

"I'm with you now, ladies; just had to put some beers in the fridge and sort them. I'm so sorry about your wait."

Dora gave him a little wink. "Don't you be worried about that, luvvie. I'm not one bit sorry about my weight. I love being me, a plus-sized queen of fabulosity."

"Err...n...no...no." The man stuttered, a red flush sweeping up his neck and colouring his cheeks. "I didn't mean that. I just meant that there was no one at the bar to serve you when you arrived, and you must have been waiting a while."

I shot Dora one of my warning glares. There she went again, trying to be funny. I really wished she could just turn down her fabulosity ever so slightly.

"Ignore my sister, she knew exactly what you meant."

Dora held up her hand in mock contrition before leaning across the bar so he could shake her hand.

"Guilty as charged, I was just pulling your leg, my darlin'. Tell me, what's your name, young man? I'm Isadora, but you can call me Dora; and this miserable old biscuit beside me is my much older sister Evelyn. And I must say you remind me awfully of a young Harrison Ford, and he's my very favourite actor, I'll have you know".

He shook her hand warmly, although I wasn't sure he even knew who Harrison Ford was. "Pleased to meet you, Dora...Evelyn, and I'm Jake."

I smiled tightly back at him. Please tell me my sister wasn't actually flirting with this youth. I shuddered at the very thought.

Dora cast her eyes around the interior of the pub. "It's a bit quiet in here though, Jake. When do things liven up a bit?"

He shrugged his shoulders, his face now returning to a more natural shade. "Dunno, maybe around Christmas, if you're lucky."

Dora hooted with laughter. "Ah well, never mind, it's like no man's land in here, and what men there are you would need a power cut to make attractive. But as I'm not on the pull tonight and just having a drink with my sister, it makes no odds. Talking of which, what's your poison, Evie?"

They both turned their heads towards me expectantly.

I looked along the optics above Jake's head. What did I fancy? I wasn't really one for mid-week drinking in pubs. Should I have a gin and slimline, or perhaps a soft drink would be wise. Keep a clear head and within my calories too. Oh, what the hell, let's throw caution to the wind.

"How about a nice chilled glass of chardonnay?" I suggested. "Or a vodka lime soda might be nice?"

Dora pulled a face. "Might be nice... might be boring. How about a cocktail? Do you do cocktails by any chance, Jake?"

"Indeed we do, ladies; they're pre-made, I'm afraid though, although you do get a full three units of alcohol in each jug."

Dora's face fell about a mile. "Three units of alcohol? Pah, there's more than that in my pee at any given moment. Speaking of which, please excuse me for a moment; I really need to answer Mother Nature's call and have myself a quick tinkle."

She clambered off the stool, with all the grace of a dustbin lorry reversing up a back alley, and trotted off towards the ladies' lavatory leaving a few tufts of orange fur and her heady perfume in her wake.

"I must apologise for my sister, Jake, she's quite a lot to take on. I find her exhausting and I've known her for over sixty years."

Jake held up his hand. "No, please, don't apologise. I think she's amazing, like a bright firework display of a woman exiting and exhilarating; and her outfit just makes me happy."

Oh well, there's really no accounting for taste. And yet again it was clear to see that Dora had found another young fan.

"Well, we'll just have a bottle of the chardonnay then, Jake, and two glasses. No cocktails this time; and a couple of menus please if you're still serving food."

"We are." He grabbed two large fake-leather-bound menus from behind the bar and passed them over to me, promising to bring the wine to our table.

I found a nice secluded spot in the corner, well away from any other patrons. I felt sure they would thank me for that later.

My sister was soon back from her ablutions and joining me at the slightly rickety wooden table.

"That's better. I was so desperate my back teeth were floating. Oh goody, you've got some menus. Give us a gander then; I'm so famished my stomach thinks my throat's been cut."

She pulled a pair of what I can only describe as drag queen spectacles from the depths of her handbag and began to peruse the menu, tutting and sighing all the while.

"No...no, don't want that. Three bean salad: why on earth would you? I mean, one bean is bad enough. Eugh, grilled goat's cheese, no thank you very much; if I wanted to lick a goat's hairy balls I would move to a caravan on the Isle of Wight."

I grimaced at her coarse language. "Really, Dora, do you have to? Goat's cheese is delicious; in fact I might have the goat's cheese and caramelised onion tart myself."

"Well, you do you, no judgement from me." But from the expression on her face, she was evidently acting judge and jury and had found me guilty of being bat-shit bonkers.

Jake arrived with our bottle of wine. He blew a tuft of curly dark hair from his eyes so he could see better, then filled our glasses before depositing the near empty bottle back in the ice bucket. What was it with the youth of to-day? Why did their hair always have to be so unkempt? In my opinion young men looked so much more presentable with a nice short back and sides.

"Are you ladies ready to order?"

"We are, thank you. I'll have the goat's cheese tart with salad. What about you, Dora?"

Dora shut her menu with a resounding snap. "I fancy the steak and ale pie with triple-cooked chips; though why you'd cook your chips three times baffles me. Did the electricity cut out the first couple of tries? Just put another quid in the meter, Jakey."

She was off laughing again, as did Jake. I kept a stony silence.

"Ha ha, no, it's the way chef does them. They're really nice, though; just the right side of crisp. But I don't know if you'd really want a whole pie; the ones we've ordered are from a new butcher in the village and they're more like family-sized than one portion."

Dora was seriousness personified now, all joking abandoned. The matter of food was something she took very seriously.

"How big exactly are we talking here, Jake? Dinner plate size, or what?"

He made a gesture with his hands to demonstrate how big the meat-filled pastry would in fact be.

My sister's face lit up with delight. "That'll do me champion, Jake. That's not family sized in my book. Why you'd never fit a family of four in a pie that size!"

She erupted with laughter again. Jake was laughing to himself as he returned to the bar, promising our order would be with us very soon. I worried that this meant our food was destined for a quick spin in the microwave.

"He's a little smasher him, Ev. Never mind my pie, I could just spread him on a slice of Kingsmill and have him as an appetiser."

"Dora, do you have to? He's nearly young enough to be your grandson."

"Oh, do hush up, sis. I'm only saying he's a good-looking young man, like knitting pattern gorgeous. It's not a crime to find a man attractive, you know. Does it get really windy up there where you are? Right on top of your very high horse."

"I just think you should act your age a little more, that's all I'm saying."

"What, like you? In your sanitised sepia cell of a home, no thank you very much! I will carry on just as I am; and why would I want to act my age anyway? I know we're not getting any younger, Evie, and before we know it the grim reaper will be swinging his blade; and when he does, there's no point ducking. So until that day comes, I will be squeezing every bit of fun I can out of my life."

"All I'm saying is that a little refinement would go a long way. If you adopted a demurer ladylike demeanour, it wouldn't mean you were boring. And after all, ageing isn't the enemy; you know that age brings knowledge and great wisdom."

"Does it really?" Dora's words were dripping with cynicism. "All it seems to bring me is chin hairs and boobs I can wear around my waist like a swimming aid."

Unfortunately, Jake chose that very moment to return to our table and his cheeks flushed scarlet again. He was carrying piping hot plates of food and was relieved to deposit them on the placemats in front of us. He blew on his fingertips, probably wishing he had worn oven gloves for the trip from the kitchen.

Dora's pie was in fact, as we knew it would be, huge. I had little doubt, however, that she would polish the whole thing off. The chips looked delicious too. But rather than looking impressed, Dora's face appeared a little perturbed; maybe the portion was too big for her after all. Truth be told, if she did consume it all, she'd better have a good supply of antacids for when we got home.

"Decent portion of pie there, Jake; can't fault you for that. But the crust appears barely cooked – it's very anaemic-looking. Is the chef in the kitchen rowing with his wife or something?"

Jake looked confused. "Err, no, I don't think so. As far as I know, his wife is in Tenerife. She ran off a month ago with the man who delivers the pork scratchings."

"Sounds like she might have been scratching more than his pork then." Dora hooted with laughter at her perceived wit. "No, what I mean is that this pie crust is so pale and pasty it looks as if it's been cooked under a heated argument."

I sighed inwardly. I had a feeling this was going to be a very long night.

Chapter 5

• ♥ • ♥ • ♥ • ♥ • ♥ •

Our food was actually quite delicious. I tried to ignore my sister's queasy glance at my goat's cheese tart. It was superb and complemented perfectly by the fresh green salad and balsamic dressing.

I noticed that for someone who wasn't enamoured by the shade of her pastry crust, or the origin of thrice-cooked chips, my sister's plate was scraped within an inch of its life, empty bar a swirl of tomato ketchup reminiscent of a Jackson Pollock painting.

"It's a pity there's no decent fellas in here tonight, Evelyn," she grumbled, casting her eyes around the motley assortment of men. "I'm always looking for myself, obviously, but I would so like to get you fixed up with someone nice."

Oh, dear I didn't like the sound of this at all. This needed stopping dead in its tracks.

"I'm completely fine as I am, Dora." I hoped my stern tone would prevent her from delving any deeper.

Of course, "completely fine" wasn't exactly true. I was in fact lonely. That said, the thought of my sister fixing me up with a suitable gentleman would be as sensible as inviting an alcoholic on a bottomless brunch and then a quick nightcap after.

I cast my eyes around the haphazard collection of men-folk on offer in the Swan and Key. It was fair to say that this barrel of bachelors had been well and truly scraped. Though I couldn't help but notice that amongst all the detritus there was one chap who wasn't half bad, all things considered. And if I had been on the lookout, which I most certainly wasn't, he would have definitely received more than a cursory glance.

He had just returned to his table from the bar, carrying a large glass of red wine, and had settled down at his table to read his copy of the *Independent*. He was tall, probably about six foot two, and perhaps in his mid-sixties; his long legs were crossed at the ankle and encased in dark blue jeans. He had a pleasant half smile on his face as he turned the page of his paper; completely unlike the ginger-moustached man who still appeared to be royally pissed off. Maybe it was just the male equivalent of resting bitch face, and maybe contrary to all appearances "Mr. Angry" was in fact a very pleasant chap. The gentleman I had my eye on, though, unlike "Ginger Moustache", looked completely approachable; he had plenty of wavy salt and pepper hair swept back from a rather handsome face, just the right side of craggy, and a definite twinkle of Tim Robbins about him.

Dora hadn't missed a thing: she'd evidently noticed me clocking him.

"Don't even think about it, Evie. He would be more interested in the ginger whinger over there than he would be in you, believe me. He's definitely a confirmed bachelor of the highest order."

I didn't understand what she was getting at, but then slowly, like one of those coin fall machines at Minehead beach, the penny finally dropped.

"How would you know if he was gay? You've never even met him before."

"Just trust me, I have a nose for these things."

My own nose let out an unattractive snort of derision. "What do you mean, a nose for these things? Maybe you just need to get your sinuses checked."

She tutted at me as if I hadn't the first clue about any-thing.

"Well, first of all he's wearing a cologne with definite undertones of sandalwood; that's a dead giveaway, straight away. And secondly, check out that hint of mankle poking out from beneath his immaculate jeans; those pink socks are gayer than a flamingo farting a unicorn."

She was struggling up from her stool now and heading for the bar. "Gonna get us another bottle; that pastry has left my throat drier than a week-old Weetabix."

I nodded to her, my eyes still on the elegant chap en-grossed in his newspaper. She was being ridiculous: how on earth could she tell the sexual orientation of a stranger at first glance? Suddenly I realised my eyes must be boring into him like a sniper with their gun trained, the little red dot clearly fixed on his forehead, as he suddenly looked up and locked eyes with me. He smiled, a lovely crinkly smile with straight white teeth and full lips that made my tummy turn a somersault. I quickly looked away, feeling guilty at having been caught ogling at my age. But then again, maybe it was just the goat's cheese causing my tummy to quiver; it had been rather rich, and I wasn't always good with dairy, prone to gastro issues at times.

Dora was on her way back from the bar. Instead of the bottle of wine as promised, she was carrying a couple of martini glasses. From the slightly viscous liquid within and the olives, I surmised she had decided to change the order to dirty martinis – her drink of choice. I had never particularly cared for them myself, although I did think they looked quite elegant in films. I remembered Daniel Craig had seemed especially debonair sipping one in *Casino Royale*. I quite liked him as an actor, but there would only ever be one true Bond for me: Sean Connery.

"Stroke of luck, young Jake knows how to make a mean martini; I'm telling you, that young man is gonna go far."

She placed the glasses carefully down on the table, to ensure not a drop was spilt. "There you go, my darlin', a salty drink for a salty broad."

I lifted the martini glass to my lips and took a tentative sip before wincing. Blimey, it was strong. I would only be having one of these, that was for sure.

"Yep, that's quite the pour, young Jakey's got: more than three units of liquor in one of these bad boys; it'll sure put hairs on your balls. And talking of balls, you see what I mean about Mr Debonair over there?" Her eyes flashed over to the gentleman engrossed once more in his newspaper. "I'm telling you, sis, unless you've sprouted a cock and a couple of hairy plums under your sensible granny pants, he would never be interested in you in a gazillion years."

I tutted at her and took another sip of my heinously strong drink. "Would you just shush up now? You don't know a thing about that man and you're making me feel extremely uncomfortable. If you don't stop it, then I'm going home. You're very unfiltered, Dora, and this is not the sort of conversation I ever wish to have."

She shrugged her shoulders. "All I'm saying is don't waste your time looking. That one couldn't even walk straight if he tried."

I shot her a warning glance, ready to grab my bag and be on my way. "I'm telling you, Dora, you'd better zip that lip."

"OK, OK, I'll be good, I promise. But you do know, all jokes aside, you really should consider dating again. Andrew has been gone a long time now and I hate to think of you rattling around that big house on your own. I don't just mean for sex, although it must have been a hell of a while since you last saw any action; but for the companionship and the conversation. And if you met someone and got on splendidly, then it wouldn't hurt to blow the dust off the banister and have a nice little ride, don't you think?"

I scowled at her. My face felt a little warm, whether from the strong liquor or the blunt conversation. I had a feeling I might be blushing as rosily as young Jake had.

"I'm fine as I am. I see Lottie for coffee and lunch now and again, there's my bridge club, occasional coffees with Belinda, and I still get to Waitrose and the library plenty; so my life's very full, thank you very much. I think you'll find I'm doing just fine."

Dora looked utterly appalled. "Library? Supermarket? Coffee with boring Belinda? It's hardly living life on the edge, is it? And what is it I always tell you: if you're not living life on the edge, you're taking up too much space."

I was too polite to say her gargantuan arse was always taking up too much space wherever she chose to sit.

"Where's the excitement, Evie? Where's the passion?"

I took another sip of my drink. I wasn't going to tell my sister that the over 60s lunch club was having a matinée showing of *Gone with the Wind* tomorrow at the local cinema, and that was about as much passion as I could probably handle.

"Look, Dora, I really don't want to discuss it. Men just aren't on the cards for me now, and if I'm completely honest, I don't think they ever will be. I've had my time. I had my love, my Andrew, and I'm not going to find that again, am I?"

"No, you don't have to, but there's sometimes more than one lid for every pot; you could find love again, it might not be the same, but it might be wonderful. There's not necessarily only one person for everyone."

"There is for me."

My sister gave me a little knowing look as if to say, "We'll see."

"And why does it have to be about love anyway? You could just date, you know. What is it the young ones say these days: hit it and quit it? You're the one always going on about getting enough daily exercise, and casual sex is an excellent sport to get your heartrate up."

I shushed her again. "Dora, stop it, I'm warning you. Honestly, I sometimes wonder how you and I are even sisters."

Dora drained the remainder of her martini glass with a little burp.

"Ooh, excuse me, that pastry has got some hang time. But honestly, Evie, there's no need to get all aerated. Just chill out a little. Life doesn't have to be so serious. For once consider taking an evening off from being a stuck-up prude and perhaps crack a smile, I'm enjoying myself here, and it wouldn't kill you to do the same. It pains me to say it, but you really are a right old misery guts, you know."

From the smile on her face, it didn't seem to pain her in the slightest.

I felt my shoulders rise huffily beneath my jacket. "You need to stop with all the criticism, Dora. If I were looking to be judged, I'd dig up our old Headmistress, Miss Hardcastle, and I'm sure that old harridan would soon have a few choice words to shut you up."

My sister shuddered visibly, remembering the tyrant teacher from our middle school, even though we hadn't clapped eyes on the woman in over fifty years.

But surprisingly, Dora's words had struck a chord in me. Maybe it was the vodka in the martini or the fact that I did really love my little sister, but I felt my heart soften somewhat. Was she right? Was I in fact being a prude? Or was she, as I still believed, a bit of a walking disaster zone with a filthy gob on her? Either way, I could at least try and enjoy myself a little more. What was the harm in that?

And that was exactly what I did. One martini swiftly led to another, which soon became three, with the third sliding down so smoothly that I was tempted to have another.

I fiddled with the cocktail stick from my glass. I was suddenly seeing my life through others' eyes and feeling forlorn; a mournful mist seemed to linger in the air, along with the smell of cooking oil and my sister's perfume. It was a strange sensation; I wasn't often given to introspection or navel-gazing, but then again I wasn't often one to imbibe so much liquor on a week night either. No, martinis and melancholy weren't the usual modus operandi for Evelyn Weaver.

I turned towards my sister, whose eyes were half closed, and I realised she was on the edge of nodding off. I gave her a little poke in her orange cardigan. There was something I needed to say. And it took the truth serum currently masquerading as a martini to give me the courage to say it.

"You are right though, Dora. I do get lonely at times. I feel there is a hole in my life, a big hole that really needs filling."

My sister's eyes were wide like saucers at this. "Well, in that case ..."

I cut her off before she could fully respond. Stopped her dead in her tracks.

"No! Before you say something filthy, you know exactly what I mean."

She nodded her head slowly, understanding clear in her watery green eyes, the green eyeshadow around them now streaked and patchy like bad army camouflage. I hoped my make-up was withstanding the rigours of the evening better than hers was.

It might just be prudent to check. I fished my compact out of my handbag and gave myself a quick once over. Fair to say that, like Dora, I wasn't exactly looking my best. My face was marginally more intact make-up-wise than my sister's, but that wasn't saying much; and my eyes had a definite bloodshot tinge to them.

"Oh no, look at the state of me," I groaned.

"Yep, fair to say you're drunkety drunk drunk. I'm thinking we may have had one too many martoonies."

She reached over, took the compact from me, snapped it firmly shut and dropped it into my open bag.

"There is a time and place to look into the mirror and berate yourself for your poor life choices; but that time is not now, that time is tomorrow morning when you're staring into your bathroom mirror and wondering who the old bag is that's glaring back at you. Now is the time for us to have some fun."

And that's exactly what we did – we had fun. We didn't order any more drinks; we were both steaming as it was. But we talked, talked like we hadn't since we were young. It seemed just a mere moment of time before Jake was ringing the bell for last orders at the bar. I couldn't believe it was nearly 11 p.m. We had been in the pub for nigh on five hours. It was certainly time we were on our way home. The allotment crew were long gone, and the only person remaining apart from Jake, who was collecting glasses, was the ginger-moustached fella with the slight serial killer vibes. Dora and I had decided earlier that he was a definite wrong 'un: he'd ordered a chip butty from Jake, and insisted it be on brown bread. That was clearly psychopathic behaviour in anyone's books.

"Come on, Dora, it's time we were making tracks home."

Her bottom lip jutted out, but she didn't argue. She was winding her scarf around her neck as I spoke.

Once her scarf was firmly wrapped, she was on her feet and we made our way tentatively towards the door, Dora holding onto the furniture as she went, as if she was on an ocean liner in a particularly savage storm. She had nearly made her way to the exit when she lurched into the ginger chap who was also vacating the premises, a black beanie hat pulled firmly down on his bald pate in preparation for the chilly night air.

"Oooh, sorry, love, didn't mean to knock into you like that; seems I'm a bit unsteady on my pins. I nearly did a swan dive in the Swan, can you imagine?" She let out a gassy giggle cum hiccup at this.

His face was absolute thunder; anything but amused.

"Watch where you're going, lady. Does the nursing home know you're out this late?"

Drunk or not, Dora was far from impressed. We were both of the same old-fashioned and perfectly right opinion that men should behave like gentlemen when they encountered a lady, even if said lady was as inebriated as a fart.

Dora let go of the collar of his fleece jacket that she had been using to steady herself, and adopted her best "don't mess with me, mate" tone.

"I beg your pudding, sir?"

I noticed that Jake had returned behind the bar, put down the tea towel he'd been using to polish glasses and shot a concerned look towards us, ready to intervene if necessary. But Dora was made of sterner stuff; a prematurely bald man in his early thirties with a bad attitude was not going to get the better of her.

"Get stuffed, mate, stuffed with all the trimmings. That's no way to speak to a lady, and I am a lady, but you most certainly are not a gentleman."

"A lady?" Mr Beanie Hat gave us the most scathing look I'd ever encountered. "I'm sorry, love, but I don't see no ladies around her. All I see is a couple of silly old women."

He fixed his beady eyes right on Dora, his eyebrows slanting aggressively.

"And one of these women is in the most ridiculous get-up I've ever seen, making a right show of herself. Grandma needs to get home for a cocoa and calm down as soon as possible if she don't want no trouble."

Dora's smile was as enigmatic as the Mona Lisa's as she swung her hefty handbag right into his downstairs department. He went down like the final pin in the bowling alley, the wind well and truly taken out of his sails. What was it they said? The bigger they came, the harder they fell. Well, he went down like a sack of King Edwards, and it was high time we got the hell out of dodge.

I half dragged my sister up, her handbag which had spilled across the floor and all its contents needed scooping up and flinging back in. There were bottles of pills – her many supplements she insisted on taking – along with items of jewellery and, bizarrely, a half-eaten packet sandwich which was more fluff than filling. I finally dragged her out of The Swan as she regally waved to a stunned Jake, hiccuping as she went.

"Toodleoo, Jake, we will miss you muchly, but we will miss your martinis even more."

The heavy oak door swung shut behind us with a bang that echoed in the silence of the night. The sharp frosty air sobered me up like a slap in the face. I hooked my arm through Dora's to lead her on the short walk home.

"Come on, we'd better make our way. You do know that was a little uncalled-for, Dora? You can't just assault a random man in the pub with your oversized tote because he was rude to you."

"No, it was completely called for. That's the problem, these days; there's no respect any more. Once you're old, it's like you have no value. And anyway, what am I talking about? I'm not even old, I'm in the prime of my life. But he treated us like there was something wrong with us enjoying ourselves because were over sixty. And calling me Grandma: that sealed his fate for sure. He earned himself a hoof in the balls for that, good and proper and no mistake."

Her words were unwaveringly confident, but I couldn't fail to notice the tears collecting in the corners of her eyes. It seemed the altercation had affected her more than she was admitting. Either that or the super-strength cocktails were making her a little maudlin too.

We fell into step beside each other, each lost in our own thoughts. Suddenly I felt my mobile phone vibrate in my coat pocket. It was rather late for messages, so I felt inclined to check it.

"Hi Mum, sorry for messaging so late, there's no problem at all but would it be OK if Lila and I popped around to see you tomorrow after lunchtime? We have a favour to ask."

Of course I was delighted at the prospect of seeing my daughter. I had a real soft spot for Lila, her best friend, but as was my nature I couldn't help but feel a fizz of apprehension. What could possibly be this favour they wanted to ask?

I was still mulling this over as Dora and I wandered down the road homeward bound. Suddenly I felt her sharp elbow nudge me in the ribs.

"Ouch, what the heck?"

I turned to face my sister, who had an excited glint in her eyes. She was pointing further down the street. "Look, Evie... look who it is."

I squinted into the darkness. What was she talking about? It was then that I saw the handsome *Independent*-reading gentleman from earlier making his way towards a smart car parked further down the road. We watched as he opened the door, slid his long, elegant legs into the passenger's side and reached over to drop a tender kiss on the cheek of the driver. A man.

"See?" Dora announced triumphantly. "I'm always right. I told you so, didn't I? He just loves the cock!"

Chapter 6

• ❤ • ❤ • ❤ • ❤ • ❤ •

The sun was high in the beautiful cloudless sky, and I was meandering along the pure white sands of the most stunning beach, hand in hand with my perfect man. Daniel Craig smiled lovingly down at me, his clear blue eyes crinkling at the corners. He was dressed casually in slacks and linen shirt unbuttoned to the waist, while I was elegantly chic in capri pants and a Marks & Spencer swing top of muted pinks and taupe.

"Evelyn, my darling, it has always been you." Daniel stopped dead in his tracks and turned towards me, his eyes darkening with unbridled passion and desire. "Since my first days as Bond I have only ever dreamt of you. I tried to fight it, I really did, drank far too many martinis trying to erase you from my memory, but it was no good. Even Connery said I was a fool, and I should forget you. I'm embarrassed to admit I punched him in the chin for that. I *must* have you, I simply *must*. Please say you will be mine, my love; to have you by my side for eternity would make all my dreams come true."

He leaned down to kiss me tenderly, but I put my hand to his full lips to prevent ours from touching.

"But Daniel, your wife, your child; I could never break up a family." I turned away from his embrace, my shoulders sagging. "And even if you were single, I'm years older than you; what would people say?"

"Pah, my darling. Who cares what fools would say? What is age but a mere number when there is a love like ours. I know I must leave my wife; it's regrettable, but a passion like ours comes along only once in a lifetime, and who are we to deny it? Our love is like the angels singing its utter perfection, its fate, its destiny... well... it's simply the best."

He pulled me into his arms once more, desire swimming deeply in his eyes. I felt helpless against their magnetic pull so felt myself surrendering to the inevitability of our kiss.

Suddenly a herd of cats were running towards us at speed, sand flying, whiskers twitching, tails poker straight behind them and razor-like claws ready to do some serious damage. Front and centre was Feline Dion, and she looked ready to cause a right ruckus. She was a snarling blur of tortoiseshell fur as she dashed towards us, stopping to give an ungodly wail before launching herself at Daniel.

A cry of pure anguish ripped from my throat as Feline ripped into his. My romantic rendezvous was turning into a bad B horror movie before my very eyes.

Suddenly the beach was gone, Daniel was gone, and thank the Lord the zombie cats were gone. Disorientated and unsure of my surroundings, I looked tentatively around me in the gloom. The semi-darkness surrounded me like a heavy cloak, almost pinning down my limbs beneath the weight of the duvet. I was in bed. I must have been asleep. Scrambling to my left I felt for the plastic alarm clock that had lived on the bedside table for years: 10:20 a.m. I never slept so late, not unless I was ill. Was I ill? I certainly felt like I might be. My head was woozy and there seemed to be a rock concert playing just behind my eyes.

I gingerly rose from my pit and opened the heavy drapes to let some light sweep into the room. What would the neighbours think with my bedroom curtains closed at this time? It was unheard of for me to sleep so late.

I had been dreaming, a weird fever dream brought on by an ungodly amount of booze. But what a dream it had been. Although I knew it hadn't been real, the memory of being embraced like that remained imprinted on my heart. It had felt wonderful, really wonderful. What didn't feel quite so wonderful was realising that for the first time in years I was suffering from an almighty hangover.

I couldn't help pondering on why such a perfect dream had descended suddenly into such a nightmare. And what had woken me with such a start? It was at that moment I heard the sound of cats once more: the blood-curdling wailing straight out of my dream. But this time it was emanating from somewhere outside my imagination, probably inside the house. To be precise, it seemed to be coming from the kitchen.

It wasn't a bunch of feral strays after all: it was in fact my sister singing along at the top of her lungs to Tina Turner blasting out of the portable radio.

"You're simply the best…better than all the rest."

I fought the impulse to stuff my pillow over my head and attempt to return to dreamland. The deafening din sounded just like a bunch of stray alley cats, if such cats had been let loose on karaoke.

This simply wouldn't do. I had the most horrendous headache. I *never* woke up with a headache and I *never* slept so late. I prided myself on being an early riser and "up with the larks", as my mother would say. I was a creature of habit, and it was my habit to be dressed and at the kitchen table eating my toast and marmalade by 8 a.m., listening to the *Today* programme on Radio 4. To sleep in until after 10 a.m. was unheard of for me. But then again, drinking martinis like my life depended on it wasn't my usual behaviour either.

I couldn't believe I had a hangover. What was I thinking, getting into a state like that at my age? Even in my sixties, my little sister could still lead me astray. But part of me couldn't deny the fact that I had enjoyed myself; had even enjoyed what had been lacking in my life for the longest time...fun.

With much more effort than was the norm, I struggled into my pink fluffy dressing gown and wedged my feet into a pair of burgundy zippy slippers. I had to keep sitting down as the waves of nausea that assaulted my stomach were reminiscent of an ill-advised trip from Hull to Rotterdam on a ferry crossing, back in the 1980s. The sea sickness had been brutal, and this felt pretty much the same. It took me over twenty minutes and a Herculean effort to make my way gingerly downstairs to put on a pot of coffee and fix my toast and marmalade.

My mood didn't improve when clapping eyes on the state of my lovely kitchen. It wasn't lovely any more; no, now it was an absolute mess. We must have decided to have a late-night snack of cheese on toast when we'd got home from the pub. There was grated cheese all over the worktops and the pickle jar was missing its lid. In sympathy, I felt my top might well blow at any moment too.

My sister was completely oblivious to my presence as she carried on her caterwauling, her hips swaying from side to side as she sang; well, "sang" might be a bit of a stretch. I couldn't be sure if that was what she was in fact doing, or had she stubbed her toe on the kitchen counter and was wailing in agony? She was dressed in a black vest top decorated with smiling avocados and a pair of pale pink silky French knickers. It was not suitable attire for breakfast, in my opinion.

"Dora, would you look at the mess!"

She jumped slightly and thankfully the singing ceased as she turned to face me. My eardrums were considerably happier, even if I wasn't.

"Oh, I know, Evie, it seems we were ravenous when we got in. We must have been talking to way past two. I know because I sent a cheeky WhatsApp to a gentleman friend at quarter past, so I know I was still awake then. It seems we polished off half a pound of your best aged Somerset cheddar on toast. But don't worry, once we have our brekkie, I'll get the whole place shipshape and Bristol fashion in a jiffy."

I could do without the nautical talk, especially as my feeling of seasickness seemed to have returned. We had been up talking until after 2 a.m.? No wonder I was resembling one of the walking dead in nightwear this morning.

I collapsed on my kitchen chair with a gusty sigh. I needed a little rest before I could even think about preparing my breakfast.

"I've been up a while myself, but I thought you might need a bit of a lie-in, so I just let you be."

My sister was looking as fresh as a daisy. How was that even possible when I felt like a trampled dandelion in comparison?

There seemed to be a slight buzzing noise coming from my head. I gave it a little shake to clear it, but to no avail. It took me several seconds to realise the noise wasn't in fact inside my skull; it was coming from the combination oven in the corner of the kitchen. Plus, the delicious aroma wafting from it was a bit of a giveaway too.

"Are you cooking something, Dora?"

"Ah yes, I'm always starvacious when I've had a wee drink the night before. I didn't think you'd mind if I fixed myself a hot breakfast. I can't be doing with all that dry cereal that you seem to favour; it's like chewing a bowl of Feline's cat litter."

I was nothing if not the gracious host, so I smiled thinly at my sibling and nodded my head in agreement. Truth be told, I was low-key annoyed; the kitchen was already a bombsite without adding more mess to the mix, and honestly I was rather proud of my selection of boxed cereals. It was so extensive there must have been at least one she would have liked. My larder bore the whole complement from Mr Kellogg's: everything from the ubiquitous cornflakes to the bowel-friendly All-Bran. I even had a box of Frosties for when Jacob came to stay, but clearly it was not cereal that my sister fancied as her morning repast.

I sniffed the air again like a hungry bloodhound. The smell was making my tummy rumble: meaty and cheesy and possibly double-stuffed crust.

"Are you cooking a pizza? Why on earth would you cook a pizza at 10 a.m.?" My voice was high and shrill. I sounded like one of the bolshy types from *Coronation*

Street and probably resembled one too, especially in my dressing gown and messy morning hair.

Conversely my sister spoke softly and slowly as if explaining something to a young child or someone of less intelligence than herself.

"Well, when you think about it, it's just cheese and meat and bread, so technically it's no different from having a continental breakfast; and you do love one of those on holiday. It's just heated up, that's all, so it slides down better with a mug of tea."

I suppose on some level what she was saying made some sense. But really who put a pizza in the oven for breakfast? It just wasn't the done thing.

I slowly rose from my chair feeling in my nineties rather than sixties, and filled the kettle from the combination tap. I was going to have instant coffee this morning; I really didn't have the energy to grind beans. I felt my gears were being ground as it was. I popped a couple of slices of wholemeal into the toaster and flopped down onto the chair again, exhausted from my endeavours.

"Are you going to have a slice of the pizza with me when it's out?"

I shook my head firmly. "Absolutely not, I'll be having my toast and marmalade as always."

"OK, well once I've finished my brekkie I'm going to have a bath; a nice soak is just what my old bones need. You know you really should have some of the pizza, live a little; marmalade is so boringly basic. Honestly, you're like the poster child for the breakfast of the elderly."

I felt outraged. How dare she malign my beloved breakfast conserve.

"It absolutely is not the breakfast of the elderly; I've been eating toast and marmalade since my early twenties."

Her eyebrows rose as if I had just proven her point perfectly. "I know you have, and until today I didn't even realise it came in more flavours than just orange. Your pantry is coming down with jars of the stuff: lime, lemon, grapefruit even pineapple marmalade, though why any bugger would want to eat that is beyond me."

I scowled at her before picking up the post from the table where Dora must have deposited it in a messy heap. Same boring stack of brown and white envelopes as usual. I thumbed through it and then put it back, this time in a neat pile. I couldn't be bothered with opening any of it in my current state.

"Anyway, never mind talking about my collection of marmalades. Can you just make sure you don't use too much water in your bath? Last time it was so deep when you got in that it caused a tidal wave and dripped right through to the kitchen. I fancy one too this morning and the emersion takes an age to heat, so just have a couple of inches in the bottom or I will marmalise you!"

I held my half empty jar of thick-cut Seville in front of her face to elucidate my point.

Dora shot me a bright smile. "Good one, sis, and yes, only a couple of inches in the bottom is more than enough, as the bishop said to the chorus girl."

She roared with laughter, her shoulders rocking as she skipped over to the oven, reaching for the oven mitts to extract the perfectly cooked pizza. I had to admit it did look good and the aroma was making my mouth water; my stomach let out another little betraying rumble of hunger. I coughed to cover the sound and got busy spreading marmalade on my rather burnt toast.

The sound of the butter knife against the toast and the noise of my sister chewing the pizza crust was enough to make me feel my head might explode and possibly leave little fragments all over the kitchen, along with the grated cheddar and chunks of chutney.

It took Dora all of two minutes to demolish the entire 12 inches. "Well, that hit the spot perfectly." She let out a little satisfied belch and rose to her feet, making for the door while leaving her plate with a few crumbs abandoned on the table. "Right, bath time. Do you happen to know where my make-up bag is, by any chance? It's got my face in it, and you know me, I'm not at my best without my slap on."

"For some reason, you left it on the coffee table in the lounge yesterday. Can you please keep it in the bathroom or your bedroom in future? Please make sure you don't keep helping yourself to my stuff: my skin's very particular, and so am I about you using my lotion."

I had found her two fingers deep in my Estée Lauder the other day and had not been impressed.

"Yes, sorry about that. I couldn't find my bottle of Nivea so didn't think you'd mind too much."

She started singing again. Her dulcet tones were enough to tip my headache into a full-blown migraine.

"Would you just be quiet, Dora?" I snapped. "I'm used to peace and quiet and a little radio of a morning, not X Factor auditions; my head is absolutely killing me."

Dora stopped in her tracks, turned and sank down in the chair opposite me. She was clearly in no mad rush to join her bubble bath.

"Sorry, sis, I'm just naturally a morning person. I sometimes forget not everyone else is."

I liked to believe I was a morning person too, but being so perky after the amount of booze we'd guzzled just couldn't be normal, could it?

"Sorry for snapping, Dora, it's just I have this headache from hell and a sore throat too. I think I might be coming down with that cold that's doing the rounds."

Dora gave me a knowing look. "Nah, I think your sore throat will just be from the olive stone I tried to Heimlich out of you last night at the bar. I thought you were a goner for a minute. If I remember correctly, your face went the exact same shade of purple as the beetroot in your goat's cheese tart and salad."

I blanched at this. Things must have been even more rowdy than I remembered. I had no recollection of choking on an errant olive, or of us walking home, or of us scoffing down enough cheese and white sliced to put us into food comas. There was also something else I had forgotten, something that was niggling at the corner of my mind. What was it? I was sure there was something happening today. I felt convinced of it. But for the life of me I just couldn't remember. I reached for my diary from the top drawer of the mahogany bureau and checked it carefully. I was a stickler for recording every social event and appointment in my paper diary, but there was nothing in for Wednesday 16th March. There was a new series of *Vera* starting that evening, but apart from that there was nothing planned. So what was tugging at my memory then?

"I thought I might pop out to the baker's on the High Street and get a few sweet treats for the girls coming. I seem to have eaten all the sugar in the house, whoops, naughty old me." Dora giggled as she smacked her hand as if scolding herself. "Can't have my favourite niece come around and not spoil her with something yummy! All you've got are those low-calorie wholewheat things, like chewing on a piece of garden decking; I wouldn't give those to my worst enemy."

She was right. She had polished off anything delicious that had been in the house; even the Belgian chocolates that I had won at the bridge club Christmas raffle. OK, my high-fibre sugar-free biscuits might not be mouth-watering as such, but at least they were healthier, and they made sure your bowels were regular, and you were drinking your daily water allowance. You needed a whole pot of tea just to get one of the buggers down, they were so dry.

But what had Dora been saying something about her favourite niece? Lottie was her only niece, and that was it! I remembered now. I'd got a message from my daughter when we were walking home from the pub saying she was coming to the house later today with her friend Lila as they wanted to ask me something. I checked the kitchen clock: it was now just on 11 a.m., but Lottie had said they would come after lunch.

An unsolicited thought popped into my head. What if I went back to bed for a bit? I couldn't do that, could I? I had been doing a few things out of the ordinary since my sister had come to stay, so really what was one more? I headed back to bed for an hour, the siren call of my comfy duvet and cool pillow just too much for me to resist.

I left the mess in the kitchen exactly as it was, shutting the door firmly behind it. Out of sight, out of mind. I was not one normally to leave a room messy, but I simply had to get my head down. I sank back against my pillow with a contented sigh as I heard the distant rumbling of the bath filling, accompanied by Dora who was now singing what I believed to be Iron Maiden.

I awoke from a dreamless sleep with a start: it was the front door being slammed shut. Dora must be back from the shops.

I rose from my cozy bed for the second time that day, feeling a little better but still rather like Nosferatu rising from his tomb. The bedside clock confirmed it was just after 2 p.m.

Dora was in the kitchen, the radio on once more, but this time she was listening to Steve Wright on Radio 2 and thankfully she wasn't singing. Also thankfully, the kitchen was now pristine. Wonders would never cease. So contrary to what I had previously believed, Dora could actually get handy with a cloth and detergent when needed.

"Ah, there you are, Evie. I must say you're looking a lot brighter than before."

"Thank you, I must say I'm feeling a lot better. And talking about brighter, the kitchen looks like a new pin."

"Yes, I gave it a quick once-over after I had my bath. See, you just thought I was a goddess; you didn't realise I was a domestic one too."

Dora was busying herself sorting out a selection of the most decadent-looking cream cakes on our Grandma's antique crystal cake stand. Her round face bore a look of complete concentration, her tongue jutting out of the side of her mouth. My sister took the matter of baked goods very seriously. Cream cakes were one of her greatest passions in life, and they needed to be arranged perfectly so the first sight would always delight.

"Don't they look amazing, Evie? I can't wait to sink my teeth into one of those eclairs."

I had to admit they did look mighty good. But not for me, thank you very much. I had no plans to consume the high-fibre wheat biscuits Dora had scoffed at, although never actually scoffed, but I did have an unopened packet of rich tea biscuits, that my sister had also scorned; a couple of them would do me quite nicely.

Dora picked up the stand reverentially as if she was lifting the crown jewels.

"I'll just take these into the lounge ready for the girls' arrival. I've also got a couple of iced fingers for us for later in front of *Vera*. Do you remember how we used to love those with Nanny?"

I did. My mind was instantly back to warm summer days many decades before, with home-made lemonade and cakes in the garden.

Dora looked wistful for a second. "Yes, I've always loved a cheeky finger in the garden."

Chapter 7

"Do you think we should have one now while we wait?"

Dora had been eyeing up the plate of cream cakes the way an oily-suited businessman would eyeball an exotic dancer, desire clear in her bright green eyes.

"I think those vanilla slices are drying out a touch."

I shook my head firmly. "Absolutely not; we're waiting for Lottie and Li..."

The shrill ring of the doorbell cut me off mid-sentence, before I had a chance to finish. Dora's eyes lit up with obvious delight.

"Oh goody, they're here, shall I let them in?"

I nodded my head. To be honest, I was still feeling a little delicate, unlike my sister who bounded to the front door with all the exuberance of an excitable puppy.

I heard her cursing slightly as she struggled to locate the key to unlock the door, followed by a startling screech of delight. I couldn't hear the visitors apart from a few muffled words. Clearly Dora was embracing them both to her ample bosom.

"Here they are."

Dora walked back into the lounge, a delighted smile lighting up her face. Lottie and Lila followed in her wake, also smiling.

My heart soared as I clapped eyes on my daughter. She was looking good. Life was treating her well. Everything in her demeanour and body language was relaxed and radiant. No longer did she have the perpetual crinkled look of concern that had once haunted her pretty features, the gloomy heaviness that had settled above her like a rain cloud. No, now she was as sunny and light as a summer's day. This lifted my mood and made me feel lighter too.

It was amazing what a new career and a wonderful new man could do. Giving her philandering ex-husband Daniel the heave-ho had been the best thing she had ever done. I gave her a warm hug; my hand patted her blonde curls.

"Hello, darling, you're looking beautiful."

She returned my hug tightly.

"I'd like to say the same, Mum, but you look a little under the weather. Are you feeling alright?"

Dora reached over to give her niece's arm a reassuring rub.

"Don't you worry about your old Mum, Lots, she's absolutely fine. She just had a little too much of the lady fuel last night; nothing one of these cream cakes and a gallon of tea won't cure. But she's right about one thing: you do look smashing, love."

She gave her niece another twinkly smile. It did my heart good to see how clearly my sister adored her.

"I was overjoyed when I heard you'd got rid of that hubby of yours. I always said to your Mum that if there was an Arrogant Twat party, then Daniel would have been the founding member. So when I learned you'd given him his marching orders, I must say I had a little dance of delight around my dining room with Feline Dion in my arms. And when I saw the stuff about him online, well let's just say I nearly broke my toe in my haste to get to the comments section on Facebook."

She let out one of her booming laughs that I'm sure could be heard in the next village or three away.

"Anyway, your Mum says you've got a lovely young man now. Leo, eh? Quite the looker apparently and a handsome bank balance to match. It sounds like you've landed with your arse in the butter, my love. But to be fair, anything would be an upgrade on your ex; he really was a festering old dog turd of a man."

Lottie blushed slightly, her cheeks tinted pink; it made her appear even prettier. There was no love lost between her and her ex, but she still didn't like to slag him off too much. Even though he had chosen to eat out on a bit of scrag end when there was a beautiful hot dinner waiting for him at home, if you catch my drift. They had tried to keep things civil for the sake of my grandson. Well, Lottie did anyway; Daniel was only ever concerned with himself.

Lottie was nodding her head slowly; clearly there was much she could say, but she still wanted to remain somewhat loyal to her ex.

"Well yes, Daniel could be an arrogant git, that's for sure. I was heartbroken when I found out he was cheating with that girl from his office, but now I realise it was the best thing that could ever have happened, I'm just so happy now: happy with life, happy with work, and more than happy with my Leo."

Lila nodded in agreement and winked at her best friend. "Yes, you wouldn't have believed it at the time, but that Roxy did you a right favour in the long run. She didn't steal your man, she took over your problem."

"Amen to that." Dora's voice was somewhat distorted by the chocolate éclair she was snaffling, a look of rapture evident on her face.

I cast her a reproachful look. We hadn't even poured the tea yet.

Lottie cleared her throat; I could tell she was keen to steer the conversation away from talk of her love life.

"Oh, so you've been leading Mum astray on a week-night, have you, Auntie Dora? You know Mum likes to be tucked up in bed with a mug of cocoa and Hercule Poirot by 10:30 pm."

My sister clapped her hands together in delight. "I bet she does, the filthy minx."

Dora was off laughing again, little bits of choux pastry pebbledashing the front of her lime green cardigan – another one of her bold fashion statements. She helped herself to a cup of tea from the porcelain pot to wash down the crumbs before continuing.

"I'm afraid I did lead her a little astray last night, so guilty as charged."

I threw my sister a stern warning glance. There was absolutely no need for her to do a full post mortem on the carryings on the previous night.

To distract her, I poured the tea and handed round the cups. Lila accepted hers with thanks before taking a dainty sip. It beggared belief how she could be wearing such a vibrant scarlet shade of lipstick, yet not a trace of it transferred to the rim of the cup. It must be some kind of voodoo or make-up that was seriously outside my price range.

"And how are things going with Seb?"

I had met Sebastian: Lila's colleague, and the man she'd been dating for a while. He really was a very sweet man: quiet, with impeccable manners, and clearly devoted to his glamorous girlfriend. He had loved her from the sidelines for many years, and now they were officially an item he still seemed rather in awe of her; as if he couldn't quite believe his luck.

There was a twinkle in Lila's clear blue eyes. Like Lottie, she was in a happy place too. She ran her hand through her glossy shoulder-length blonde hair; it fell perfectly back in place as if it had a memory all of its own. It was fair to say that Lila Glover cut a very glamorous figure.

"Oh, he's an absolute doll, Mrs W, no bother at all. I know I can be a lot to handle at times, but he honestly seems to think everything I do is perfection."

She made a little high-pitched snorting sound, but even that couldn't make her appear unappealing. I'm sure if I had made that sound, I would have been mistaken for a side of bacon.

"It's unbelievable really, but true: he never so much as rolls his eyes at me when I make him turn off the sci-fi channel to watch *Don't tell the bride.*"

Maybe he was hoping the programme might give her a bit of a hint matrimonial-wise, that he wanted to get the woman of his dreams down the aisle.

Dora's head was bobbing up and down like a nodding dog at this point.

"You're lucky there, Lila. It sounds like Seb's a definite keeper; there's not many men can take on a firecracker like us. My Ossie could, and we made the prefect pair: me the wildly exotic and emotional one, and him so calm and cool as a cucumber."

She took a long sip of her tea before continuing. "Do you think this could be second time lucky and you might marry him?"

Lila choked on her tea, her composure for once completely gone.

"No fear. Once is more than enough for me. I've never been a fan of wedding cake anyway; give me a big chunk of tiramisu any day."

"Yeah, you're right there, love. Marriage is like a lottery; you're not guaranteed to win it, no matter how promising it seems. Mind you, I hit the jackpot with my Ossie; I wouldn't be so lucky to get that again. That's why I just keep my gentleman friends nice and casual, nothing too heavy. I do have one fella I see quite regularly, just to get my loyalty card stamped, if you know what I mean."

There was no need for the salacious wink. We all knew exactly what she meant in referring to her neighbour Keith. I dreaded to think what went on at their Scrabble and sherry shindigs on his formal leather recliner.

"Well, whatever you and this new fella of yours are doing, it's looking good on you. It's not just my niece who's glowing; you look as radiant as a twenty-year-old. What's your secret? Have you got a painting hidden away in your attic we should know about?"

Lottie chimed in at this, grinning at her friend. "No, but she's got just about every anti-ageing remedy known to man in her bathroom cabinet."

Lila held her hands up in mock defeat. "Can't deny that, but if they actually worked, I'd be back in primary school. Enough about me; you're looking fabulous too, Dora."

I smiled at them all. It was so nice when women complimented each other. There was so much negativity in the world these days, it was good to lift each other up.

Dora batted her hand in the direction of Lila with a snort of her own. Much more inelegant than Lila's had been.

"Nonsense, child, I'm as wrinkled as an old walnut. But you know what? I've earned every one of my lines, and I wouldn't change a thing. I've had the best life ever."

I paid close attention to my sister in that moment. She was clearly thinking back over her years, a wistful smile playing at the corner of her mouth. Could I say the same? I didn't regret my life, of course I didn't. But it hadn't always been fun being the steady sensible one; the one that got depended upon; the dull one, in fact.

I had loved being a mother to Lottie, a wife to Andrew. But the last few years? I sometimes felt I was just treading water, stuck in limbo waiting for something. But waiting for what? Death? Surely not, there must be more to my life than that. Another chapter just waiting to be written. I sincerely hoped so.

I gave my head a little shake. I needed to stop being so maudlin. Probably the after-effects of over-exuberance on the cocktails last night. What did the young ones call it? Hangxiety?

I watched my sister help herself to a jam and cream scone. So far, she was the only one tucking in. Dora could never be referred to as dull or dependable, especially in her over-indulgence in Devonshire scones.

I rose slowly from my chair; with every hour I was feeling a little better, but still wasn't back to fighting fit by any stretch of the imagination.

"I'm going to make some more tea if everyone would like another cup."

"Well, I'd rather have a nice gi....."

Dora stopped abruptly. It was obvious to me that she was going to suggest a hair of the dog by way of a gin and tonic, before remembering she had drained the last of the bottle the previous night. "Ah yes, Evie, tea would be lovely. Industrial strength for me, please. After last night, I reckon we both probably need it."

"So where did the two of you go last night?" Lottie leaned forward in her chair, keen to know the details of the previous night's shenanigans.

"Nowhere really; we just took a little stroll down to the Swan and Key and had a very nice dinner."

My tone was nonchalant as I carried the tea tray out of the room to the kitchen.

"How lovely. Was it as quiet as always?"

I shot a warning look at Dora as I left the room. There was no need for Lottie to know that we had both got horrendously drunk and then her Auntie had decked a man with her ten-ton handbag for daring to disrespect her.

I could clearly hear my sister's voice as I busied myself in the kitchen, filling the kettle from the combination tap and adding milk to the jug.

"Yes, pretty quiet, I'd say. We just had one too many drinks while reminiscing about the past, but an uneventful night overall."

I was glad my sister was being non-committal; she clearly could keep her counsel once in a while. Just a pity she didn't do it more often.

"Can I help you with anything, Mrs W?"

I turned with a start to face Lila, who had followed me into the kitchen. She was now propped up against the fridge freezer, scrolling through her phone. Work, no doubt; she was one of these high-flyer lawyer types. I was always a little in awe of her. Although twenty years younger than me, she could still make me feel a little awkward and unsophisticated. She didn't mean to, of course; she was in truth a lovely girl: headstrong and sure of herself, and not likely to ever feel intimidated by anything or anyone, and that was something to be admired. "A bit of a pistol", my Andrew used to call her.

"No, my dear, that's quite alright. I'm just fixing the tea. Actually, on second thoughts, would you be a sweetheart and just reach up to the top cupboard?"

I gestured to the cupboard above the mugs and glasses. "My rich tea biscuits are up there. I keep them high up so they're difficult to get at; less chance of the temptation to snack. Doesn't always work, of course."

She quickly slipped her phone into the pocket of her smart slate-coloured trousers. They looked as soft as a cloud and probably cost her a small fortune.

She gave me a little wink. "No need for you to cut down on the biccies, Mrs W. You've got the figure of a model, and no mistake."

I blushed, despite myself. Then she effortlessly reached up to the top cupboard and located the blue packet with ease, hardly having to stretch at all. But I couldn't help but watch with concern. It seemed these days that I could pull a muscle simply by waking up in the morning.

"Careful, dear."

"Don't you worry about me. I'm not scared of heights. Have you seen my shoes?"

I glanced down at her glossy black stilettos. They had a pair of heels on them that could serve as a lethal weapon.

"I like my men like I like my shoes: absolutely nothing under five inches."

Dora had just appeared with the empty cake plate and deposited it in the sink. I couldn't help but wonder if she'd polished off the whole plate by herself.

"You and me both, my darling. If they're not packing down south, they can just keep walking. But not in our high heels, eh?"

Lila laughed along with her, but a look of alarm passed briefly across her glacial features. I knew she must have been thinking back to her disastrous date, the one when her charming beau had appeared out of the bathroom resplendent in her sexy slingbacks. Lila had told me this story herself when Lottie and she had taken me out for brunch to Olive Affair a few weeks back. But Dora didn't know about that, just an off the cuff comment that hit a bit close to home.

I couldn't help thinking, and not for the first time, how much alike Dora and Lila were. One could be mistaken for thinking *they* were related. They certainly had the same confidence and craic, even if that craic was as coarse as a hair vest at times.

Once the tea had been brewed and the biscuits arranged on my best china, we headed back to the lounge. Steaming hot mugs were handed round. I couldn't help but notice my biscuits went untouched, well, apart from the broken half I nibbled on.

"Biscuit, anyone?"

I offered the plate around for a second time. I had always prided myself on being the best host. Even Dora shook her head, obviously none too impressed by them.

Lottie shook her head too as the plate was proffered to her, the blonde highlights in her shoulder-length locks catching the light that streamed in through the bay window.

"Not for me, Mum, thanks, I'm saving my appetite. Leo's making me a curry tonight."

She stretched her legs out in front of her so we could all get a look at her flat nude-coloured ballet pumps.

"Unlike Lila, I'm wearing my flats. Leo gets a bit gung ho with the spices when he's cooking, and some of his curries are hot enough to blow a hole in the roof of your mouth. Honestly, they could strip the palate straight off you. So I only want one part of my body to be burning tonight: my mouth, and definitely not my feet."

"Well, two parts," Dora corrected her. "If his curry is Madras hot like you say it is, I'll be betting your arse will be burning too."

"Too right." Lottie laughed in agreement. "My arse will be burning like molten lava."

I shot my sister another one of my famous warning looks. It was not like Lottie to use such coarse language, but I knew the reason. Once in the company of Dora, it seemed like all bets were off. She just seemed to bring the naughty side out in everyone.

"No fear of that with Seb, he's a very basic eater. The hottest curry I've tempted him to try is a bhuna, and even that had him nearly convulsing and gulping milk like a newborn. But to be fair he comes out in a sweat if he sucks an extra strong mint, so I don't know what I was thinking."

Dora was shaking her head. "Oooh, I love a bit of spice in *all* things, if you know what I mean? And why be boring when you can be spicy and extra hot? Not like our Evie here, a liberal splash of Worcestershire sauce on her cheese on toast is about as adventurous as it gets. Heaven knows what she'd do if she came face to face with a huge portion of Hari Mirch."

Never mind Seb convulsing over his curry; Lottie and Lila could barely breathe for laughing at my sister's teasing of me. I just didn't understand why Dora felt the need to bring the conversation down to smutty talk every opportunity she got. I had no idea what a Hari Mirch was, and had no intention of finding out.

Lottie grabbed a tissue from her shoulder bag and dabbed at her eye make-up, clearly concerned it was sliding down her cheeks.

"Anyway, much as Lila and I would love to sit here and chat about Auntie Dora's sexploits all day..."

"I'll say," Lila interrupted.

Lottie continued, her composure restored. "Mum... the reason Lila and I are here is we want to ask you a favour."

Here it was: what their visit had been leading up to. All the small talk had just been building up to this very moment.

Chapter 8

I put my teacup down on the arm of the chair and sat up straight: as if I was about to face a firing squad or a serious telling off from the headmaster.

Lila mirrored my body language and with a quick cough to clear her throat she began.

"You see, Mrs W, I've met this young girl through work; she's a lovely lass, went to school with my Thomas. She's twenty years old now, and been in a relationship with this lad Alfie for a few years. He's a bit of a bad sort and she's fallen out with her parents over it all. She's in a real pickle and needs a place to stay for a few days. I would have her myself of course, but as I could be representing her as my client, there would be conflict of interest..."

Lottie chimed in that point. "And I would have her at mine, but there's just not the room, not with Leo there half the time and all my clothing stockpiled up everywhere. I even thought of Ivy, as she would normally relish the company, and she's missed me and Jacob since we've moved; but she's putting Jo and David up for a couple of days as they're having the kitchen knocked into the lounge to open the downstairs up and there's dust everywhere."

Jo and David had bought Lottie's old house. I couldn't understand why anyone would want to mess about with such a nice old property, but then again people always liked to stamp their own mark on a place. Make their home a representation of themselves.

Lottie smiled to herself, her eyes twinkling. It was clear that she was thinking fondly of her old neighbour.

"I know Ivy's enjoying having them to stay, but she's enjoying having Mr Scruffy, their little Border Collie, even more. That poor pooch has his legs walked off him the number of times she drags him out to have a gander at what's going on in the neighbourhood. So unfortunately, that's me out of options for where Bella could stay; and with Lila not being able to have her, we thought of you as our obvious next choice."

Lila went on to explain the whole situation to us. It seemed that this young girl, Anabella or Bella for short, had fallen in love with the local bad boy. Although I had always been a sensible sort when it came to all things romantic and would never fall for the wily charms of a ne'er-do-well scoundrel myself, I knew that this was common with plenty of women.

There was a certain appeal in that sort of fella, a mistaken fancy that you could perhaps change them or somehow save them from themselves. Apparently, this Alfred was not keen on changing; and after leaving school, or rather being expelled, his bad behaviour had worsened to serious criminality.

He was now on a disturbing and dangerous path: dealing and consuming hard drugs and running with a crowd that would make the Krays appear like the Chuckle Brothers. Bella had realised much too late that he wasn't the hero in her love story. He would never change; and she was in far too deep.

She loved Alfie, but he certainly didn't love her. She was just another accessory, like the many gold chains he wore around his neck. He treated her with little to no respect, openly ridiculed her in front of his friends. Although they rented a little house in the estate his parents lived in, he would order her daily to leave "his" home in the vilest language. However, when she did eventually pluck up the courage to leave, all hell had broken loose. She was his property until he decided otherwise. Nobody left Alfie Dodds. Nobody.

But it was clear that Bella shouldn't be merely portrayed as a victim: she was so much more than that. She was made of sterner stuff then he had ever imagined. Leave she had, and point blank refused to return, even with promises of him changing and the allure of lavish gifts.

She stayed strong, returned the gifts and blocked him on her phone. Alfie wasn't used to not getting his own way. He ruled his local neighbourhood like a hateful despot, and even at his young age was feared throughout the estate and beyond. Even his own family didn't cross him. So, Alfie had turned *really* nasty, He found other ways to harass her: bombarding her with abusive emails, turning up at her family home and making a nuisance of himself. It had caused a rift with her own family, and she could no longer stay with them either.

Then he decided to play his trump card. He had intimate photographs of Bella on his phone that she had sent him at his request in happier times, when she believed she could trust him. She had felt uneasy sending them, but

Alfie could be so charming and persuasive when he wanted to be, and she had believed he loved her too.

Now he was using these images to try to control her. And unless she returned to him, he was going to send them out to everyone: her family, her friends, even put them on adult sites for the whole world and his dog to see. Anything to get her back, and more importantly to get his own way and not lose face.

I was shocked. I could see from Dora's expression that she was too.

"He sounds like a right nasty piece of work; it sounds like he needs a right good kick in the sticky bun."

She reached into the pocket of her voluminous maxi skirt to extract a paper bag with an iced finger inside.

"Speaking of which, I'll just take little bite of this; shock and stress always makes me want to eat."

I raised my eyebrows at her. What didn't?

Lila was nodding at Dora. "You're right: he does need a swift kick, and I'd gladly hoof him in the balls with my Balenciagas given half a chance, but as I could be representing Bella that wouldn't be such a good idea. We really need to do this by the book. He's avoided jail by the skin of his teeth so far, but if he goes through on his threats against Bella, this could see him banged up. He needs to realise there's consequences to actions in life. A little stint in prison could teach him that. I like to think everyone is capable of redemption and can change, and I'd hope he can too but as things are now, he really is the most horrible cretin, a deeply flawed individual, cruel, a bully and has all the charm of haemorrhoids up an itchy arsehole."

Lottie nodded her head in agreement. "Yeah, he's even worse than Daniel, and that's saying something. It seems this Alfie does the most horrible things and always seems to get away with it. He needs stopping, and we're going to see that he does. I'm telling you, he thinks he's got a charmed life. If there was a nuclear winter, Alfie Dodds and cockroaches would be the only creatures that survived."

Lila laughed, but there was no humour in the sound.

"It just beggars belief why a lovely girl like Bella would hook up with such a scumbag. She's a beautiful girl and Alfie Dodds, well, he's got a face that only a mother could love; and I seriously doubt whether she does, after all the trouble he's brought to her door. I suppose he can turn on the charm when he wants, but looks-wise, he resembles something that's been wading in the bottom of the gene pool since birth, and about as handsome as a turd that just won't flush."

Her face was red, I could tell she was angry and annoyed at the injustice of it all. "Anyway, Mrs W, what do you think? Are you able to help a girl out? We'll make sure Alfie doesn't know where she's gone so there's no risk at all."

All eyes turned towards me, waiting for me to make my decision. I felt exhausted by it all. Between talk of floating turds and nuclear winters, I could do with heading back to bed for another nap. Ah yes, the chance to return to that beautiful sandy beach, strolling hand in hand with Daniel, but without the bloodthirsty cats of course.

As it was, I already had an unexpected house guest – my sister. And heaven alone knew how long she was going to stay. The last thing I needed was a young girl to enter the mix. She sounded as if she might be quite damaged too. I really felt for her, I truly did, but this was my home, my sanctuary, my safe place. Did I really need the hassle?"

Dora reached over and took my hand in hers. "Remember, sis: evil triumphs when good women do nothing."

I let her words sink in for a few seconds. Maybe she was right. Maybe this was my one time to make a difference in the world, even in just a small way.

"And anyway, Evie, wouldn't it be nice to have a youngster around the house for a bit? It might blow some of our cobwebs away."

She looked at me pointedly. Clearly, she thought I was the stuffy one that needed a whirlwind to blow my cobwebs away.

Against my better judgement, I felt myself nodding at the women. I thought about my life, the safe security of it, my quiet little existence. It was a good life. But boy, was I bored.

"OK, tell her she can stay in Jacob's room, but only for a few days."

Chapter 9

·♥·♥·♥·♥·♥·

It was the following day, and I kept going back over my decision. Was I right to agree? I really felt for the plight of the girl, but let's face it, I wasn't a fan of change. Was I going to regret saying yes so readily? But the second I came face to face with Bella, my worries melted away.

She was standing on the doorstep, Lottie beside her, with her hand protectively on the girl's arm as if to stop her from running away. The first thing I noticed was the worry evident in Bella's eyes; and the second was that she was exceptionally pretty: dressed demurely in baggy blue jeans and a high-necked sweater, the blue wool perfectly matching the azure of her eyes. She had shoulder-length hair like spun blonde which cascaded onto her slim shoulders. I couldn't help being reminded of Cinderella. I had loved the 1950 original cartoon version as a child, believing in the magic of it all: that fairy tales really did come true. Looking at the frightened young woman before me, I realised, not for the first time in my life, that sadly those fairy tales weren't real.

Bella smiled up at me timidly and I returned the expression with a pleasant one of my own as I ushered her into the house and through to the lounge to sit down.

Lottie mouthed "Thank you" as she followed the slightly stooped figure of the young woman through the door.

"This is Bella; Mum and Bella, this is my lovely Mum, Evelyn."

"Hello, Bella, it's lovely to meet you, my love."

She caught my eye for a mere moment before her gaze shot down to the floor as if fascinated by the swirly pattern on the carpet.

"Why don't you take your coat off and make yourself nice and comfortable."

She nervously removed her thin jacket, far too flimsy for the current chill in the air. Her body was slightly hunched, as if scared she might be taking up too much space in the world. There were a few faint bruises on her upper arms, and I shuddered to think how she might have got those.

We sat in silence for a few seconds, as if all of us were scared to be the first to speak. Suddenly Dora bustled into the room, a vision in shocking pink tracksuit with a silver beret atop her mass of grey curls. For once I was pleased to see her. Her perennial cheerfulness could only be good in this situation.

She gave a little whoop of surprise and rushed over to hug Bella. I cringed inwardly. Would this be too much too soon, invading the girl's personal space like this? But if anything, my sister's boldness seemed to put Bella more at ease.

"I never heard the bell; I tell you I'm as deaf as a post these days."

She let go of Bella momentarily and stepped back so she could take a good look at her, her eyes sweeping over the diminutive figure crouched against the sofa cushions.

"Bella...it's so lovely to meet you, my darling. And aren't you a beauty? Why, you remind me of a young me back in the day. I bet you're a real heartbreaker. I'm Isadora, but you can call me Dora, all my friends do, and I know we're going to be great pals."

Bella blushed slightly, but I shot Dora another one of my famous steely glares. She really shouldn't be mentioning Bella being a heartbreaker. It was clear to see the girl's heart was broken already. This really wasn't the way we needed the conversation to be going.

Bella studied Dora for a few seconds. Clearly, she was not sure what to make of this older woman dressed in such a flamboyant manner.

"Hello, Dora, it's so nice to meet you. But no, I've not really been that popular with boys. I've only ever had one boyfriend, and we got together in school. He's called Alfie."

I could only imagine that the reason boys had never shown much interest in her was due to said Alfie scaring them off. You would have to be blind to fail to notice how beautiful she was.

Bella seemed to sink even further back into the sofa cushions. Her mentioning her ex-boyfriend's name had brought tears to her eyes.

"I really thought he was so nice when I met him: he treated me good, he did; but then it all started to change...*he* started to change, and now I'm scared of him, scared of what he might do. I had to leave him, leave our home together, I had to...had to get away."

Her words tumbled out as the tears ran rivers down her cheeks. Lottie put a comforting arm around her shoulders.

"It's OK, Bella, they know everything. Lila and I explained what's happened."

Dora's green eyes had darkened somewhat, like there was a storm brewing. "Of course you had to get away, dear, you couldn't put up with being treated like that. Who could? And I tell you something else, I really hope you ass-cracked his toothbrush as a parting gift on the way out."

Oh no. Did my sister always have to be so inappropriate? But to my surprise, Bella burst out laughing. The tension in the room evaporated like the storm clouds from my sister's eyes.

We all sat in silence again for a few moments. I did the only thing I knew what to do in that moment: I offered to make everyone a cup of tea. We were Yorkshire after all, and there wasn't any situation that couldn't be made better by a good brew. I glanced at Bella again. Never mind tea, though; I couldn't help but wonder when the girl had last had a decent meal.

"I'm going to make sandwiches, toasties in fact. Would you fancy a ham and cheese one, Bella? I could put a dab of pickle on it too if you like."

On second thoughts, I remembered how the dried-up jar of pickle with its lost lid that had mysteriously vanished the night before.

"Or maybe just the ham and cheese?"

Bella's face lit up prettily. "Yes please, that would be lovely. I was so nervous about coming today that I didn't have any breakfast. But Lottie and Lila said you would be nice, and they were right, you really are."

Dora was shaking her head as if in shock. Clearly the idea of someone missing breakfast was an alien concept to her. "Well, that's not right; you must be famished. Breakfast is the most important meal of the day, that's what our mother used to tell us, wasn't it, Evie? And you really can't beat a nice bit of sausage of a morning, or a nice slice of pizza, eh, sis?"

I groaned inwardly as Dora laughed at her own jokes. I shot Bella a little wink, as if to say my sister was a bit of a nut and to just ignore her. The smile she returned was genuine and not forced in the slightest. It seemed we were making some headway with the girl; helping to put her at ease.

I had known that Bella would like Dora. Let's face it, everybody did. It didn't matter how inappropriate she was, or how many blue jokes tripped off her tongue, nobody ever seemed to take much offence. She had the likeability factor going on in spades, and that just seemed to give her a hall pass. Well, apart from the chap at the bar the previous night. He hadn't seemed too enamoured by her or her drunken behaviour. I couldn't help but wonder if he had regained the feeling in his testicles yet.

Unlike my sibling, I seemed to be much more of an acquired taste; but if people needed to acquire more taste to like me, then so be it.

I left them making small talk and busied myself in the kitchen, buttering bread and slicing cheese. When I returned to the lounge, I was pleased to see everyone appeared relaxed and at ease with each other. I passed the plates of food around. I had made enough ham and cheese toasties to feed half of the village. Lottie took hers gratefully.

"My Mum really makes the best toasties. Whenever I was a little girl and felt upset about anything, one of these and a big mug of tea would sort me right out."

Dora nodded at her niece in agreement. "That she does, Lottie. I've eaten my not inconsiderable body weight in them since I've been here."

She turned her attention to Bella, who was staring at the thick doorstep butty and its oozing cheese as if overwhelmed and not sure where to start.

"You get your chops around that, Bella, love; you can't beat a nice bit of cheese and a thick slice of hand-carved ham to perk you right up."

Bella's eyes began to fill up again, fat tears tumbling down her cheeks. Her happy demeanour from five minutes before had evaporated. She looked like a young woman on the edge of despair.

Dora reached over and patted her arm affectionately, once again keen to lighten the mood. "There, there, my love; there's no need for tears. My sister's cooking isn't that bad, you haven't even tasted it yet."

The girl sniffed and dabbed at her eyes with a paper napkin. "It's just that I really love him...loved him... and he's hurting me so much, threatening to...to do things, and then there's these...these... photos."

It was hard for her to get her words out, and she blushed again. it was clear she didn't want to tell us, two much older women, about what we already knew.

Dora handed her another napkin to replace the one she already had, which was getting soggier by the second.

"Look, you may think my sister and I are a couple of old relics, and we couldn't possibly understand what all of this means, but you'd be wrong. I might be more of a Queenager than a teenager these days, but I like to think I keep my ear to the ground; there's not a lot that goes on in this world that would shock me. Well, apart from Simon Cowell's trousers; he really needs to learn where his waist is. Anyway, we understand how Alfie having these pictures of you could go; it could ruin your reputation, your relationship with your family and friends. Mud doesn't just stick, my girl, it spreads too. But we're not going to let anything bad happen to you. When us women stick together, there ain't nothing we can't overcome."

She paused for a second and checked that Lottie and I agreed with her. We did.

"This Alfie is all you can think of now. It's like he's living rent-free in your brain because he's all you've known for so long. You love him or at least you think you do, but it won't always be like that. You can't see it now, but believe me, life's a long time and this is only a little blip on your lifeline. In a year's time you'll barely remember his name. He thinks he's the shit, but you'll soon come to realise that in fact he's barely a fart."

I wouldn't have used the words my sister had, but I couldn't deny she was spot on. Men like Alfie Dodds had been around since the dawn of time, some of them hiding in plain sight. We believed their lies, wanted so much to believe in them, so we dreamed of a better life, a better man. But when our dreams die, they die hard; and then all that is left is for us to pick up the pieces.

Bella was going to stay with us until this was all sorted out. And sort it out we would. We had to. In life we sometimes accepted the love we thought we deserved, even though it would leave us broken. Bella had chosen to get out of her toxic relationship, and that was to be applauded.

I was glad to see the girl had managed to eat most of her toasted sandwich. Only a few random crusts remained on the plate. Her face was much less pale now too. It really was amazing the restorative powers of a good chunk of cheddar and a pep talk from Dora.

"Thank you for the sandwich, Evie. Lottie was right, it really was delicious. And thank you for helping me by letting me stay here, it's so kind of you."

"You're welcome, Bella, you really are."

It was edifying to see how much more relaxed she was again, and certainly much more than when she had arrived. I had a feeling it had been a while since anyone had shown her any care or kindness. Even her body language had improved, and she was sitting up straighter now. I thought back to our bygone Headmistress, Miss Hardcastle. What had she always said? Poor self-esteem equals poor posture. Well, old Hardcastle should have known; as Dora used to say, she always walked ramrod straight, as if she had her broomstick stuck up her bony arse.

Bella picked up her mug of tea from the coffee table beside her and drained it. Even her hands were steadier now. I had tried to not to stare earlier, keen not to draw attention to it, but her hands had been clearly shaking when she had taken her plate of food from me.

"I know I'll be alright; I have to be." She glanced around at us all in turn: Lottie then Dora then finally me. "It's just I feel like a piece of me is missing now that I'm not with him. But I understand that staying with him is the worst thing I could do. It's just hard when he's all I've known. I just don't know how to be single."

Dora winked at her affectionately and rubbed her hands together, causing the many plastic bracelets on her arms to rattle like a windchime on a stormy day. "The only thing that's been missing with you, my love, is a bit of common sense. But believe me, you've remedied that now; and as for being single, pah, that's the fun bit. I've made being single into a veritable art form; you stick with me, lass, and we're gonna have a ball."

Chapter 10

· ♥ · ♥ · ♥ · ♥ · ♥ ·

And stick together they did. In the few weeks after Bella arrived, she and my sister became pretty much inseparable.

I had to admit that having Bella around was no hardship. In fact, so far so blooming good. She was a sweet-natured girl, and nothing was too much trouble for her around the house. She would help with the cooking, even though her liking for plasticky cheese slices was never going to persuade me to ditch my mature cheddar any time soon. But it made a nice change from Dora, who point blank refused to cook. It was even a battle of wills to get my sister to heat up soup in the microwave. She was adamant she was no Nigella in the kitchen, and so it was best she avoided all things culinary. After all, she would only give out negative vibes around the raw ingredients. And bad energy in good food simply wouldn't do.

Also, unlike Dora, Bella knew how to use the washing machine. And she never needed to be asked twice to lend a hand when the washing up required doing; whereas when there was a sink full of dirty dishes, Dora would be notable by her absence, or if she was in the vicinity would adopt a deaf ear, probably for the best as I wasn't even confident she knew one end of a dishcloth from the other.

I had first thought that Bella would only be with us for a couple of days, but a week passed and then another and another, and actually I was more than happy for her to stay for as long as she wanted. She was simply a pleasure to have around, and I was confident she was enjoying her time with us too. Maybe not exactly living the dream, but certainly less of a nightmare than the reality she had escaped from.

I knew she missed her parents and her younger sister though, and was hoping perhaps to return to her family home. There had been an ongoing rift between them caused by Alfie, but now that she was away from his clutches, bridges were slowly being built. I felt genuinely pleased for her. Family was everything. And even though I sometimes heard her crying at night, missing her ex-boyfriend, I knew that this would lessen in time too. With each day that passed she would become stronger, more aware of how toxic their relationship had really been.

Dora seemed in no rush to be heading homeward-bound any time soon either. She did phone her neighbour Keith every few days, just to check on her beloved Feline Dion: whether the miserable moggy had bitten off yet another flea collar, or in fact bitten the Bullmastiff again from next door. That poor canine lived in fear of Feline's fangs.

I couldn't help but notice that when my sister was on the phone to Keith, she always excused herself and scurried away to her room for a bit of privacy, shutting the door closed tightly behind her. I was beginning to wonder which one she was missing more: her pet or her "neighbour".

Although Dora was proving to be just as chaotic and messy as always, it didn't seem to bother me so much lately. Maybe I was becoming more tolerant in my old age; learning to breathe in and out and embrace the chaos. The first few days of her visit had been hard, to say the least. My anxiety levels had been off the scale, and her constant singing was like a cheese grater to my nerve endings. But now I could say with all sincerity I was happy to have my sister around. Yes, of course, she was still a nightmare at times and messier than a truckload of teenage boys, but she certainly brightened up my days. Put simply, my sister was just good fun to be around.

Although everything was smooth sailing now, I had found the first evening with Bella more than a little awkward. Lottie had stayed a while, ensuring that Bella had everything she needed packed in her one small suitcase and scruffy backpack. But then my daughter had been on her way, lavishing us with hugs and kisses before heading for the door, calling over her shoulder to Bella to insist that she ring her or Lila if she needed anything.

Once the door had shut with a resounding bang that echoed throughout the narrow hallway like a judge's gavel hitting the bench, we had turned to face each other. Now we were three.

I had excused myself to do the washing up in the kitchen, whilst Dora ushered Bella upstairs to help her unpack and settle into her new room. It was the same room that Jacob would stay in when he came to visit from Uni, or when he was younger where he would arrange his army of soft toys on the nights I babysat, those rare occasions when Daniel and Lottie had a night out.

It still had Jacob's posters pinned to the walls: those bands he loved that sounded more like painful wailing to me, as if the lead singers had a nasty case of trapped wind – the Red Hot Chilli Peppers and Foo Fighters to name but two of his favourites. Not my cup of tea at all, and certainly not a patch on The Beatles or Sir Elton John. Apart from the posters on the magnolia emulsioned walls, the rest of the room was a bit of a blank canvas. It was cosy and clean with nice neutral bedding and accessories. Dora had informed me that my soft furnishings were the exact shade of undressed tripe. I strongly disagreed, as I knew for a fact that the range went by the name of "vanilla dream".

Bella had followed Dora up the stairs to her new room. She hung back slightly as they went up. I knew the poor girl must have been a little concerned about how she was going to fit in with a couple of unattached old biddies in a semi-detached in a quiet street in a sleepy little village.

I was just drying up the last of the plates when there was a loud banging noise from above my head. I dropped the towel in my haste to get upstairs and see what the heck was going on. It sounded like an earthquake had shaken the house's very foundations. I reached the landing as quickly as my pink fluffy slippers would allow. What on earth was going on?

Dora and Bella were in the middle of the bedroom, hand in hand dancing, while Taylor Swift sang out from Bella's mobile phone on the bed. Her suitcase had been left abandoned half unpacked with piles of clothing messily heaped on the bed. They had clearly stopped working so that Bella could teach my eager sister some new dance moves. I watched them for a few seconds, unable to drag my eyes away, rather like when you know you shouldn't look at an eclipse put you find yourself sneaking a peek. There was no chance that Dora would be selected for *Strictly Come Dancing* any time soon. They were both laughing, having fun. I couldn't help but smile. Taylor's voice was petering out now, replaced by an up-tempo dance track. I had the dubious pleasure of watching my sister attempt to twerk, clearly something that did not come naturally to her, despite her ample derrière.

They both fell back onto the bed in fits of laughter. Once again, Dora had made a new friend. It was the story of our childhood all over. Me the demure, austere one, some might even say prickly; and Dora the life and soul of the party, who everyone gravitated to no matter who they were. Everybody loved Dora.

It was amazing to see how within a couple of hours the timid-looking lass who had arrived at my front door had morphed into this relaxed young woman, seemingly without a care in the world. I knew that wasn't true; she was enjoying herself now, but later, in the early hours, when alone in the dark in the single bed unable to sleep, then she would be dwelling on things. But she was happy now, and that was good.

Seeing Dora and Bella dancing together reminded me of Lottie: how she would have her friends over at weekends for sleepovers. They would laugh and dance, eat ice cream and talk of boys until the early hours. It had been over thirty years since then, but for a second it was as if those years had simply melted away. Dora grabbed my hand and for a few moments I was back there too, dancing and laughing like I hadn't done in years.

Later that evening, after a supper of quiche and salad, we had settled down to watch television. I had insisted that Bella choose the programme, just to welcome her and make her feel more at home. I needn't have worried though; she seemed perfectly at ease sitting beside Dora, both in matching green facemasks and wearing near identical unicorn-emblazoned pyjamas – proving my point that my sister dressed ridiculously young for a woman of her age. If it hadn't been for my sister's unruly grey curls next to Bella's blonde locks, they could have passed for sisters.

I sat in my armchair, as was the norm, whilst they stretched out on the sofa. In lieu of any gin, Dora had found my poorly hidden bottle of Baileys left over from Christmas and had split it between three large tumblers. Dora and Bella were drinking theirs whilst noisily crunching on a family-size bag of fancy country cheddar and caramelised onion crisps. Dora was helping herself to large handfuls, despite the fact she had grumbled earlier that day about their strong flavour, insisting they were less cheese and onion and more cheese and bum crack. She had no choice though; she had finished all the other snacks in the house. I was forever finding notes stuck to the fridge reminding me to stock up on Beefy Monster Munch and Mr Kipling cakes. Her diet was more appropriate for a child at a birthday party than a woman in her early sixties. It was clear to me there was not an additive or e-number my sister couldn't get along with.

I was reading my library book, the latest thriller from Ann Cleeves. It really was a cracker and much more to my taste than the drama unfolding on the television set. Dora and Bella were engrossed in the latest season of *Emily in Paris* on Netflix. Dora insisted she was watching purely for Paris, which happened to be her favourite city. I was not convinced this was the only reason she was so engrossed;

she was practically drooling over the two leading men on the screen, and I doubted if she had even noticed the Parisian backdrop. I'd heard on Radio 4 that morning that we were due a full moon tonight, and I knew my sister was prone to getting fruitier than an orchard of apples once it cast its celestial glow.

I was glad that Dora and Bella were becoming so close, although sometimes I felt slightly envious of their friendship and just how easy and natural it was. On occasion I had a little pang of regret, feeling that I was surplus to requirements. I would walk into the lounge looking for the newspaper and they would both fall silent. Clearly, I was not privy to their conversation. I was glad that Bella had someone to confide in, I really was, but I couldn't help feeling a little left out.

It was some days later when I discovered the reason why I hadn't been included in their conversations. We were just finishing our supper of chicken pie and salad; it had been delicious, although Dora hadn't stopped grumbling about the lack of chips accompanying it.

"Look, Evie, Bella and I have got something we need to tell you, but it's important you don't go mad."

On no. What was it now? I put my knife and fork down neatly on my plate and turned my attention to the two women, bracing myself for whatever was coming.

"We've set you up on a dating site."

Chapter 11

•♥•♥•♥•♥•♥•

"You've done what?" They had clearly lost the plot, and I doubted whether I had a map which would direct them safely back to common sense.

"A dating site? Have you gone mad? I can't speak, I'm speechless... completely speechless."

"Well clearly that's not true." Dora laughed a little nervously and Bella's face flushed, her eyes glued to her empty plate, anywhere to avoid meeting my eyes. My sister however brazened it out.

"It's what everyone's doing these days, sis."

"Is it? Who exactly is doing it? Nobody as far as I know. I can't imagine anyone at the bridge club doing it, or Belinda...or"

"Bugger Belinda and the bridge club and what they think. This is something you need to do, Evie. And as for not knowing anyone who's done it, you're dead wrong there. You know me, don't you? And believe me, out in the real world, I was having no luck at all with men. In fact

I could barely get a dog to bark at me, never mind show me their juicy bone. But online, I'm catnip for the gents. I tell you I'm dropping more boxers than Tyson Fury."

I had a feeling Bella's face might well be mirroring the shock on mine. The poor girl looked discombobulated in the extreme, clearly not expecting someone of Dora's vintage to be still interested in bedroom activities. The girl had a lot to learn.

In truth I was somewhat less shocked than Bella. The amount that Dora talked about sex, it stood to reason that she was still engaging in that sort of thing on a fairly regular basis. I had imagined it would be with just the one gentleman, namely Keith; but from the sound of it her dance card was well and truly full, and we were talking the horizontal mamba with many eager partners.

I had assumed that any "friendships" she had with the other sex were due in part to her confidence and charisma and a dash of good old-fashioned luck. I didn't realise there was a computer app involved too. It took some getting my head around.

"So, let me get this right, you're on a dating app?"

"No...I 'm on dating *apps* plural. I always find the scattergun approach works best: cast your net wide enough and you're sure to catch some fishes. Mind you, there'll be plenty you want to chuck back."

Bella was nodding her head in agreement. "And catfish too, there's always a few of those knocking around that you need to avoid."

I had no idea what the girl was talking about. Weren't catfish those whiskery creatures they consumed fried in the southern states of America? What could they possibly have to do with online dating? I looked at both women in confusion. This was bonkers. I wasn't even au fait with technology, for goodness' sake. OK, I was more technologically savvy than I had once been, thanks in part to Jacob and his "trying to bring his granny into the 21st century"; but I was certainly no Bill Gates. The idea of putting me on a dating site was frankly ridiculous. I was adamant on this: Dora could simply put me down as a "never gonna happen".

My sister looked me dead in the eye, giving me the chilling notion that she could indeed read my mind. "Look, this *needs* to happen. Andrew's been gone a long while now, and it's time for you to find yourself someone to love."

I felt my eyes fill at the mention of my late husband. Even thinking about meeting someone new felt like a betrayal, but I knew in my heart that wasn't true. That was just me and my loyalty. Andrew would never have wanted me to end up alone, and I knew without a shadow of a doubt that Lottie didn't want that for me either.

Dora's tone softened upon seeing my watery eyes. "You're lonely, Evie. You've admitted that, and neither I nor Bella are going to be here forever. What then? You'll be rattling around this place like a pea on a drum, talking to yourself or answering back to that blasted radio. You've got more to offer than that. You're a beautiful, intelligent woman; you need to get yourself back out into the big wide world."

I wasn't sure about that. Quite frankly, it all sounded a bit too scary and out of my comfort zone. And yes, I scrubbed up OK, I supposed, and I definitely was a whizz with a sudoku and a bit of small talk; but dating? Surely I was too long in the tooth for all that nonsense. And even if I wasn't, would I really have the nerve to do it? Get myself back out into the world as a single woman?

"You'd never have had the nerve to do this yourself, which is why Bella and I took control. And you might as well agree now, because if you don't, we will just nag you relentlessly until you give in. So come on, I'll pour us a little sherry and we can show you your new profile."

I looked wearily at the dirty plates abandoned on the kitchen table, and the baking tray soaking in the sink. For once they could wait. My curiosity was getting the better of me. Against all my better judgement, I needed to see this profile they were talking about.

A few minutes later, we were all squashed up together on the sofa. No longer me cast adrift in my armchair, now I was slap bang in the middle of the gruesome twosome, Dora to my left with her laptop balanced precariously on her colourful lap and Bella to my right offering her advice and insights every time my sister nearly deleted the page.

Despite myself, I needed to know what these two had decided was a fitting profile for a retired woman in later life such as myself, and the whole process was taking too damn long.

"Come on, Dora; enquiring minds, more precisely my mind, wants to know what you've written."

I could have been mistaken, but for a second a fleeting look of concern passed over my sister's face. Just a second, and then it was gone.

"Err...OK, Evie, but first, just out of interest, what would you have written if you had been doing it for yourself?"

I thought for a few seconds. It was a good question. After all these years as a widow, how would I market myself in this strange new world?

"Oh, I don't know exactly, but maybe something along the lines of... sophisticated lady, late sixties, enjoys reading, knitting and playing bridge, seeks a gentleman friend for nice walks out, the occasional lunch and some good conversation."

I nodded to myself. I had been thinking on my feet, but I had to admit it summed me up and what I would require in a relationship to a tee.

Dora and Bella locked eyes momentarily and Bella let out a small nervous laugh. "Well...it's a little like that, I suppose."

This wasn't sounding promising at all, but if they hadn't veered too far away from my version, maybe it would still be OK.

"Show me."

Dora cleared her throat. Perhaps she was playing for time? She took a deep steadying breath and began to read. "Foxy femme fatale, late fifties..."

"Late fifties – I'm 69!"

"Yes, well, everyone shaves a few years off their age, you know."

"But that's knocking off a decade; that's less shaving and more ripping it asunder."

Dora ignored me and carried on. "Foxy femme fatale, late fifties, looking for Mr Right, or at least Mr Right Now, who can misbehave in all the right ways. A glamorous girl with a flair for fashion and a need for passion. Swipe right and let's misbehave together."

The silence that settled over the room was deafening. It took me a few seconds to regain the ability to speak, but when I did, I let rip.

"Oh, good grief, I can't believe it." I was up from the sofa and pacing around the living room carpet. "That's terrible, simply terrible."

"No, it isn't. Look, you've had loads of messages already."

Dora pointed to the laptop screen and I could see she was right. There were twenty-two messages keenly waiting for the foxy femme fatale, aka me, to answer.

"Of course they've messaged: you've made me sound like a right strumpet."

"What's a strumpet?" Bella enquired, clearly puzzled and not having a clue what was going on.

"A strumpet is a slattern.... a... harlot, a floozy a trollop." I paused for breath. The poor girl was none the wiser.

"A skank," Dora offered.

"Ahhh." Bella understood perfectly now.

Despite me clearly being the injured party here, Dora looked seriously put out, none too pleased that I wasn't happy with their dating app endeavours.

"Well, we can change it, I suppose," she grumbled, "to something you feel is more appropriate. But please, not too much about bridge or knitting. Talk about a passion killer; you'll never get a pickle pic with chat like that."

I had no idea what a pickle pic was, but I could hazard a guess, and I was confident I didn't want one of those dropping into my inbox any time soon.

Chapter 12

· ♥ · ♥ · ♥ · ♥ · ♥ ·

An hour later and several glasses of sherry down, we had a profile I was at last happy with.

Elegant, young at heart lady, mid-sixties, loves crosswords, great books and fine dining. Seeking a refined gentleman for walks, conversation and the possibility of romance.

"It's a bit dull," Dora grumbled. "I really think we still need to spice it up a little."

I reached over and took the laptop off my sister to prevent her for from sprinkling any spice on what was now already perfection. "You're spicing nothing up. It's staying strictly vanilla."

I had finally relented to shaving a few years off my true age and making myself mid-sixties. I had to admit my actual age was a little too close to seventy for my liking.

Then, with trembling hands, I clicked on the first message. It was from a man who laughably claimed to be 52, but had a face boasting more wrinkles than Methuselah.

82 would have been closer to the mark. Maybe Dora had been right after all, and I should have lopped a couple of decades off my age if this was the game they were playing.

His message wasn't too terrible. He just said how he liked my profile. I had a sinking feeling that he was probably referring to the first one, and had not seen the new and improved version. He claimed he would love to take me out for a drink and "do lunch" as a chance to get to know me better. Nothing too scary there. The only frightful thing was his photo. I clicked on his profile: no scratch that there was something even more terrifying – his bio.

"Young at heart 52 looking for that special someone. I like fast cars, fast women and making love slowly. Let me take you for the finest steak dinner with all the trimmings and let's see where it goes."

Dora had been reading over my shoulder the whole time and was now making obvious gagging sounds. "I think I've just been sick in my mouth a little. Oh dear me, no "Salvatore 53", you're far too oily by far, and I can only hazard a guess at what 'the trimmings' with your steak dinner would be: a glass of Rohypnol Rioja, no doubt, so you're comatose for a night of his geriatric mattress activities."

Bella looked shocked in the extreme. "He's about a hundred years old, looks a lot like my mate Leesa's great grandad. I really hope it's not him." She shuddered and wrapped her arms around herself as if to keep out a sudden chill. "He's forever hanging around the betting shop and smells of pee. That's not him, though...I hope not anyway; but imagine if it is. He's always in the local Wetherspoons getting the OAP specials."

The local Wetherspoons? Was this where I was to have my finest steak dinner? Well, he might enjoy a flutter down the local bookmakers, but he would be on a losing streak if he was betting on a date with me.

Bella shook her head as if to clear it from all troubling thoughts. "Whatever, though, even if he's not Leesa's great grandad, he's still got a face like roadkill."

I nodded my head in agreement. "Indeed, and never mind his face looking like a scabby cabbage; I could never date a man who says 'do lunch'; it's just so naff."

So "Salvatore 53" was quickly forgotten. Bella was now all but bouncing up and down on the sofa cushions beside me, excitement evident on her pretty face and in her energetic body language. "Oooh, check this one out though, Evie, you've got a message from 'Dan' and he's insanely hot."

My eyes shot back to the screen: "Dan 32". She must be mad. 32? I could nearly be his grandmother, for goodness' sake. Not so much an age gap, more of an age chasm.

Dora was actually licking her lips, as if she'd spotted a cream-filled meringue. "Ooh, that's definitely more like it. I'll say, colour me impressed."

But then she clearly changed her mind and shook her head, ready to impart her knowledge on all things dating. "Very nice but not for you, Evie; he's after a cougar, that's not you at all."

I slowly looked at them in turn, trying to alert them to my ignorance. Catfish and cougars? It was beginning to sound more like a wildlife documentary than a dating site.

Dora went on to explain: "Some men like a cougar – an older, more experienced woman who can show them a thing or two in the boudoir. It's quite a compliment really, when you think about it."

Was it? I couldn't help but think it was a wee bit creepy, like this Dan must have a bit of a granny fetish or something. It definitely wasn't something I was interested in pursuing. My sister could clearly sense my reluctance.

"I suppose it might be worth considering, Evie. A great way to check everything is in good working order below the border, if you know what I mean. It's been a long while since you gave the bed springs a good old rattling, after all. And what better way to test things out than with a hot young guy with whom you definitely don't want a long-term relationship? A sort of hit it and quit it arrangement, as the youngsters say. And let's face it, after a night of bonking with that gorgeous young specimen, it wouldn't be so much a walk of shame, more of a victory lap."

I shook my head again firmly. Bella reached over Dora and tapped the screen.

"What about this one then?"

I read the bio from "StanTHEMan007". Did he really fancy himself as James Bond? Looking at the picture of the toothless chap grinning gummily out at me, he clearly wasn't licensed to thrill. More Double O heave my guts up.

"Looking for that special woman—classy, clean-living, and family-oriented. If you've been slammed more times than an Uber door, you can just scroll on by. I want a fabulous thoroughbred, so no fuller-figured fillies please. I like my women like I like my racehorses: in peak physical condition. So if you like to browse the buffet too often, you're definitely not the one for me. But if you're a fan of suave and sexy men, then message me. I'll make all your dreams come true."

Dora looked fit to burst. She was clearly furious, red dots of rage high on her cheeks. "The bloody nerve of him, no fuller-figured fillies indeed? That's out and out fat shaming right there, to veto a whole section of fantastic females right off the bat. As if he could handle a real curvaceous woman, anyway. Look at the bloody state of him. Make all your dreams come true? Pah, don't make me laugh. A date with him would be a living nightmare, and no mistake. Sex with him? No thank you very much, I'd rather be in bed with a head cold."

"He certainly seems to like to reference horses a lot though," Bella noted. "Maybe he owns a couple."

Dora snorted unattractively. "I sincerely doubt it. His photo's clearly been taken outside the local working men's club and he's carrying an Aldi shopping bag. It hardly screams wealth and sophistication, does it?"

Bella and I couldn't argue with her logic.

"And as for suave and sexy, he must be having a laugh; he's got fewer teeth than my tangle tweezer hairbrush, and it has to fight its way through my curly mop every morning."

"Maybe it's his idea of a joke. It does say further down that he's got a great sense of humour," Bella noted.

"Well, with that face, he'll bloody well need it."

All in all, this online dating malarkey was proving to be as disastrous as I had known it would be. There wasn't one man here I would even nod at in the street, never mind spend an evening with. They all had faces that could trigger a panic attack, or photos that were clearly decades out of date. And the ones that looked passable seriously let themselves down with their bios and messages. There was even one called "BigBen10", and alas, I quickly came to the conclusion he didn't work in Westminster but was in fact referring to his own hanging pendulum. That really conjured up all sorts of visuals I seriously didn't need.

Anyway, as Dora had helpfully pointed out, if and when I did decide to have a physical relationship, I would be much better served by choosing a man of moderate equipment, so to speak; more fun size than supersize, so I wouldn't find the whole experience overwhelming. As she whimsically put it, an "inbetweeny weenie" was just what the doctor ordered.

On the back of this, I quickly scrolled past "Debonair Drew", as he claimed to have an impressive penis. The sheer audacity of the man announcing that to all and sundry! It wasn't until I re-read it that I realised he had in fact written that he was an impressive pianist. But alas, he lived in Edinburgh, and I really didn't want to travel that far north. The weather could be even chillier than Yorkshire, and I wasn't a fan of my family tartan; it really washed out my complexion. The furthest I would be going up north was to Specsavers on the High Street, as I clearly needed another eye test.

And "Noman-loves-numbers" didn't fare much better either. I had a quick gander at him, but to no avail. He claimed to be a retired accountant who loved fine wines and was aged like one too. Unfortunately, I think that was a bit optimistic on his part, as looking at the balding man grimacing out from his profile picture, I felt he was aged more like a chunk of ripe gorgonzola than a fine burgundy. However, his nose was so scarlet and veiny it was clear he hadn't been lying about his liking of the vino. He claimed his other hobbies were stamp collecting and watching Nazi documentaries, which gave me the distinct feeling that, rather like blue cheese, a little of him would go a long way.

There were a couple of chaps whose faces were pulled so tight they looked like overblown balloons and fit to burst at a moment's notice. I had never been one for the aesthetics needle myself, but knew plenty who did; I could see no harm in it if that's what you wanted. But some of these chaps had clearly had more tweakments than the cast of all the *Real Housewives* franchises combined. I had old Tupperware in my kitchen cupboard less plastic than them. What was wrong with a man ageing with a little grace and refinement? There could be something very attractive about wrinkles and grey hair. It showed maturity and a life well lived, their story etched upon their face. From "Salvatore 53" to these baby-faced beaux, it was really the sublime to the ridiculous.

I was beginning to feel seriously exhausted with it all. What had started out as a bit of fun was beginning to lose its sparkle. It felt like trawling through the wonky veg on the reduced aisle at Tesco, rather than searching for a life partner. As games went, it felt more like Snake Charming than the Trivial Pursuit of love.

But just as I was about to shut the laptop lid and call it a night, a certain someone caught my eye. My stomach lurched a little and I knew it wasn't from the chicken pie: it was from something far more delicious, the image staring out at me from the screen.

Dora and Bella had been so adamant about this, and maybe they had been right after all.

I turned the computer screen towards them with a triumphant smile.

"I've found him, I've found the one."

Chapter 13

•♥•♥•♥•♥•♥•

*"**W**idowed ex-solicitor, 62, looking for a lovely lady to share life's good moments—travel, great meals, cinema nights, and deep conversations long into the night. I'm a genuinely nice guy, old-fashioned and loyal in the best way, kind to the core, and ready to find someone special to enjoy the rest of my life with. If you appreciate good company and a touch of class, let's see where this goes."*

I read Jonathan's dating profile for what must have been the thousandth time as I walked on unsteady legs towards the wine bar where we were meeting. We had been messaging each other for a few weeks, and tonight was the night when we were finally meeting up.

Of course I was nervous. Strike that; I was petrified. The unsteady legs weren't just down to the high heels that Dora had insisted I wear, but the multitude of butterflies flitting around in my tummy. My sister had suggested drowning them with gin to take the edge off. So, I had taken her advice and had a couple of small ones before I ventured out. Although I had never been to Amsterdam, I was a big fan of Dutch courage.

I had high hopes for the evening. Jonathan and I hadn't spoken yet, or Facetimed for that matter, though looking at his photo he definitely had a face I would certainly enjoy spending time with. We had messaged though, many, many messages. I felt I knew him already. We had just clicked.

We were due to meet at Olive Affair, a chic tapas wine bar in town. It was a firm favourite with Lottie and her gang, and they had dragged me there a few times despite my protestations that I would prefer a quieter venue. I had always enjoyed myself though, and I really hoped I would tonight. It felt like safe ground for a first meeting.

I took another quick glance at his photo. He was staring out from the screen, and it was enough to make my knees tremble. Mind you, that might still have been down to the six-inch slingbacks I was tottering along on. Dora had said they gave me "legs for miles" and my fella would be "knocked bandy when he got a good gander at me". I hoped this was a good thing. Only time would tell.

I reread Jonathan's bio and then had another quick glance at his profile pic. He was six foot three, sported a thick thatch of salt and pepper grey hair and a neatly trimmed beard, a shade or two darker. He was smouldering out from the screen; his grey eyes were so magnetic I felt they could look into my very soul. He was smiling, his mouth closed but with full sensuous lips. I felt excitement and fear in equal measure. Please God, let me be doing the right thing.

Bella had given him her seal of approval. Obviously, him being 62 meant she was over forty years younger than him, so there was no fear of her drooling like a love-struck schoolgirl the way Dora had. In fact, my sister had commented that he was so dreamy, given half a chance she would ride him until the wheels fell off.

Bella had smiled at me and simply said he looked very handsome and could be considered a "stone cold silver fox", which I decided had to be a ringing endorsement in anyone's books. She had also been in favour of my choice in footwear; told me to strut into my date with poise and purpose. Since leaving Alfie, she was hooked on motivational podcasts and self-help books. I couldn't knock them; they seemed to be doing her the world of good. As I left the house, she had called out to me, "Don't forget, Evie, you're the SheEO in your own life; you go and boss it, babe!"

I actually didn't have the foggiest what she was talking about, but I gave her a cheery wave as I headed off in my taxi.

I was wearing my favourite little black dress, even though my sister had done plenty of tutting and rolling her eyes when she'd first clapped eyes on me in it. She said that calling it "little" went against trade descriptions, as it was skimming past my knees; and with its high neck and elbow-length sleeves it was as seductive as a day-old Yorkshire pudding. I strongly disagreed: it was elegant and sophisticated, and finished off perfectly with a single string of our mother's pearls and my hair caught up in a chic chignon.

I had to hotfoot it out of the house to avoid Dora with her armfuls of jaunty scarves and costume jewellery, advising me that if I really wanted to impress a man, I needed to dress more festive and fun. Apparently, colour was key when it came to catching a man's heart.

But now, here I was: Evelyn Weaver, a few inches taller and a few years younger (than was on my birth certificate anyway); standing outside the restaurant, ready to meet the man and just hoping beyond hope that he would like me.

With a deep breath and all the confidence I could muster, I pushed open the heavy wooden door that stood between me and the start of my new life, my dating life. The warmth of the bar within was welcoming. The time was now.

I spotted Jonathan straight away. He was sitting at a corner table, looking relaxed, with a large glass of red wine in front of him. He hadn't seen me yet, he was engrossed on his phone, tapping away on the screen. It gave me the opportunity to give him a quick once-over. I wished I had my glasses on. But even without them, he was looking damn well dishy. And now I knew what a catfish was, I was just relieved he was the man from his picture: elegant and empirically good-looking.

I took another deep breath, repeating the affirmations in my mind that Bella had taught me from her latest tome on self-belief: "I am confident...I am enough.... I shine like a thousand suns." As I walked confidently over, without wobbling on my high heels, I had more than an inkling that this was going to be a simply marvellous night.

Chapter 14

• ♥ • ♥ • ♥ • ♥ • ♥ •

"Jonathan?"

His head snapped up from his phone and I saw him look around a little startled. His eyes lit up when he saw me standing before him. And what beautiful grey eyes they were too, all the better for smouldering with. This was a very good start.

"Evelyn, there you are, how lovely. Please sit down. I've been so looking forward to meeting you."

I smiled back at my date, barely believing my luck. Ding dong, he was mighty fine.

He jumped quickly to his feet and rushed around the table to pull out my chair. Excellent manners, and I was a sucker for a chivalrous man. But I couldn't help noticing he wasn't the six foot three he'd claimed to be; in truth more like five foot nine. I hastily pushed this from my mind. After all, wasn't I guilty of knocking a few years off my age? So I couldn't be too shocked that he had chosen to fudge the truth on his bio a little too. He was a tad shorter than six foot three, and I was a tad older than mid-sixties. Really, where was the harm?

I accepted the seat gratefully, quickly removed my trench coat and slipped down into my seat in one fluid movement. So far so good; I was appearing quite elegant. Most unlike at home, where I was often to be found tripping over my own shadow, notably when wearing my fluffy slippers.

"Let me get you a drink, Evelyn. What would you like? Are you a confident cocktail drinker, or perhaps a red wine; this cabernet sauvignon really is quite sublime."

"A gin and tonic would be lovely, thank you, Jonathan."

Best to stick with what I had already started, although I really wasn't one for too much liquor. My mother had always called gin "mother's ruin", and I couldn't help thinking of that famous image from Hogarth's "Gin Lane". Also, as I always told Lottie, "Don't mix grape with grain." I was nothing if not sensible, so I would be sticking to my own advice.

Two double gins later, and my senses had all but left me entirely. Jonathan was talking ten to the dozen, and alas my perfect man was turning out to be a perfect bore and not at all what he had proclaimed to be.

Over the preceding weeks, we had exchanged so many lovely messages, his exceedingly witty and charming, that I had fallen completely under his spell. How could that be the same man now sitting opposite me?

Firstly, there was the fib about his height, which I could overlook. (In fact in my heels I could have overlooked him just about anywhere.) But then there was the matter of his teeth, or lack thereof. OK, he hadn't lied about them as such; he hadn't mentioned them at all, and his mouth had been shut in all his pictures. Truthfully, he was missing more teeth than my old zippy slippers. And even if I could look past a few missing molars, which I hoped I could, had the man never heard of Colgate whitening? His gnashers, along with being few and far between, were not so much the colour of pearly white as wet concrete.

This was most likely down to the amount of red wine he guzzled. He had necked three large glasses in quick succession, and there was still no mention of us ordering any food. Too busy flapping his gums, bragging non-stop about himself and his many many achievements to eat.

It was so strange: I had felt I knew this man before I even met him; imagined little scenarios of our possible future together, felt I would recognise his voice instantly, the lustrous timbre of his speech that I was sure he would possess. Nothing in fact could have been further from the truth. Jonathan had a very high-pitched voice and one hell of a lisp. In fact, his recounting how he became so successful a snowboarder had me wishing I had an umbrella tucked away in my clutch bag, anything to save me from the shower of spittle that was misting my face like setting spray. Jonathan definitely had some difficulty pronouncing his "s" words.

Without ever having to ask him a question, I discovered so many things about my date: the biggest being that he was a braggart of the highest order. Each accomplishment that rolled off his tongue was followed by something even more astonishing. I doubted very much whether all (or in fact any of it) was true.

Before his retirement, Jonathan had been afforded the largest executive corner office in his company, much to the chagrin of his jealous subordinates. He was also an excellent squash player, and his golf handicap was not just low, he in fact played off scratch. He was also gifted in the kitchen, after having learned the art of French cooking from a Michelin-starred chef in Paris, no less.

He extolled the virtues of live music, having seen most of the greats over his lifetime. In fact, he had just been down to Colchester to see his all-time favourite band, The Eagles, in concert. They had been playing at the castle. Of course, he had been the one person selected out of the huge audience to appear on stage with his idols.

He was also a keen rambler, which made sense as he had been rambling on for eternity. He droned on and on about the best hiking locations and types of terrain. I half expected him to whip out a Powerpoint presentation on it all. There was good walking to be had in Colchester, apparently; he had visited the nearby Fingringhoe and had saved the life of a fellow walker in the park. The poor chap had suffered a heart attack, so Jonathan had slung him over his shoulder as if he weighed less than a bag of sugar (oooh, that lisp) and carried him to safety. He clearly was quite the hero.

"That's unbelievable, really quite unbelievable." And I meant it.

He shrugged his shoulders nonchalantly. "All in a day in the life of Jonathan Handcock."

At least his name was apt. To use my grandson's vernacular, this wassock was an out and out wanker.

He went on to tell me about all his philanthropic endeavours. He gave generously to a wide array of charities. He paused to tap on his phone again. The only time he broke off from his monologue was to silence his constantly buzzing phone with a well-timed finger.

I did hope he was being truthful about his charity work, though. Never mind the rest of his tall tales, someone who could lie about supporting charities really was the lowest of the low. But even if all he said was true, and he really had Bob Geldof on speed dial, I certainly wouldn't be ringing the palace any time soon to suggest a knighthood for him too.

Whether his stories were just cavalier posturing or else out and out fiction, I did not know. Perhaps it wasn't all blatant lying, but there was definitely more than a pinch of bullshit peppering his many tales.

Eventually, thankfully, he ran out of steam. He fastened me with a wide wolfish grin. It went well with the red wine fangs around his mouth. He even had a little vin rouge staining his beard.

"So enough about me, Evelyn. I seem to have been talking too much. Tell me about yourself. I really want to know everything about you. First off, you're a widow, right? But are you a merry one? What exactly does a beautiful lady like you do for a little excitement?"

I felt a little thrown by this. I had already told Jonathan so much about me. In all the messages we had exchanged he had asked me many questions. So different from how he was tonight. I had been happy to send him lengthy, heartfelt replies, opening myself up to him completely. That charming man seemed so unlike the chap sitting across from me now.

"Well, you already know that I enjoy walks, good films, reading."

"Ahhh...yes." He was clearly not listening, distracted by his phone as he feverishly tapped away on it. I felt my stomach sink as I got a quick glance at this phone screen, realising he was logged into the dating site. Is that what had been happening all night? He'd been receiving messages from other women while on a date with me? It seemed to be the case. But I had believed that when we were messaging, neither of us was contacting anyone else. Well, I certainly wasn't, and he had led me to believe the same of him.

The waiter, a soft-spoken young man of no more than twenty, was back at our table clearing his throat in an attempt to attract my companion's attention. He had already tried to take our food order three times, but each occasion had been fruitless. Jonathan had merely wafted his hand at him, as if batting away an annoying bug, a gesture rudely informing the young man that we were still not ready to order.

I had cringed each time, feeling acutely embarrassed for the poor guy who was only trying to do his job. The optics weren't good. It was just plain rude of Jonathan, and I couldn't help but notice a few other diners eyeballing my date with simmering hostility. It was clear that Jonathan just liked to drink. I, on the other hand, needed something more substantial than a breadstick to mop up all the gin. It had gone straight to my head, and that never boded well; a good slice of bruschetta would do the job of sobering me up quite nicely.

"I'd like to order some food, please." I shot the waiter my brightest smile, and hoped my eyes conveyed my regret at how rude my date had been. He smiled down at me kindly; I could almost feel the waves of sympathy for my situation tumbling off him.

"Of course, madam, what can I get you?"

After a quick perusal of the thick leather-bound menu, I selected the goat's cheese bruschetta, some arancini balls and the gambas pil pil.

The waiter turned his attention to Jonathan, pad in hand, eyebrows slightly raised as if ready to be rebuked again. Jonathan looked none too pleased at the interruption, but took a cursory glance at his open menu.

"I'll have a large glass of the Sangiovese, the sun-dried tomato bruschetta, salade niçoise and calamares."

The waiter kept his head bowed as he noted it all down. Although I didn't know the young man, I felt proud of him: how he managed to keep a straight face and his composure was beyond me. It was certainly not funny to laugh at someone's speech impediment; but hearing my date make his menu choices was beyond funny. Who'd have thought ordering a few tapas dishes could be such a minefield for a lisper?

"OK, that's all grand, food will be with you shortly, folks, and if there's anything else you need, just shout."

He had his back to us now as he hurried away towards the kitchen. I could clearly see his shoulders shaking, no longer able to keep the laughter in. Jonathan, thankfully, hadn't noticed. He was too busy checking out the menu once again.

"I'd have liked to plump for the charcuterie board too, but decided against it; I find cured meat really makes my gout flare up."

As sweet talk went, I had heard better. His phone pinged again, and my eagle eye flew to the screen: another message from a woman. I suddenly had a rare moment of clarity. He was a dating dog, a romancer of many, possibly addicted to dating sites.

"Jonathan, are you talking to a lot of different women?"

Chapter 15

•♥•♥•♥•♥•♥•

"**W**ell... erm...one or two."

Perhaps I was being unreasonable, after all, after the last hour or so I never wanted to see this cretin again. I couldn't help but feel hurt.

"Jonathan, you said you'd only speak to one person at a time to try and establish that special connection; your bio was clear on that too...what did it say? Something along the lines of 'looking for that special one to spend the rest of your life with'."

At least he had the good grace to look a little sheepish. A stark contrast from the wolf who had been sitting across from me previously.

"Well...ah... yes, I am looking for the one ultimately, but I'm a fine specimen of a man, I'm sure you'll agree, so I have to keep my options open. I mean, let's be honest, it wouldn't be fair to all females everywhere if I just limited myself to the one lucky lady."

There was so much wrong with that statement. Firstly, I strongly disagreed that he was a fine specimen; more likely something yucky and gross to be studied under a microscope. And secondly, I think all females everywhere would breathe a collective sigh of relief if he was fished out of the dating pool for good. I smiled politely at him. I was nothing if not polite. He had clearly been using Dora's scattergun approach when it came to dating. But how had he managed to send so many messages to me? To appear so interested? The penny finally began to drop. He was probably copying and pasting the same messages to all these women. I wasn't anybody special; wasn't special at all. Just another one in a long line of gullible women.

I felt utterly deflated. Not because I wished to be with this man, perish the thought, but gutted that I had built him up in my mind so much. I had thought I had won the lottery, my first date in years and with a fabulous man to boot. But now I just felt worthless.

The waiter returned with our food. He placed the prawns and other tapas in front of me, the plate of crustaceans steaming hot, in stark contrast to the frostiness now hanging over the table like a cloak. Once all the plates were in front of us, there was to be no sharing, Jonathan had already informed me of this; he didn't like to share his food. It was tapas, for God's sake; wasn't the whole point to share? The waiter, who was clearly a sensible chap, beat a hasty retreat to the kitchen.

I speared a sizzling prawn on my fork, imagining it was part of my date's anatomy. Clearly he had cottoned on to the fact that all was not going as splendidly as he thought. From the lack of conversation coming from me, I could have been mistaken for a mime artist. And if I was, I would mime being trapped on the date from hell.

"Look, Evelyn, I feel I may have put my foot in it somewhat, so let's not talk of other people. It's just you and me tonight, and I feel there's a definite spark between us, an affinity if you will, like souls finding their true connection."

I doubted this massively. He was sounding as he had in the many messages he'd sent me, buttering me up like a hot crumpet, which I suppose to him I was. He clearly had a BA in all things bullshit. I let him carry on as I wolfed down my food. At least this evening I was going to enjoy a good meal.

He threw me a little suggestive wink. "I know you believe it too; I really feel we're so alike, I can definitely see a little of me in you."

I had to take a large gulp of water to dislodge the prawn that was stuck in my throat. Not a chance in the world was any part of him going in any part of me.

Jonathan leaned across the table and lowered his voice seductively. "Let's put our cards on the table. There's no denying you're a fine-looking woman, but let's face it, you're no spring chicken either. You must have thought all your birthdays had come at once to be sitting on a dinner date across from me."

Well, that wasn't right; in truth more like sitting slap bang across from a firing squad. And his words might as well have been bullets, not physically damaging, but hurting me nevertheless. How bloody rude of him. How could I have thought for a second this man was charming, when clearly I was sharing small plates with the embodiment of all earthly evil. He really was beyond repellent.

Jonathan took my ongoing silence as reason enough for him to plough on with his misogynistic nonsense. Was he always this much of a bore? Or was it exacerbated by how much red wine he'd thrown down his neck?

"And I know I said that I was a one-woman man, and strictly speaking I am, if I can find a real cracker. But I do like to hedge my bets a little; after all, I don't want to plump for just one lovely and find there's a new and improved version just out there waiting for me. It's rather like my golf clubs." At mention of his beloved sport, his eyes misted over a little. It was clear where his true love and affection actually lay, and it was not with a woman.

"'I'll keep my woods and putters for however long they're performing well; but once they're not up to scratch any more, it's high time for a replacement.'"

If I hadn't already been stony silent, I would have been rendered speechless. Did the man ever listen to himself? He must seriously think he was catnip to women. Not to me of course; I suddenly felt a kinship to Feline Dion, as I would happily scratch this cretin's eyes out, given half a chance.

His dating bio had been a work of pure fiction, knowing that a loyal man was like the Holy Grail to all singletons out there. He had fibbed his way into the affections of many females. But this man was in no way looking for commitment, though I'm pretty sure he needed committing to a facility somewhere.

"You know, Jonathan, you really should be more cognisant of the way you speak to people and how you're being perceived. The way you've talked to me just then is disrespectful in the extreme, and you were just as rude to our poor waiter."

Suddenly a startled look crossed his features. I couldn't fathom whether he was choking on his salade niçoise (sorry, nith-ois) or was perhaps rethinking his appalling behaviour over the last hour. It was neither.

Our waiter was walking past our table on his way to deliver a jug of water to some diners seated behind us, and Jonathan clicked his fingers loudly – a sound that reverberated around the restaurant and startled several diners.

"Waiter, here, now."

I knew in the pit of my stomach he was not going to apologise. The waiter, professional as always, tended to the other table promptly and was back to us in a flash.

"Yes, sir?"

Jonathan had pulled his wallet out of his suit pocket; it was a mock snakeskin affair and a bit poncey. No surprises there.

"Look here, laddie, I have a voucher somewhere in my wallet for forty percent off the meal if ordered before 8 p.m. I forgot to give it to you earlier."

I saw a fleeting look cross the young man's face. He was weighing up his options. We all knew that we had ordered the meal way past the 8 p.m. cut-off, but did he really want to go to war over it with this belligerent bellend? Probably like me he was half hoping Jonathan would lean over the table, get too close to the candle and the fumes from his red wine breath combined with the naked flame would see him go up in a whoosh.

The waiter simply nodded. The poor guy looked exhausted; it probably wasn't his first rude customer of the evening, and a fight with this boozed-up bore would simply not be good optics.

I felt myself cringe inside my beautiful crepe dress. Vouchers on a first date? Call me old-fashioned but that really wasn't the done thing, I was feeling awkward and unappreciated before, but now it was a thousand times worse. This date had been a disaster of epic proportions.

Jonathan was looking as pleased as punch. "Righto, well I'll just whip it out then."

My heart sank into my shoes. He'd better still be talking about the voucher. But after the way the date had gone, I half expected him to pull out his penis and plonk it on the table to be admired by all and sundry. After all his boasting, it was bound to be at least ten inches and a thing of beauty. Relief was not the word when he extracted a tatty folded-up print-out from his wallet and slapped it down on the table. "We'll have the bill too; we've finished eating."

Well, he might have done, his plates all scraped clean, although he had whinged his way through each plate – too spicy, not spicy enough, his calamares too "squiddy". How was that even a thing? But I still had some of my food left. To be fair, my appetite had pretty much deserted me, so I put my fork down and mouthed "sorry" to the poor waiter as he commenced clearing the plates away.

I glanced around the darkened interior of the restaurant. It was Friday night, so most of the tables were occupied by couples. I felt a wave of envy to see them huddled together, so romantic, so happy. Jonathan had noticed too.

"Oooh, look at them all billing and cooing over each other. Maybe they've got the right idea. Say, why don't you slide your chair a little closer to mine and we can do a bit of the same."

Absolutely not. I shook my head forcefully.

"Are you OK, Evelyn? I've got to say you've been very quiet. I feel I've had to keep the conversation going at times."

Keep the conversation going? The cheek of the man. It had been impossible to get a word in edgewise. "Actually, Jonathan, I'm feeling a little unwell. It may have been the prawns. I really think I might need to go home."

He was not impressed. In fact, his face was positively peevish. I half expected him to stomp out of the restaurant in high dudgeon, but thankfully he paid the bill first, and without whipping out his calculator to divvy it up to the exact penny, which was what I had expected, with me obviously having to pay more as I had opted for the expensive seafood option, or "she-food" as he had called it.

I suppose him paying the bill was the first thing in his favour. However, he paid it to the exact penny. There was no tip.

We made our way out of the establishment and onto the pavement beyond. The night sky was densely black and an owl hooted somewhere in the distance. It had an almost eerie feel to it. At least Jonathan still had good manners enough to help me into my coat, but I cringed all the while, scared he might try and cop a feel. He didn't. Possibly because he'd decided it wasn't worth the bother. I wasn't exactly blessed in the boob department, more flat-packed than fully assembled, if you know what I mean.

"Well, thank you, Jonathan, it was very nice to meet you."

I really was a good liar when I wanted to be. What I really should have said was that he was the most repulsive individual I had ever had the displeasure to meet in many a long year, and could he do the world a favour and take a night off from being a crashing bore and an arrogant twat.

"Well, how about we do it again sometime?"

Was the man actually insane? I needed to get away from this fool as soon as I could. "Oh, I'm sorry, Jonathan, I really don't feel very well. I simply must get some fresh air."

He looked from side to side. "What on earth are you talking about? We're outside?"

I gave him a hard stare. There was so much I wanted to say to him, but I just couldn't be bothered. Would he even listen anyway? There was only one person Jonathan found worth listening to, and that was the face that looked back at him from his bathroom mirror. Certainly not me.

"Sorry...I just can't... bye."

And on wobbly legs, in part due to the gin and the ridiculous high heels, I ran like a pair of cheap tights into the night. And out of Jonathan Handcock's life forever.

Chapter 16

O r so I'd hoped, but it seemed it wasn't going to be quite so easy as Jonathan had other ideas. I had barely slammed the door on my Uber (nice chap, good review imminent) when my phone vibrated with an incoming message. I fished it out from the depths of my handbag. No doubt it was from Bella or Dora keen to find out how the evening had gone. They would just have to wait a couple of minutes until I'd got into the house and out of my coat, and then I could unburden myself of all the juicy details. But alas it was neither of them, it was from Jonathan. There was a photo with an accompanying message that simply read, ***"a little something to whet your appetite."***

I couldn't quite work out what I was looking at. I turned the device around several times to try and get a better understanding. On first glance it appeared to be a baby mouse asleep on top of a ginger wig, but oh no, it was something far less cute than that. In fact, it was enough to knock me sick.

I felt repulsion sweep through me right to the tips of my toes. I really needed Lila's sci-fi fanatic boyfriend Seb here with me to perform a Jedi mind trick to expunge this visual image well and truly out of my head.

I opened the front door with shaky hands. As usual, Dora had forgotten to lock it. I was always nagging at her to make sure it was double-bolted of an evening, but she simply shrugged as if to say, "Whoops, forgot again."

"Dora...Dora... where are you?" My voice was high and shrill to my ears.

I heard some movement from the floor above, and my sister's muffled voice, "I'm in the bathroom."

"Well, what are you doing? I really need to speak to you right now." She spent hours in there, exfoliating and moisturising and all manner of other stuff, and her bubble baths spanned whole evenings.

"Well, truth be told, I'm having a little shit. But that's a detail most people don't require."

She was right, I didn't. A few excruciatingly slow seconds ticked by on the hall clock before I heard the rumble of the toilet flush, followed by my sister flinging open the bathroom door and hurtling down the stairs, simultaneously spraying a can of air freshener. It was after 10 p.m. so she was dressed in her night attire: leopard print shortie pyjamas, and her curly hair held back in a matching scrunchie. She was by my side in a flash, literally fizzing with excitement, all bright-eyed and with a lingering odour of forest pine about her.

"So how was the date? Tell all."

I rolled my eyes, a dead giveaway that it hadn't been all hearts and flowers, and made my way into the kitchen as she followed in my wake. I wasn't trying to build tension, I just really needed a nice strong cup of tea after the evening I'd had. Once the kettle was on to boil, I turned to face her with a sigh. "Honestly, I don't even know where to start."

Dora settled down on one of the kitchen chairs. I caught her giving me a quick once-over with an amused expression dominating her make-up-free face. I felt sure the same could not be said about me: no doubt my lipstick was a mess and mascara was streaking down to my collarbone. I must have looked a right fright.

"You're drunk, aren't you?"

I thought about this for a few seconds. I'd certainly had a fair bit to drink, but was I drunk? Not really. "Well, I may have had more gin and tonics than I should have, but I don't think I'm drunk, more sedated against the pain of the date from hell. But actually I'm more upset by what I've just received."

Dora's face instantly changed as her mouth settled into a concerned line. "Why, what's happened? Is it Lottie or Jacob? Are they ok? Or is it that Alfie? Has he done something with those pictures of poor Bella?"

I shook my head firmly. "No, nothing like that...but it is a picture and quite a horrific one at that."

I passed my mobile phone over to her and she scrutinised the image, like I had, turning the device around several times so she could better check it out from all angles.

"And this is from him?... Mr Perfect?"

I laughed bitterly. It wasn't a pleasant sound. "Believe me, he was anything but perfect. In fact the date was perfectly horrendous. He bored the very giblets out of me."

"Well, it can't have been that bad, my dearest, as it appears you have received your very first meat mail."

"Meat mail?"

"Yes, a dick pic. But why on earth he's sent you a picture of it all flaccid and slumbering like that is beyond me."

The phone vibrated again. I nearly jumped out of my skin. Dora, however, kept her composure and was nodding to herself. "Oh, hold on...yes...yes... that's more like it."

She turned the screen around so I could see. Another message had come through, this time a clear shot of an erect penis with the accompanying message:

"See what you're missing."

"He's definitely a grower." Dora sounded impressed. "Not manscaped, more's the pity, but that's the trouble with older men: they're not always up with the latest trends. But ginger pubes aside, I've got to say those are some aesthetically pleasing balls...very nice."

I grabbed my phone back from my sister with a stony glare. What fresh hell was this? What on earth was Jonathan thinking with an image like that? It should be illegal to send a picture of your meat and two veg to an unsuspecting lady. It was not something I wanted in my inbox, or any box for that matter. But for some reason I couldn't drag my gaze away from it. It was like a horror film when you're appalled by what you see and dearly want to hide behind a cushion, but you can't tear your eyes away.

Dora was clearly amused. "Yep, don't look too long at it or you might get dicknotised."

"That's disgusting... why would he even think that was an appropriate thing to do? The date was a disaster. I literally legged it away from him with the excuse of impending diarrhoea. What on earth was the man thinking?"

Dora nodded towards my phone. "*He* wasn't thinking, something else clearly was. And anyway, it's really not that big of a deal; he's just a chancer trying his luck. You know, like a friendly dog waving his tail at everyone and hoping someone, anyone, will pet him. He's got a big juicy bone and he's not afraid to share it. It's clear you don't want to tickle his pickle, so just block and delete. He probably won't be all old school and try to call you, too busy with his hands down his pants no doubt, but at least even if he tried, he wouldn't be able to get through if you've done the old blockeroo."

I guessed she was right, but blocking seemed a little drastic. Was that not just plain rude? It was as if my sister could read my mind.

"And it's not bad manners to block someone when they send you an unsolicited dick pic; sometimes you can be just too bloody nice, Evie. I realise you haven't got a nasty bone in your body." She broke off as she had started laughing and needed to regain her composure. "Well, you could if you wanted to, we've both seen the picture."

"Who's getting blocked?" Bella had appeared in the kitchen, also in her pyjamas, and wandered over to the fridge to get herself a bottle of water. What was wrong with the young and getting a good old glass of Adam's ale from the tap?

"Hello, darling, Evie's date from tonight seems like it was a right disaster. Haven't heard all the details yet, but he's sent her a couple of photos of his coc...crown jewels."

Bella's nose wrinkled up at in disgust. "Oooh no... really? The dirty old bugger."

So, we sat at the kitchen table and dissected the events of my disastrous date over cups of tea, bottles of water and a few slices of Battenburg cake. It was true what they said about a problem shared. I was beginning to feel much better about things. Could even see the humour in it.

"He sounds like a geriatric player to me," Bella noted wisely. Clearly at twenty years of age she was the most sensible out of the group. She nodded towards the few cake crumbs abandoned on the plate in front of her. "He wanted his cake and eat it too. Fancied you as a bit of a side piece."

Dora nodded in agreement. "Yep, he was a bona fide spunktrumpet all right."

I ignored my sister. She was clearly making up words at this point. "What do you mean, a side piece? Like a portion of onion rings or a slice of garlic bread?"

"Exactly, he's probably already got a girlfriend, or even a wife, but just fancies a bit on the side. You know, when you order the same thing every time you go to a restaurant, it's nice but it's a bit predictable; so you get yourself a bowl of cheesy chips on the side, just to liven things up a bit."

Questions circled frantically in my head, foremost why anyone would want to put cheese on top of their chips, but I think I knew what she was getting at. And she was probably spot on. I felt my good mood slip a little into despair. Nobody wanted to be thought of as a bit on the side, like a dollop of mayonnaise clinging to the crust of a burger; an afterthought, in all likelihood to be scraped into the bin. I was better than that. And Jonathan, well he was clearly the devil's own work and no mistake.

"But at least you've broken your duck."

I looked at my sister in confusion. What on earth was she going on about now? "I'm sorry, my duck?" As far as I was aware, the only thing that was broken was my spirit.

"It's a cricket turn; Keith just loves his cricket."

Bella and I exchanged a quick glance. We both were of the opinion that Dora and Keith were definitely an item, even though my sister was still adamant that wasn't the case.

Dora helped herself to the last sliver of cake. "You've got your first date under your belt; granted, it was a major fuck-up and old Jonathan sounds like he needs a hoof in his not unappealing balls, and so boring paint probably watches him dry. But if you think about it, things can only get better from here."

Bella nodded. "Yeah, things can only go up."

I thought of the picture I had received from my date and shuddered. I really hoped not. And would I really want another date after that fiasco?

Anyway, I was tired now; the effects of alcohol and adrenalin leaving my system hit me hard. I was keen to change the subject. Picking apart my date now felt about as much fun as picking nits out of eight-year-old Lottie's hair had been at primary school all those years ago. Plus, I was acutely aware that talking about these pictures from Jonathan could be triggering Bella to consider what was going on in her life. I turned towards her. She seemed happy enough, no obvious cause for concern.

"So, Bella, still no news from Alfie?"

"No, fingers crossed, it seems he finally realises that it's all over between us, and carrying out his threats of posting those pictures would see him get into so much trouble that even he isn't so stupid as to think it would be a good idea."

The fact was that Alfred Dodds could land himself in jail for up to two years if he carried out his threats.

"Well, that sounds promising, love. Let's hope he continues to keep his distance."

She nodded and took another sip of her water. I hoped she was as confident as her body language conveyed.

Bella had really come on in leaps and bounds since arriving. The shy, timid lass who could barely get through a cheese toastie and a mug of tea without crumbling into a sobbing mess was now a much more confident and happier person. It did the heart good to see. She had even secured a few hours working in a local children's clothes shop in Leeds city centre, run by Lottie's old boss Diane. Bella was apparently excellent with the customers, and she had a real affinity with the little kids too. Truth was, they all loved her. She had shyly told Dora and me that she had hopes of being a mum herself one day. And I knew beyond a shadow of a doubt that she would make a fabulous one. Just not with Alfred.

Dora gulped down the dregs of her tea and clapped her hands together. A veritable call to action. "Well, time to get back on the whores, I think."

My sister had whipped out her laptop and I could clearly see the familiar red flame logo of the dating site. My heart sank into my slingbacks. I really wasn't in the mood. And whores? I knew Jonathan clearly fancied himself as a bit of a gigolo in the making, but I really wanted to steer well clear from that kind of man in future.

"Seriously, Dora...the whores?"

Dora collapsed onto the table with laughter. She was crying so hard she was what she called "snot sobbing".

"Not *whores*...horse...get back on the horse. Just because your first date in years fell flatter than a flabby fart is no reason to throw in the towel."

She clicked on one image, and a dour-looking chap appeared. His bio informed us he was "DaveBehave65". Not a good start. Apparently he considered himself a dashing gentleman, but by the look of him he hadn't dashed anywhere in many a long year. His bio also claimed he had the heart of a poet but from his cold stare I worried it may be in a jar on his mantlepiece.

I let out an exaggerated sigh. My bed really was calling me. My sister took no notice, and before I could say "goodnight" and make a dash for the stairs and the safety of my duvet, another image had replaced Dave's.

"DisneyFanDan" was only marginally better: a chubby fella with a kind face smiled out from the photo. At least this one appeared less like a serial killer. Trouble was he also appeared to be in dire need of a good wash. He was giving off scruffy vibes from his long greasy hair down to his *Lion King* sweater, which bore several holes in the fabric, as if Mufasa himself had taken a few hearty bites out of it.

"Oooh, if you went out with him, you could be in your very own Disney film, *Lady and the Tramp*."

My face was like thunder, so wisely Dora moved on to the next man. "LegalEagle007", she read from his bio, nodding slowly to herself.

"This sounds more like it, even if he does have a chin as weak as the gin you serve. Alex, 64; retired barrister from Bradford, enjoys fine dining, long walks, James Bond films and his model train collection."

I looked over her shoulder to get a good look at Alex. He was smiling and holding a pint of dark ale, his sandy hair an obvious comb-over. He had a thick Argyle-type sweater and a bit of a boozer's nose. "A retired barrister, you say?" I looked at the photo again. "Can't see it myself. I certainly wouldn't peg him as being a barrister."

"Me neither...in fact I wouldn't peg him at all." Dora shuddered to herself. "Model trains, I ask you. What a passion killer that is."

She wasn't ready to give up just yet. Next up was "HeadingleyHarveyLooking4Luv". As was obvious from his bio, he hailed from Headingley and was as keen as mustard to meet his Miss Right. And he wasn't choosy. He was 38 himself, but had requested his date's age range be anywhere from 35 to 78. His picture showed him standing proudly in a river, the water waist high, casting his tackle with a hopeful look in his eye. He listed amongst his hobbies that he thoroughly enjoyed "fisting", and after seeing the photo I rather hoped that was a typo. But by this stage, who knew?

They really were a motley bunch. I wasn't exactly spoilt for choice. It was like picking the lowest hanging fruit in the orchard, the ones literally dragging on the floor, like some of these men's knuckles surely were. Dora clearly knew what I was thinking and jumped in.

"I know you wouldn't be interested in any of these chaps. You're a discerning lady after all. Hell, I'm hardly choosy, and I wouldn't have this bunch even if they were gift-wrapped and their peckers spurted out shots of Baileys. But I'm not letting you give up, Evie; there's no way I'm throwing my betting slip away just yet."

My sister really *didn't* have a way with words. "Look, Dora, I'm not saying I won't go on another date, potentially... eventually I will. I'm just saying not yet; at least let me have time to recover from the debacle that was the first one."

Dora shook her head like a petulant toddler, her bottom lip jutting out. "But if we keep looking, I'm sure your knight in shining armour could be just a few clicks away, just polishing his hardware and waiting to meet his maiden Evie, and for you to live happily ever after."

"Yeah, fat chance of that." I really was exhausted now. I scowled at my sister, my face like thunder – dark and foreboding.

"What's nagging at you?"

I gathered together the plates and mugs, ready to do the washing up. I had no intention of leaving it until the morning, not this time.

"There's only one person nagging at me, and I'm looking at her."

Chapter 17

Of course I relented. It was just easier that way. Dora had a way of nagging and niggling at me until it was just easier to give in and let her have what she wanted. It had been the same since we had been children. If I had a toy she wanted to play with, damn right she was going to get it. I guess I was just a bit of a soft touch at times.

And truth be told, although I had suffered through every excruciating millisecond of the date with Jonathan, I didn't want to throw the towel in just yet. So, against my better judgement, I promised her I would at least go on one more date.

His name was Philip, and he was a retired civil servant. I didn't exactly know what that meant in the real world, but I imagined some sort of stuffy grey character in a badly fitting suit. So that said, I felt him a safer bet than my last date. Boring might make a rather pleasant change of pace. He enjoyed cooking, detective shows and walking in the countryside. Nothing earth-shattering there, but nothing to alert the church elders either.

I arranged to meet him at Olive Affair. It was fast becoming my go-to place for candlelit liaisons. I didn't know if this was a good idea or not. Maybe the staff would see me as some later life floozy and discuss me around the dessert trolley in hushed whispers. But the truth was I just felt more comfortable with familiar surroundings, and knowledge of the quickest escape route was a bonus too.

I clocked him as soon as I entered the dining area. He was sitting in a rather relaxed manner at a table near the door. Jolly good, not too far then if I had to make a quick dash for it. He waved cheerily over to me. Thankfully he looked exactly like his photo – which according to Dora was often not the case. Apparently, some men had the nerve to send photos at least fifteen years out of date, and then not seem to understand their date's disappointment when they'd arranged to meet Tom Hardy but Tommy Lee Jones rocks up instead. Saying that, a date with Tommy Lee Jones would be plenty good in my book. And Dora had warned me about dates with men sporting the most lustrous locks in their profile pics, only in person to have a few wispy strands slicked into a ridiculous comb-over; and these men could never understand why she had an issue. Starting off a relationship on such an obvious lie could never be a good thing.

Thankfully, Philip looked exactly as I had been expecting. A not unhandsome face, nice and smiley, with a little grey hair neatly brushed back; and dressed smart casual with a pale blue shirt, blazer and dark indigo jeans. So far so good.

I was decked out in my outfit from the other night, sans the high heels. I had opted for my sensible flats this time.

Much easier to run screaming for the nearest exit in flats than on stilts; and as Lottie said, if I was going to be in pain thanks to the date, I didn't want to have sore feet too. And let's face it my last date had been so very painful.

I walked over to his table. There was still a little voice in my head screaming "What are you doing? Are you mad? You're far too old for this nonsense; run, woman, while you still have the chance."

But it was too late.

He was out of his chair and holding out his hand for me to shake. Thankfully his hand was bone dry; a clammy palm like a damp haddock at this juncture might very well have seen me running screaming for the door.

"Hello, Evelyn, do take a seat. And I must say you're looking especially splendid tonight. I always believed the hottest thing known to man was the sun, but I have clearly been mistaken as the hottest thing simply has to be you, my dear."

Oh no. He was Jonathan mark two. Here we go again.

Chapter 18

• ♥ • ♥ • ♥ • ♥ • ♥ •

As it turned out, Philip was nothing like Jonathan. It was such a relief to be proven wrong. Unfortunately, I still realised within the first few minutes of the date that he simply wasn't for me. And I would hazard a guess that he felt the same, but nevertheless he was good fun and made for quite charming company. So good in fact that the night was simply flying by.

OK, his sense of humour left a lot to be desired, so cringey I felt my toes curl inside my ballet pumps at times, but despite this I found him to have a certain boyish charm. Like when he told me, in an excited tone, to order absolutely anything off the menu as it was his treat, even suggesting a bottle of champagne to accompany our tapas dishes.

I had swept my eyes briefly over the drinks menu, shocked by the price of bottles, but he had merely shrugged his shoulders and invited me to touch the sleeve of his blazer. "Do you feel that, Evelyn? I tell you, girl, I'm made of money, so don't worry yourself; the night is on me; your money is no good here."

We ordered a plethora of dishes – seafood, meat and paella too, and Philip was more than happy to share. We had the same waiter who had served Jonathan and me, but unlike that date, Philip chatted pleasantly to him and was perfectly charming. The young man caught my eye at one point and given me the thumbs up. I smiled back at him. We knew what the other one thought without having to say a word. He had given his vote of confidence on my choice of date for the evening.

It was just a shame there was absolutely no chemistry between Philip and me. When you think about it, it's funny how attraction works. Sometimes someone might seem a good prospect on paper, but in reality there just isn't that *je ne sais quoi* that would pull you together as if by magnetic force. But magnetism aside, it still felt good just to be in the company of a nice man for the evening, and one that actually seemed interested to find out a little more about me.

"So, tell me about your husband, Evelyn."

Philip leaned over the table and refilled my glass of fizz. He only had one small glass himself, saying he wanted to keep a clear head as he was up early in the morning walking in the Yorkshire Dales with his rambling group. I felt comfortable in the knowledge that at least my date for the evening would remain sober, unlike Jonathan who had been unceremoniously pissed as a fart for the entirety of our night.

I took a long sip of wine. It was simply delicious; I savoured it as I thought about how best to answer. In all honesty if felt weird, almost disloyal, to talk about Andrew to another man. But if I was going to continue to date, it was something I was going to have to get over.

"Andrew was...well he was a wonderful man, we had a lovely marriage. It wasn't perfect by any stretch, but then again whose is? I was devastated when I lost him so suddenly...a heart attack."

I paused and took another sip of my drink, desperately trying to compose myself. I had felt the sudden onslaught of tears threatening, and I really didn't want to cry in public. It was strange how grief worked. You could be feeling fine, even enjoying yourself with another man, and then suddenly out of nowhere it would hit you like a punch to the stomach, not physically painful but excruciating none the less.

"My...my sister and my daughter think it's high time I got myself back out there again, you know, started dating, hence me being here tonight."

He nodded, understanding clear in his kind brown eyes. "They're right, you know. You can love someone and lose them, but it doesn't mean you need to be in mourning for the rest of your life. I'm sure Andrew wouldn't have wanted that for you, and in truth going on and living a happy life is a great testament to the love you shared together; the fact that you're willing to take a chance on love again. It might not be the same love, perhaps not glow as bright as the one you shared together, but still a light in the dark, something good in your life."

I appreciated his words. He really was a very nice man. He was right, of course. I didn't ever think I would love again like I had with Andrew. But my life wasn't over. I might still have another twenty odd years in front of me, and I knew now that I didn't want to spend it completely alone.

I lightened the mood by telling him about my disastrous date with Jonathan, and in turn he had me in stitches relaying a few stinkers of his own from the dating site. Some of them were clearly not interested in love, just looking for a free lunch. He was a generous soul and there were plenty of gold diggers around; as he explained in his own words, plenty had plundered his gold mine. But like he said, he set his sights low, so he was rarely disappointed. But then again there was always the odd occasion that could reduce him to shudders.

The most recent such date had been with a 62 year-old grandmother who drank pints of lager all night and then demanded everyone in the fine dining restaurant arm-wrestle her. They had to be politely asked to leave, which she had taken great exception to, and had finally to be escorted from the building by two burly wait staff with her shouting, "Thirty quid for a sliver of steak that tasted like it had been marinaded in a wrestler's jock strap, you robbing bastards! I'm off to find myself a doner kebab and a tub of garlic sauce."

He had cringed at this part of the story, and lowered his voice a few notches. "I really don't like to use the "c" word in front of a lady, but she really was quite... common."

Maybe my date with Jonathan hadn't been quite as bad as I'd thought after all.

I was pleased that Philip had the good grace to look appalled when I told him about the "arty" shots of male appendage Jonathan had sent me. He shook his head, clearly baffled by it.

"I just don't know why some men do that. I suppose teenagers – young guys maybe, they've got all the hormones raging and haven't grown up enough to realise that it's not the done thing, but a man in his sixties? OK, if a lady requests one, then fair enough; but just to send a picture of your crown jewels, no, that's just wrong. It's not something I would ever do. I would imagine most women would have a visceral aversion to getting one of those unexpectedly pop up, so to speak, on screen."

I nodded in agreement. "Absolutely, it sent a shiver right down my spine."

He took a sip of his mineral water and gave me a wink. "In all fairness, probably not the shiver he was hoping for. You should have messaged him straight back with something that would have put the wind right up him, told him you were forwarding the picture to his wife or that you had submitted it to a Facebook group, 'small dicks of the world unite', or something like that. After all, you know what they say: 'karma has everyone's address', and I'm betting he's probably married and has a todger like a tadpole."

I hadn't expected him to say that, and I couldn't help but laugh. In fact, I think a little bit of the champagne dribbled out of my nostril. Not terribly attractive, I think you'll agree.

"I'm sorry, Evelyn, am I being inappropriate? I know my sense of humour gets me in trouble at times."

"Inappropriate? Oh, I think we may have passed that mark some time ago."

I smiled at him, reassuring him I wasn't offended. Talking about Jonathan's naughty photos had hit a chord though. I couldn't help thinking about poor Bella and the threat she had been living under: constantly worried that intimate pictures of herself would end up on random websites. It didn't bear thinking about.

Philip offered me some more paella, but I declined. I was fit to burst — another sign that I was feeling relaxed on the date. If I had been ill at ease, there would have been no way I could have gobbled as much as I had. He scraped the remaining rice and chicken mix onto his plate. "The food's lovely here, I must say. Great choice, Evelyn."

He shovelled the rice into his mouth with gusto, mopping up the stray oil on his plate with a big chunk of crusty bread.

"But talking about that chap sending you a text of his tackle just seems so alien to me. To be fair, there's not much rumpy pumpy going on in my life these days, not with my sciatica." He laughed and took another hearty swig of water. "In fact, unless the lucky lady hops on top, it's really not worth the effort. Regretfully, I think my days of heavy lifting are over."

He gave me another cheeky wink, probably to check I wasn't too appalled, before carrying on. "It wasn't always like that though. I used to be quite the stallion back in my youth, I'll have you know. My ex-wife and I used to have the most amazing marathon sessions, love-making that went on for hours. Mind you, that consisted of me begging for a couple, and then ten minutes of lacklustre action."

He really was the limit. But I found his cheeky humour refreshing. Because we would only ever be friends, it didn't offend me in the slightest. It probably meant I'd been spending way too much time around my sister, and coarse language was now just water off a duck's back.

"Yes, I was what was commonly known as a sex object: I wanted sex, and the wife objected."

"Ha ha, yes, well, that joke is nearly as old as you are, and about as painful as your sciatica."

He held up his hands in mock contrition. "Touché, dear lady, touché. But look, as for you dating, just go for it, girl. No man's perfect, we all have a few design faults, but I've got to say you make a very pleasant dining companion and it would be a shame to rob all menfolk of your company. And if that date with joyless Jonathan was hitting rock bottom, there's only one way to go."

Clearly, he had the same opinion as Dora and Bella.

"You know, Philip, you're right, and I really am enjoying myself. I know there's no spark between us, but it's just been so much fun tonight, and fun has been a bit lacking in my life of late."

He gave me a look of mock devastation, his bottom lip trembling theatrically. "So, what you're saying is you don't find me completely irresistible. I must say I'm mighty aggrieved to hear that. So, I'm physically repugnant, am I? Well, I'm mortally wounded."

He picked up his dessert spoon as if he was going to plunge it into his chest.

"Stop it now, you're putting words into my mouth."

"Dear lady, I'm putting nothing in your mouth." He laughed again and the cheeky wink was back. "To be honest, if I had a fiver for every woman who had found me unattractive in my life, they'd be starting to find me attractive by just about now."

I smiled at him. I really appreciated his self-deprecating nature. After Jonathan, it made for a refreshing change of pace. OK, perhaps he was trying a bit too hard, like a stand-up comedian always trying to find the spotlight and get the biggest laugh, but I couldn't help but like him.

He was as good as his word when it came to paying. There was no hassle this time over money-off vouchers. In fact, the whole procedure was seamless. There was a generous tip for our lovely waiter too.

It was after 11 p.m., way past my bedtime. Although not always the most tactile of people, I felt the urge to lean over and give him a friendly hug.

"Thank you, Philip, I really have had the nicest night."

"So would you like to see me again, Evelyn?" His eyebrow was raised, looking at me expectantly.

The truth was, although I had enjoyed myself, I had no intention of seeing Philip again. We would only ever be friends, and I really wanted to find my special someone who would be much more than that. Trying to lighten the mood again, I gave him a wink of my own. I hope it mirrored his cheekiness, not suggesting I was suffering the onset of a stroke.

"Well, Philip, I think you'll find I'm kinda seeing...anyone else but you."

He threw his head back and roared with laughter. "OK, but how about a little bit of slap and tickle then? Is sex definitely off the cards?"

"In your dreams and in my nightmares."

He laughed again. He had a nice laugh. I couldn't help but wonder if I had said yes, would he have taken me up on it? I felt he was joking, but was he still trying his luck? He was a man after all, and according to Dora they were "always on the sniff for a bit".

I needn't have worried as his next words put me at ease. "I know I'm a relentless tease, Evelyn, but I really would like to see you again – just as friends. I know there's not going to be anything romantic between us, but I would like to take you out again. Not everyone gets my sense of humour the way you do."

I smiled at him warmly. He was right, I had really enjoyed his company and his wit. So much for me being the stuffy severe Evelyn Weaver I had always believed. Maybe you could teach an old dog new tricks after all. It was being around Dora and Bella: they had unlocked a less fussy version of me. I had to admit I liked it.

"So can I walk you to the taxi rank, my dear?"

I linked my arm through his. "Of course, Philip, I would be delighted – unless of course you want to stop off for a kebab on the way."

Chapter 19

•❤•❤•❤•❤•❤•

As it turned out, the adage about third time lucky turned out to be spot on. A few weeks after my one and only date with Philip, I met Edward.

It was an organic meeting too: no dating app involved this time. We had both been shopping and reached for the same packet of cream of chicken soup in Tesco's. Our eyes met – it was instant attraction over the instant soup. Perhaps not worthy of a Mills and Boon novel, but romantic nevertheless.

We got chatting in the "five items or less" aisle, and it progressed from there. After leaving the supermarket, we walked together to our respective cars. I had expected that to be it – supermarket trolleys that pass in the night, sort of situation, but he surprised me by inviting me to go to a local café for a cup of coffee. We shared a toasted English muffin as we sipped on our cooling cups of coffee, and we talked. Really talked.

He was my age – 69. Unlike on the dating app, I was completely upfront about my age. He didn't mind in the slightest that I was tapping at the door of 70. He said something cheesy about the older the vine, the sweeter the wine, and I smiled.

He was a retired university lecturer in English literature; he didn't exactly dress like one though. I always had the notion that retired professionals had a rather stuffy austere edge to them, but his grey hair was slightly on the long side, and he was casually dressed in a navy polo shirt and jeans in the same shade. He was an attractive man, not unlike Kevin Bacon in the looks department, which was a definite bonus; and just nudging six foot two, which meant I could easily wear my heels and he would still tower above me. Although whether I would wear high heels again was debatable.

Our first official date was at Olive Affair – no surprises there. We had the exact same waiter once more, and the exact same table. He smiled at me in recognition, a twinkle of amusement in his eyes to see me out on the town again with yet another man. I really was going to have to choose a new venue at some point.

We drank delicious dry white wine and ordered a large paella to share – chicken and chorizo.

The conversation was wide and varied. He spoke briefly of his career, his late wife whom he had lost to cancer several years before. His eyes filled up at this point, and I reached across the table to rub his arm to show my support. The poor man had been through so much.

He told me how he loved to travel, often as a solo, but wished in time to meet that special lady he could holiday with once more; make special memories with. He hoped that person would be me. We could travel to Venice, to have the opportunity to see it before it inevitably sank without trace. He wanted to float down the Grand Canal with me in our very own gondola. Unfortunately, he pronounced it as gorgonzola. I had to bite my tongue not to correct him. As misplaced malapropisms went, it was quite a doozy. I was swept away with dreams of the Rialto Bridge and St Mark's Square. I had always wanted to go to Venice. Andrew and I had planned to, but you know what they say about plans — and we never had the chance to, his sudden death had put paid to that. It was one of my biggest regrets. Would I ever get the chance to float on a gorgonzola...sorry, gondola, with a man I loved?

That was the one drawback with Edward, that he sometimes got his words confused. Like in the café when he became "fuss-strated" when his "expresso" was cold. I think you get the drift. That's not to say he wasn't smart — he really was — but he just seemed to get his words back to front or quite frankly completely wrong at times. It was surprising as English literature had been his speciality. I wondered if maybe I was just misunderstanding him, but I didn't think so.

But who was I to judge, and that aside he was simply lovely. And I agreed with him, I hoped we could travel together in time. In truth I was travelling already — in my mind, imagining us strolling down sandy beaches together, or sitting in a secluded bar drinking cocktails and gazing out towards the twinkling sea. I was seeing our future together, even though we were only a couple of hours into our first proper date.

When the night came to a close, I glanced at my watch. How could it be that hours had passed so quickly? I felt like the night had barely started. We had been sitting at our table for over four hours. The impatient staff were starting to stack chairs and blow out candles: a clear indication that it was about time for us to leave.

I was sad when the date ended, but then we had another and then another. Before I knew it, a month had flown past. We would spend hours together, walking and talking about anything and everything. There were trips to the theatre and long intimate lunches. I was a changed woman. There was a spring in my step now that came more from infatuation than insoles.

He lived only a few miles from me. I hadn't had the opportunity to see his house, though as he was currently having it fully refurbished, it was a bit of a bomb site. He had been staying with his son while the renovations took place. But I was so looking forward to seeing it when it was finished: it sounded perfect, a quaint cottage in a lovely village with breathtaking views. Edward had promised to cook for me in his brand new kitchen, and I was a sucker for a man who knew his way around a set of pots and pans.

Dora and Bella were pleased to see me so happy. They met Edward in passing a couple of times and seemed to approve. Had I fallen in love? I wasn't sure about that, but I definitely felt I was beginning to topple tentatively in that direction.

I even cooked for him at home, something I had not done for a man since Andrew passed away. I ensured my sister and Bella were out of the house, instructing them to go to the cinema for the night. I prepared my special dish of spaghetti carbonara, which Andrew had always loved so much. I stopped cooking it afterwards, but now the time seemed right to crack open the eggs and parmesan again. I cooked it the proper way, you see, the way the Italians did: no cream, just cheese and egg yolk to thicken the sauce, and the addition of cubes of pancetta to add subtle saltiness and flavour.

"This really is sublime," Edward commented, wolfing down the pasta in huge mouthfuls. "You certainly are a woman of many talents."

I blushed like a schoolgirl at this. It did my heart good to see him enjoying the food I had lovingly prepared. We followed the pasta with a home-made raspberry pavlova and then I did something even more out of character than scoff down a huge portion of dessert – I went to bed with him.

It still doesn't seem quite real. We kissed over the washing up. He had the tea towel ready to dry, and then it just happened. We kissed. OK, perhaps not the most romantic of backdrops, but it felt perfect. It was so nice to be kissed again, to be really kissed. To feel his arms encircle me and hold me close. I had always imagined if I had sex with a man again, I would be sick to my stomach with nerves. In reality it was nothing like that, it just felt so natural, so right.

Maybe the glass of port after dinner lowered my inhibitions. I don't know. What I do know is that I went to bed with him, and we made love. And it was lovely, not anxious, not awkward, just lovely. He was not as Dora would later ask "a freak in the sheets", but he was tender and giving. A generous lover, I guess you would say.

I still couldn't believe that I, Evelyn Weaver, on the cusp of her seventieth birthday, could be experiencing such feelings again, but I was. And it was everything I had hoped it would be – tender, affectionate; and I was happy, so happy.

I spent that first night together sleeping on his hairy chest, wrapping tendrils of greying hair around my fingers as if it was the most natural thing in the world. And we had done what came naturally to us. It turns out that after all the years of me checking the duvet was straightened out perfectly each morning, this old girl would still rather break the bed than make the bed.

Chapter 20

• ❤ • ❤ • ❤ • ❤ • ❤ •

I bought a brand new outfit for our date this evening, which cost a small fortune from the fancy boutique in town. It was a long satin number in hues of green and just skimmed my heels. It was a birthday present to me. Yes, I had turned seventy today.

I had point blank refused for Lottie and Dora to throw me a party. I saw nothing to celebrate in this milestone and the fact I was now officially old; I could no longer deny the fact.

I received a lovely present from Lottie and Jacob – a watercolour street scene I had been coveting in a local gallery. It was a very generous present, and I protested they were spending far too much; but my daughter just smiled and said that if she couldn't spoil her mother on her seventieth birthday, when could she? She really was the most thoughtful girl.

Bella bought me a beautiful box of Belgian chocolates; and Dora, well, Dora presented me with the tackiest set of polyester underwear I had ever had the misfortune to clap eyes on. They were scarlet and had holes where underwear should never have holes. The offending garments would be staying exactly where they currently were, hidden away in a plastic bag under my wardrobe. She told me I needed some sexy undies now I was getting some proper action. I knew that if I ever wore those underpinnings, the only action I would be seeing would be down the local hospital in the burns unit, not because my libido was on fire, but any friction against that cheap material would inevitably start a fire.

The brightest spot to the whole day was the fact that I was meeting Edward for dinner. That made the day very special. We were dining at a charming new French restaurant in the old industrial area of Leeds city centre. It was quite the up-and-coming place apparently, and specialised in wild meat like venison and pheasant. I was looking forward to sampling the menu, but packed a box of indigestion tablets away in my sparkly clutch just in case. It was an extremely chic little venue called Le Petit Gam.

I was just stepping out of my taxi when I spotted Edward waiting for me in the doorway of the restaurant, a single red rose in his hand. My heart leapt joyfully beneath my sensible cream bra.

"Evelyn, darling, you look beautiful; and may I wish you a happy birthday." He handed me the single stem and planted a tender kiss on my cheek. "A rose for a rose."

Yes, it was a cheesy line, but I couldn't help the tingle that travelled from my scalp all the way down to the tips of my toes: toes which just happened to be encased in a brand new pair of high heels. To hell with the sore feet, it was my seventieth birthday. I needed to feel glamorous; I demanded to feel glamorous.

We were escorted to our intimate table in the corner of the dark restaurant by the efficient maître d'. I thanked the man as he held my chair out for me, and slid happily into my seat. It really was an exquisite place. The hushed whispers of the other diners barely intruded on my thoughts as my eyes scanned the room, taking in the ornate chandeliers and the decadent scarlet furnishings. The room was literally fizzing with the energy of so many chic diners talking, laughing and enjoying their meals.

Once we were alone, thick leather-bound menus in hand, Edward presented me with a beautiful gift. It was so exquisitely wrapped in pink tissue paper with a large rose gold bow on top that it resembled a little piece of art itself, far too lovely to unwrap. But rip it apart I did, so keen to see what was inside. It was a small mother of pearl type box, and inside was the most gorgeous delicate gold heart pendant. I felt a little gasp escape my throat.

"Oh, Edward, it's gorgeous, simply gorgeous."

He reached over the table and deftly helped me secure the fine gold chain around my neck. "Not nearly as gorgeous as you, my darling. I wanted to get something as special as my feelings are for you. It's nine carrots gold you know, only the best for you, my love."

I let the "nine carrots" comment slide, and our eyes locked and held. My heart was melting faster than the candle on the table between us.

I felt the shivers again. He hadn't said he loved me yet. But I could feel the unspoken word hanging in the air. It would only be a matter of time.

The sound of a throat being cleared dragged us from the moment. Our waiter, a smart middle-aged man with serious eyes and bushy brows, was looking down at us intently. "Are you ready to order...sir... madam?"

The moment was broken. My eyes slid back down to the menu. There was so much choice.

"Perhaps some oysters first?" Edward suggested. "It is your birthday after all, so we should have something special; and you know what they say about oysters."

His eyebrow twitched suggestively. I felt a flush rise up my cheeks and hoped my menu was doing a good job of shielding it. What would the waiter think?

That said, I *had* ensured that our house would be empty tonight. Bella was staying at a friend's place, someone she'd recently reconnected with, and Dora had decided to take a short trip back home to Bristol. She claimed it was to check all was well with Feline, but I felt she also wanted to check in on Keith as she was missing him more. She was returning on the early train in the morning. Still no plans to return home for good yet.

I looked at the description of the oysters on the menu, where there was quite the choice: you could have them raw on the half shell with lemon, tabasco or mignonette sauce, although I had no idea what that was. There was even an option to have them baked with cheese on top.

"How do you take them? I rather like mine with a shot of tobacco."

I tried not to wince at his mistake and shut my menu with a resounding snap. "Sounds good, *tabasco* for me too then."

This wasn't in fact good at all. When he asked me how I took my oysters, I really wanted to reply, "Not at all...please just take the repulsive things as far away as possible from me." But I didn't. I just couldn't abide oysters – slimy little dollops of snot in my opinion. I'd choked a few down over the years, and was not a fan of the mucusy mollusc. But

Edward looked so eager for me to have some I didn't have the heart to tell him.

He ordered twelve of them. They arrived at our table within minutes, crowning a small mountain of ice. The waiter deposited them between us with a little nod of his head. "Freshly shucked oysters for you to enjoy."

I managed to deep throat a couple of them without chundering. Edward, on the other hand, appeared to be in heaven. His expression was pure ecstasy as he swallowed down the remaining ten. It was quite a feat in itself.

We'd then ordered the Côte de Boeuf with Béarnaise sauce for main. An exorbitantly expensive dish in my opinion, but like he said, it was a special occasion. I wondered if we would be splitting the bill, or would it be my birthday treat? I said a silent prayer, wishing to the gods of finance that I had enough in my current account to cover it.

I sipped on my cranberry and soda. I was trying it out as my new "go to" drink. Dora had informed me it was a good choice if you were trying to avoid the dreaded hangover, which I most certainly was. It was practically a health drink in her opinion; yes, you had the kick of the vodka, but with the accompanying cranberry juice you were detoxing at the same time. I really wasn't convinced by her logic, and in truth I would have preferred my vodka in a nice dry martini.

There was an elegant lady sitting on a stool at the bar in the corner, enjoying one. It looked so delicious I could almost taste the dry saltiness of the briny olive – or maybe that was the bloody oysters fighting their way back up my digestive system. The woman was a few years younger than me, but then again who wasn't. She was a waspy looking blonde type with jutting shoulder blades, an immaculate off the shoulder jumpsuit and an impeccably aloof air about her. I thought she looked simply magnificent.

Edward noticed me appraising her and leaned over to me, his voice lowered to a stage whisper. "I know; would you look at the state of her? A face so sour you would think there was pickled onion juice in her cocktail. Talk about mutton dressed as lamb, there's more than a mil of filler in that overstretched face, I bet. What is it with women these days, just not growing old gracefully? I bet she's had more work done than Notre Dame. That's what's so refreshing about you, Evelyn, you embrace your age, wrinkles and all."

He gave my hand an affectionate squeeze, but I felt my shoulders clench inside my couture. His words had touched a nerve, no surprises there. I gave my reflection a quick once over in the back on my dessert spoon. Never the best move. Maybe now I was seventy it was time I thought about a little nip and tuck myself. It could be my belated birthday present to myself. But could I really be bothered with all that fuss? Yes, I had wrinkles, and age spots on my hands. My joints ached and moaned when I moved too quickly, and sometimes I forgot where I had put my library book. But "me", that little undefinable part, my soul or whatever you considered it, still felt young, ageless if anything. I really didn't think I needed a trip to the beauty salon to feel good in my own skin.

I brushed aside Edward's tactless comment. I didn't need bringing down, especially on my birthday. It was just I didn't feel old when I was with him. In fact, if I avoided all mirrors, he made me feel about twenty again; but clearly that was not what he saw when he looked at me.

The next course arrived at our table. The beef looked amazing, served pink with dauphinoise potatoes and steamed greens. Perfection. I breathed all the mouthwatering aromas in and felt my mood instantly lift. Age spots aside, it was the most perfect night.

We ordered another bottle of wine from the sommelier. I had dispensed with the vodka cranberry and was now indulging in the crisp fruity white wine that Edward had recommended. He knew his stuff. It was delicious.

We made short work of the main course. I wasn't usually one for a lot of red meat, it played havoc with my bowels, but it simply melted in the mouth, and the creamy potatoes complemented the dish perfectly.

Edward rose to his feet, his chair scraping across the polished floor. "If you will just excuse me for a moment, I must take a turn to the little boys' room, all this wine is going straight through me."

He shot me one of his megawatt dazzling smiles, which made my tummy do a little flip; well, I hoped it was that and not the oysters making their return visit.

I watched him slowly walk away. I had loved to see him when I arrived, but to watch him saunter away was pretty spectacular too. He really did have the loveliest bum, still nicely toned and firm, not the saggy flat disaster that most men his age sported.

A shrill little pinging noise cut through the gentle jazz music that was piped through the dining room. I looked around me, confused. Where was that noise coming from? I heard it again. Then I realised it was emanating from beneath Edward's discarded napkin. I lifted the heavy linen cloth, noting its excellent quality; this really was a fine establishment to have such good linen wear.

Underneath the fabric square was my date's mobile phone. There was a little envelope icon on the screen indicating a new text message. I should have known better and have left well alone, but my natural nosiness got the better of me. I picked the device up and took a sneaky look. What I saw upset my stomach more than a thousand bad oysters ever could. I read the message, my blood running cold.

"Hi darling, hope snooker is going well. Could you pick up a pint of milk on your way home? Love you xxx"

This was bad enough, but then I saw who the sender was - "The wife."

Chapter 21

"Very fancy toilets those, decent quality porcelain and so clean you could eat your dinner in there if you wanted. Though whether anyone would want a portion of French onion soup out of a urinal is another matter, but it's certainly clean enough." He was laughing that good-natured laugh of his as he settled himself down comfortably in his chair. "I reckon that woman from the bar was checking my arse out when I was walking back from the gents' – can't blame her though, I bet you were doing the same as I walked away, eh?"

His cheeky wink was back. I fought the impulse to slap it straight off his face. I kept my expression impassive, my lips curled in a tight smile.

"You flatter yourself."

"Indeed I do, and please feel free to join in."

"Maybe she wasn't so much checking your posterior as lip reading what you were saying."

His jovial expression altered to one of surprise, bafflement even. "Eh?... Whatever is the matter, Evelyn?"

I kept my shoulders stiff. I must remain as composed as I could. I answered him frostily, a tight rictus smile fixed on my face. "Nothing's wrong, I'm absolutely fine."

He didn't look convinced, but let out a small, somewhat confused laugh. "Honestly, sometimes you're like an impregnable fortress, you're so difficult to read."

"I said I'm fine." I spat the words out, my voice firm.

In truth I was anything but fine. In fact, I felt perfectly wretched – small, pathetic and very very old. I had felt so elegant at the start of the evening, but now all I felt was tired and cheap – cheap in the most expensive outfit I had ever owned. His wife had messaged him. His *wife.* This was quite the feat, if the poor woman had been dead for years. Shuffled off this mortal coil after a particularly gruelling illness, I'd been told. Had she been so outraged at the thought of her husband out on the town with another woman that she'd travelled beyond the veil to leave a text message about semi-skimmed on his phone? Or was he in fact just a horrible treacherous liar who had conveniently "bumped off" his wife in his pursuit of a bit of extracurricular leg over?

He still looked unconvinced that I was in fact "fine", but returned to what remained of his beef, extolling the virtues of the creaminess of the dauphinoise.

Bugger the spuds, I was in shock. He had a wife – a wife. The shock that I was feeling slowly began to switch into simmering rage.

He scraped his plate, clearly loathing to leave a single scrap; in fact the way he was going, he might have the gold leaf off the dinner plate too.

"I'm so glad we chose the beef; it was simply exquisite, but there were so many other nice dishes on the menu. We must come again and try them all; talk about spoilt for choice."

"What took your fancy then, was it the gullible old trout?"

He looked up at me, his eyes wide in shock. "I beg your pardon, I don't recall seeing trout on the menu; there was a rather nice seabass I think, but trout...no, I don't think so."

"No, not on the menu; it's a nickname I'm thinking of giving myself, "gullible old trout", I'm just trying it on for size."

He laughed awkwardly, clearly picking up my meaningful micro-aggression but not having the foggiest what was going on.

Despite the perfect ambient temperature in the dining room, a frosty chill had settled over our table. It might well have been my birthday, but the evening was beginning to feel less like a party and more of a wake.

I felt Edward's eyes on me again; he was studying me as if I was a laboratory specimen under the microscope.

"Are you feeling quite alright, my darling? You're acting rather peculiar, and I must say your face is a little red."

My face a little red. Hardly surprising, seeing how I felt it had just been slapped. Slapped in my face and all my dignity stolen, that was how bad I felt. I was fuming, absolutely fuming. It was a surprise there wasn't steam coming out of my ears.

"If not gullible old trout, how about misunderstanding controlling shrew?"

He looked completely flummoxed now: glancing through the thick leather-bound menu, half expecting to see an option of roasted shrew between the bouillabaisse and coq au vin.

I pulled the napkin off the table with a flourish, like a magician producing a white rabbit. But there was no bunny this time, just his dated Nokia phone.

"Or is that how you think of your wife? How you justify cheating on her? You missed a message from her by the way, when you were busy admiring the urinals."

Now it was his turn to redden. He snatched his phone up from the table and glanced at the screen to see what the offending message said; keen to see exactly how much trouble he was in.

"I...I thought the battery was dead."

"Is the battery in your brain dead as well?"

"Ahhhh...Eve...Evelyn, let me explain."

"Explain what? That your wife doesn't understand you, that it's only a marriage of convenience, how you share separate beds? Don't bother, I read the message that sounds like someone who's clearly still in love with you and waiting for her night-time cocoa by the sound of it."

"No, I swear to God...please, just let me explain."

"Don't you go bringing God into this; there's nothing holy about what you've been up to."

"But...but..."

"You need to shut up, Edward! Nothing you say will ever make this OK. You've been caught out in the most massive lie, and because of that it now puts your every utterance into doubt."

He glanced around the restaurant looking for someone...anyone to help him out of this tricky situation. It appeared that in my anger I had been speaking louder than I'd realised, as we seemed to have attracted quite an audience of interested spectators.

There were looks of pity towards Edward from some of the male diners; maybe they too were currently out with women who they weren't wed to. A smart redheaded woman at the next table gave me a supportive nod, before fixing Edward with a look of pure venom. A waitress was currently flambéing her pancakes for dessert, and I bet she would have happily added Edward's meat and two veg to the pan, doused it with brandy and set it alight too.

Talking of Edward, he was still trying to talk me round, clearly thinking it was worth a shot. It wasn't. I had seen what a cheating spouse had done to my daughter. I wasn't going to be the one to destroy another woman's life.

"Honestly, she doesn't understand me, she's always doing her little craft projects or reading her books, and we haven't had sex in months. I just wanted to feel alive again, to have a woman who really wanted me. I've been in turmoil, you don't know how hard it's been for me."

He threw his arm out theatrically, tears collecting in the corner of his eyes. Crocodile tears, if I'd ever seen them. I really was beginning to see him as more reptile than man. And I didn't care how hard anything of his had been. That was no longer any of my concern. He was still trying to excuse his way out of it, but everything he said just made him seem even more of a prize pillock.

"It's like this restaurant, it's lovely, all fancy and that, with its à la carte menu, but sometimes we just want an all you can eat buffet. It's the same with women. I'm a good man, I really am, I'm just not good at sticking with one dish, do you see what I mean? Like when we met in the supermarket over the soup, there're so many different flavours you can't just stick with one."

I rolled my eyes heavenwards. He actually thought he was some sort of victim in all this, not his poor deluded doormat of a wife.

"Oh, please, could you at least save me your X Factor sob story."

I was on my feet, my chair scraping on the wooden floor. The sound was enough to set my teeth on edge. My teeth were already on edge, clenched tight with fury.

"What you are is a selfish worm of a man, who has a wife at home and decides he wants a bit on the side.... I'm a...a...." I desperately scrambled to find the word that Bella had used. "I'm a side piece!" I informed him more triumphantly than I felt. "Like a piece of cheesy garlic bread, and then when you've had enough of me, you'd throw me out like tomorrow's toast crumbs."

I then surprised even myself. I picked up my glass of wine and threw it squarely in his face. The look of complete disbelief as the expensive white wine dripped off the end of his nose was priceless. I heard a few random gasps and sniggers ring out around the room, and the woman at the table adjacent to ours smiled in a way that told me she was proud of me.

"I won't be seeing you again, Edward. I hope you have a nice life."

He was fumbling for his napkin, wiping the wine from his face, when another diner wandered past our table. Clearly, he had been in the gents' and had missed our altercation. He was on his way back to his dining companion, but stopped abruptly in his tracks. "Hey, Ed, buddy? Thought that was you."

He held out his hand to Edward, who now looked completely dumbfounded and shook it like it was a wet fish.

The man seemed completely oblivious to the weird atmosphere at our table and Edward's soggy face.

"How's the plumbing business going? I've just been in the bogs, and you want to see the quality porcelain in there, mate; it's top notch, I'm well impressed."

Edward was now looking more stunned than the red mullet on the menu. So, he had lied about his occupation also? Must have thought a retired university lecturer more impressive than a plumber. It made sense now. I had wondered how an English academic could get his words so jumbled up. Surely an educated man would have known that it wasn't a cheese and pickle *sammich*; but no, it turned out he was actually as thick as any doorstep butty.

I ripped the necklace from around my neck and dropped it into his half full glass of wine, where it sank slowly to the bottom, the gold reacting with the alcohol and already beginning to turn the chain green.

So it turned out that not only was our relationship fake, but my birthday present was too.

Chapter 22

• ♥ • ♥ • ♥ • ♥ • ♥ •

"I hope you punched him square in the dick."

I winced at my sister's words. She was annoyed on my behalf. I appreciated it, but there really was no need for such coarse language. I had become much more tolerant of my sister's fruity vernacular, but even so.

"Maybe after the fact I should have... ahem, hit him in the downstairs department; but I'm really not one for physical violence. The Sancerre in the face seemed to do the trick just fine."

"I know, but after what you'd found out about the little runt, a knock-down drag-out fight would have been much more fitting in my opinion, or at the very least a little well-deserved dust-up."

She rolled up the sleeves on her colourful smock top, as if prepared to track down Edward and clobber him on my behalf.

Of course I wasn't feeling my best. Newly seventy and newly single was not where I had planned to be at this stage of life. At least the girls were back. Returning to an empty house the night before had been a bitter end to what I'd thought would have been a wonderful night. Unlocking the door and being hit by the blanket of silence had taken me back to the days before Dora and Bella. A quiet life, a less hectic one, but less happy too.

But now I had my sister and Bella back. The noise, the mess, the madness, and I wouldn't be without it.

Bella wandered into the kitchen, dropping her overnight bag onto the floor, talking ten to the dozen about the amazing fun she had had catching up with her old friend Sara. They'd been out for a pizza and then the latest horror film, before talking until dawn and falling asleep on Sara's sofa.

She stopped slap bang in her tracks when she clocked Dora and me sitting at the kitchen table, my face a mask of misery and a half-eaten birthday cake sitting between us while we glumly shovelled spoonfuls of the cream-filled confection into our mouths.

"Oh no, what's happened?"

Dora turned to face her, a chunk of cake inches from her mouth. "Edward's happened, that's what; he's a lying filthy snake, so poor old Evie dumped his sorry arse before she even got a sniff of the dessert course."

Bella let out a sharp whistle from between her teeth. "No! I wasn't expecting that plot twist."

"None of us were, least of all Evie." My sister licked a big dollop of cream from her index finger before continuing. "To be fair though, in the long run I think it's probably for the best, even without the wife returning from the dead."

Bella's eyes widened at mention of a wife, dead or otherwise, and what was it with my sister? I really wasn't expecting this. I thought Dora had been as charmed by Edward as I had. I dropped my spoon; it landed on my dessert plate with a clatter that set my teeth on edge.

"What is it you're not saying, Dora?"

Her eyes darted left to right; she was weighing up if it was the right time to impart the information that was clearly on the tip of her tongue. She shrugged her shoulders slightly, proof to me that she was going to speak her mind and bugger the consequences.

"Well, truth be told, I never really liked him; found him to be a bit of smarmy one, but you seemed so happy we didn't want to burst your bubble."

"We?"

At this point Bella had the good grace to look uncomfortable, her eyes on the floor as if she suddenly found the dust on the skirting boards completely fascinating.

"Erm, he was OK, we just got a bit of a sleazy vibe off him, and the way he spoke at times was quite knobby, as if he was trying to impress us with his long words; but then he would get them mixed up, it was proper cringey."

Dora was nodding in agreement. "Yes, yes... I'm sure we talked to you about that, Evie."

"No, you most certainly did not," I replied huffily.

Dora looked confused, but then shrugged her shoulders once more. "Oh well, it must have been behind your back then, but we definitely said it. Anyway, you chucking him might be a real blessing in not much of a disguise."

This was a bit rich coming from my sister. She had dated some right chancers over the years and was never one to take a jot of advice from anyone on the matter of her love life.

"You're sounding a little cynical, Dora?"

She helped herself to another slice of cake. "It's best to be; these are very dark times, dear sister. Plus, that Edward was too fond of checking out my bosom. I know my shop front is impressively abundant, but he could at least have made it rather less obvious."

I felt my heart contract further. I had been oblivious to any of Edward's faults, well, until last night at least. My sister hadn't finished though.

Dora turned to address Bella, pushing a large slice of birthday cake onto the girl at the same time. "Poor Evie found a message on his phone from his dead wife, asking him to pick up milk on his way back from snooker. You can imagine her shock; but old Eddie boy certainly wasn't getting his cue chalked last night."

Bella sank down into the chair next to me and rubbed my hand affectionately, her eyes full of concern. "Is that why you've opened the birthday cake at 10 a.m., Evie? Her eyes travelled over the pitiful remains of what had once been a beautiful patisserie sponge from Lottie. "You said you were only going to have a small sliver every day as a treat."

I nodded glumly. "To hell with the calories; I'm trying to drown my sorrows in sponge and cream."

"Completely understandable, and is it working?"

"Not yet, I might need another slice."

I couldn't believe I had given my sister such a hard time over her breakfast pizza, and here I was scoffing down birthday cake as if my very life depended on it. In truth, I was barely tasting it. The hunger wasn't in my belly, it was in my soul. I just felt stupid and gullible and so very old.

Dora shot me a look of concern. She was not always the most observant of folk, but as sisters, we always knew when the other was not in a good way. She took my other hand and began to rub it gently. "Look, we need to cheer you up somehow. Why don't I tell the joke about the nun and the banana? It's always good for a laugh."

"Please don't." I rubbed my eyes wearily, suddenly exhausted. "I just feel so old and used. I really liked him; how could I have been so stupid? I thought he was everything I wanted. I'm embarrassed, and even now, after everything, I still miss him. Well actually that's not right, I miss what I had built him up to be in my mind. And a part of me is ashamed thinking I've made a show of myself in the restaurant in front of all those people, and in front of him, even though I know I was in the right."

Dora was shaking her head so violently that the plastic cockatoo earrings dangling from her lobes appeared to be flamenco dancing. "Look, a lioness doesn't worry about what a scabby tabby cat thinks; so put that philandering piece of pig poo right out of your mind."

It wasn't that easy though. I had thought I had found the one. But he was never going to be mine; he already belonged to someone else. Who would have thought I would have been the other woman, at my age?

I laughed cynically. "You know the restaurant was called Le Petit Gam, it means 'The little game'; rather fitting, when you think about it. I mean, Edward was playing a game with me, wasn't he?"

Whatever he had been doing, whatever games he had been playing, I knew that I for one was through with the dating game. I had given it a good enough run, but it just clearly wasn't for me. Sliding into my seventies and spinsterhood were just what was inevitable for me now. I was not putting my heart on the line again. Not being hurt like this. I wouldn't. I just couldn't.

We sat together at the table for the longest time; none of us speaking, all lost in our thoughts. When the doorbell rang out in the silence, it pulled us all abruptly from our own little worlds.

I wasn't expecting any visitors. I looked towards the other women: perhaps they were? Both Bella and Dora looked equally startled by the intrusion, but then my sister's eyes lit up. "Oooh, it might be the Amazon stuff I ordered: a lovely, framed print of David Hasselhoff in his red budgie smugglers, and a doughnut cushion for my piles; they were both on next-day delivery."

I sighed inwardly: my sister always had all manner of random crap turning up at all hours of the day and night.

Bella was out of her chair and heaving her backpack onto her shoulder. "I'll let you get it then; I'm off up to my room to unpack and have a nap. I'm shattered after last night."

I smiled warmly at her. She was a smart, thoughtful girl, and I knew that even though she would be tired, she was making herself scarce too as she thought I might need a bit of time on my own to lick my wounds. I didn't; I'd had way too much time on my own in my life.

Dora was up out of her seat too and rushing to the door, her dressing gown billowing out behind her, as frisky as an excited puppy. "I hope it's that hunky young delivery driver; I really don't mind taking a large package off him."

"Just behave yourself, Dora, you've frightened that poor lad enough already; any funny business and I'll tell him your real date of birth, not the one you give everyone with ten years lopped off."

I could just about make out her muttering "spoilsport" as she fumbled with the large bunch of keys, locating the correct one to unlock the heavy front door. I clearly heard the creaking noise as it swung open; I would have to oil the hinges at some point. And then there was silence. I really hoped the sight of my sister in all her colourful exuberance hadn't caused the delivery driver to faint on the spot, spilling his bounty of parcels all over the front step. The peace lasted a few more seconds, and then a shriek tore through the silence.

Bella was upstairs so I flew to my sister's side as quickly as my old bones and hazardous slippers would allow. I couldn't see who the visitor was, as her bulk was blocking the door. I couldn't get a look at the street either, to see if there was an Amazon van parked outside. Dora moved slightly to her left, and at that point I could see clearly who was standing at my door.

It was Bella's ex, Alfie.

Chapter 23

• ♥ • ♥ • ♥ • ♥ • ♥ •

"What do you want?" Dora's voice was like steel, her body language much the same.

Alfie sniffed unattractively, like he was in dire need of a handkerchief. He looked rather out of place on the quiet suburban street in his over-sized hoodie and baseball cap, his low-slung jeans sagging so much as if suggesting an incontinence pad underneath the denim. His many gold chains glinted in the harsh morning sun. He appeared to have walked straight out of one of those God-awful music videos that Jacob liked to watch. Gangster, I think it was commonly called.

Alfie regarded Dora and me with a look that was half sneering, half pity. He probably couldn't understand how Bella could be associating with two pathetic old crones such as us.

He turned his full attention to Dora. "Look, lady, I don't want no trouble like, I just wanna see my girl."

When Dora replied, her voice was so refined she could have been reading from a script for the afternoon play on Radio 4 back in the 1950s.

"Your girl? Believe me, young man, there is absolutely nothing here that belongs to you."

Alfie glowered at her, his eyes narrowing dangerously as he slowly sucked air through his teeth. Then he growled and all but stamped his feet, like a truculent toddler on the verge of a tantrum. He may have considered himself a hard man, but he looked just like a spoilt brat from where I was standing.

"Bella!" His voice was a roar now, reverberating around the quiet neighbourhood and startling old Mr Jenkins from number 5 who was taking his little Jack Russell, Peggy, out for her morning walk and bowel movement. He stopped dead in his tracks, took one startled look at young Alfie and dragged the poor mutt down the street by her collar in his haste to get away from the vicinity of our house. So much for neighbourhood watch.

"Bella," Alfie roared again. "Get yourself down here now...NOW!"

My heart was going ten to the dozen, and a cold chill swept through my body. The young thug had actually come to our door. He wasn't supposed to know where Bella had gone. How had he found her? And was he dangerous? He could be armed to the teeth, and we wouldn't have a clue. Despite my sister's bravado, I was feeling a sense of dread and foreboding that I wasn't accustomed to.

I heard a slight creak from above, and glancing towards the stairs I saw Bella tentatively making her way downstairs. When she saw him, she froze like a startled deer, the blood draining from her pretty face.

"Al...Alfie, how...how did you know I was here?"

He hawked up a glob of spit and deposited it on my front mat. Unlike the message displayed on the heavy brown matting, his behaviour was anything but welcome.

"A mate saw you and Sara out in town last night, and you know how loyal my boys are; they phoned me right away and told me, so I paid her a little visit this morning." He sneered, a more unattractive expression it would be impossible to find. "Unfortunately, you'd already left; but lovely Sara and me had a nice little chat."

Bella now resembled a soggy bag of rags, her face deathly pale and her body language completely defeated. "Please tell me you didn't hurt her."

"Nah, babe, of course I didn't, it's just you know how persuasive I can be. I just asked her where you were, and she couldn't wait to spill her guts."

I hoped that was just a turn of phrase, and he hadn't hurt Bella's friend. Whatever had happened, the poor girl had been frightened enough to tell him where Bella was staying.

Alfie was clearly getting impatient, but his voice took on a soothing, cajoling edge. "Darling, I just wanna talk to you, that's all."

Worried that she might acquiesce, I laid a protective hand on her shoulder. Her eyes met mine and I could see the poor girl was torn. It was obvious she was sorry she was bringing trouble to my door, but she was terrified too, that was clear.

"No, Alfie, I don't want you here...and I don't want to see you."

"I need you, babe. I miss you and I want you back. It's not the same without you, I just gotta have you back."

He shot Dora and me another one of his malevolent stares, obviously intended to reduce us to quivering wrecks, but my sister merely laughed in his face.

"That sounds like a 'you' problem to me, little boy."

Alfie looked completely outraged. He surely wasn't used to being disrespected, and never by an old lady like Dora. "Who asked you, granny? Why don't you just fuck off and let me speak to my girl. This has got nowt to do with you."

"It's got everything to do with me, this is my sister's house, and Bella is my friend, and you, young man, have no right to be here."

His face was incredulous, and he laughed – the most unpleasant sound I had heard since my sister's singing. "She's your *friend*? How is she your friend, you silly fat old bag? You've clearly lost your mind and gone gaga; probably should be in one of those old fuckers' care homes."

Dora's hackles were well and truly up. No one called her fat, and absolutely no one ever called her old, but to question her superior wit and intellect, well, that was asking for trouble on another level.

Her arms were crossed across her ample bosom and her voice was low and ominous. It was enough to send a chill down even my spine. "Go home, you ridiculous little shit, you're not wanted here. How hard is that for you to understand? Although you're most likely thicker than the earth's crust, surely even you can understand what 'bugger off' means. So clear off, back under whatever stone you crawled out from."

I pulled her back from the door slightly. This wasn't going to end well. Best I try to speak to him, calm the situation down, aim to stop it going completely nuclear. My tone was soft and measured, as if training a recalcitrant puppy.

"Look, Alfie, Bella doesn't want to speak to you. She's made it perfectly clear your relationship is over and she wants nothing more to do with you. So there's nothing here for you, and you need to leave.

"And what? You gonna make me, are you?"

"No, all I'm saying is that it would be in your best interests to just go home. They'll have explained at Fluck, Young and Glover how you're just making things worse for yourself by harassing Bella like this. You'll get yourself in more trouble, and Miss Glover will have you wrapped up in so many legal knots you'll never be able to pick yourself out of trouble."

Alfie dug around in the pocket of his jeans; they looked precariously close to falling off completely. He located his mobile phone and waved it in our faces. "Talk to me now, Bell, or I'm warning you: I'm going to send that pic of you with your gash out to everyone...and I mean *everyone*." The nasty sneer was back on his pasty pock-marked face; he really was a repugnant rat of a man.

Bella was at the bottom of the stairs now, wringing her hands together in fear. She was in such a dilemma. She didn't want to speak to him, but she clearly thought she had no choice. He had her over a barrel. If all her family and friends saw that image, her self-esteem and reputation would be ruined.

"Evie, I'd better talk to him. He'll do it, I know he will, and it will ruin my life."

Alfie's face brightened up and he slipped the device back in his pocket, thinking he'd won. "That's more like it, girl. Just get your stuff together and we can go back to mine. I've got some cans in and we can have a nice night, just the two of us. I'll treat you real nice, the way you like."

I took a step forward in my pink fluffy slippers, shoulders back and chest out; probably not quite as impressive as Dora in all her glory, but I hoped it would make for a formidable sight.

"I don't think so, old sport." Blimey now I was sounding all Radio 4 too. "She's staying in with us tonight and we're watching *Love Island* and eating vegetable lasagne, so hard luck."

Dora had returned to the kitchen while I had been trying, and failing, to talk sense to Alfie. But suddenly she was racing down the hall towards us, a myriad flash of colour in her oversized peacock-emblazoned dressing gown and tartan slippers, an empty bottle of gin in one hand and her ten-ton handbag in the other. And by the look of fury on her face, she was coming in hot.

"Stand aside, sister, I'm dealing with him." She was now literally nose to nose with the young man, narrowing her eyes and mirroring his aggressive stance. "Firstly, you will not be posting any pictures of our Bella, because it would ruin her life for a while and yours for much longer." She gave a bitter laugh. "Mind you, I don't reckon you've got much of a life to ruin anyway; and also if you send those pictures to *anybody*, it will be the last thing you ever do, sunshine."

Alfie was clearly thrown. He looked left and right down the street as if he couldn't quite fathom what was happening. This couldn't be real. An old woman daring to stand up to the mighty Alfie Dodds. Was he being set up in some sort of reality show? Maybe Ant and Dec were going to jump out from behind a conifer bush or wheelie bin and wave a microphone in his face.

"Are you threatening me, granny? Do you know who I am?" His voice was incredulous, his eyes darting around like a pinball machine.

"No, and I don't do threats. You just don't scare me, little boy. I've eaten blue cheese stronger than you; and no, I don't know you, perhaps I could look you up online. Pray tell me where I would find you? Little boy big ego.com?"

His eyes narrowed dangerously, and with a snap of his fingers his swagger was back. "Fuck off, you old bag! Come on, Bella, I won't tell you again: get your arse out of that house NOW!"

I quickly moved in front of Bella, partly to shield her, and partly to make sure she didn't obey his command as the girl was obviously petrified. Knowing how scared she was, we needed to protect her at all costs.

Dora appraised him again, as if she was looking at something particularly unappealing. I had seen my sister give the same look before, that time when she had been cleaning out Feline Dion's litter tray after the moggy had been eating kippers.

"No, you fuck off, arsehole! I've seen Disney films more threatening than you are. Believe me, I've met a lot of bullies in my life, and the one thing they all have in common is that they're cowards. You're picking on Bella because you think she's weaker; but you're wrong, she's stronger than you will ever be, buster. You don't scare me; I could chew you up and spit you out and not even get indigestion."

He sucked air through his teeth in utter contempt and then, quick as a flash, his shit-eating grin was back. "I'm going to crush you to dust, old woman, and don't say you weren't warned."

Chapter 24

·❤·❤·❤·❤·❤·

I t looked as if Alfie was about to attack, like an animal getting into the pounce position, his prey being us, within mauling distance.

Dora stood in front of him, her body language as confident as could be. She swung the empty liquor bottle around her head.

"You really don't want to mess with me, sunshine. This bottle is empty, which means I'm already pissed off; and believe me, I've got nothing left to lose. So come on, answer me back some more, you gormless little git. But just make sure that whatever comes out of your mouth next is some Oscar-worthy shit, as it's the last thing you'll ever say and it's going right on your headstone."

"You fat old cun..."

His eyes had been fixed on the empty bottle of Bombay Sapphire my sister was swinging around her hair, when thwack! Dora's handbag swung out from stage right and hit him full slap bang in the groin area. He went down like a lead weight, harder than Belinda had hit the deck on our Baltic Saga cruise after she'd been drinking holiday measures of vodka since before breakfast.

Alfie was now lying in the porch, rolling around on the welcome mat, groaning to himself. That tote to the testicles had been anything but welcome. The bag in question was now lying beside him, flung open, the clasp, like before in the pub, proving a little unpredictable, the contents lying haphazardly all around him: half-eaten packets of biscuits, a lipstick with no lid, *my* library book (I had been looking for that since last Tuesday), the lost lid from the pickle jar and Dora's various bottles of supplements. She scooped up all the errant items and gave Alfie one last withering look.

"Are you dizzy from the bag to the balls, or is it because the tables have turned? I'm sure you weren't expecting that; too used to always being the one who lets their fists fly."

She grabbed her handbag in her arms, slammed the door on him, promptly locked it and then exhaled. She may have felt exhilarated, but she looked completely exhausted.

Chapter 25

·❤·❤·❤·❤·❤·

"You've got cancer." Bella's voice was low and pitchy, her bottom lip wobbling slightly and her worried blue eyes fastened on Dora.

Dora meanwhile was stuffing all the spilled items into her bag and hurriedly zipping it up, her own eyes anywhere but on Bella.

"No, of course I don't, don't be so silly."

"You do." Bella's voice was insistent. "I recognise one of those bottles of tablets that fell out of your bag; they're the same ones my auntie took when she had cancer. I would remember that name anywhere."

I looked from one woman to the other. What was Bella talking about? Those pills were the supplements Dora took, along with all her other colourful array of vitamins. We always laughed that it was a wonder she didn't rattle when she walked with all her wonder pills. But cancer? No – Bella must have got the wrong end of the stick completely. Surely that couldn't be right? It just couldn't. My sister would have told me if she was ill. Wouldn't she?

I remember Bella had talked about an auntie she had been very close to who had passed away from cancer several years ago. It had affected her badly at the time.

Dora let out a small awkward laugh. There was little humour in it. "Did you see the look on Alfie's face? He wasn't expecting that wallop to his wedding tackle, was he? He went down faster than a bride on her wedding night. I bet he'll be limping all the way back home with his tail literally between his legs, if it hasn't dropped off, that is."

I was eyeballing my sister, my gaze never dropping from her face. She wasn't going to joke her way out of this one. "Don't change the subject, Dora. You can't have it, surely?"

Her eyes were on the floor again, as if also fascinated by the skirting boards. They could do with a good dust; my cleaning had taken a bit of a back seat lately. I felt adrenalin fizz through my system as if I had just swigged one of Bella's energy drinks.

"You do, don't you? Have cancer?"

The seconds ticked by on the old hall grandmother clock, punctuating the silence. Then my sister turned to face us, her expression defeated and tears collecting in her eyes.

"Yes...yes, I do."

Chapter 26

How had I not known? I felt sick – sick for not being there for my sister, sick at Edward for lying about his wife having died from cancer, just sick to my stomach. But I wasn't sick, was I? No, that was my sister. She was the one with the cancer.

Somehow we ended up in the lounge, although I couldn't for the life of me remember walking into the room; all hunched up together on the sofa, Dora in the middle and Bella and me on either side, holding her hands.

Bella had already phoned Sara and confirmed the girl was OK. Thankfully Alfie hadn't got physical with her. The poor girl had been so scared by just seeing him rock up on her doorstep that she surrendered the information about Bella. She was so apologetic, sorry for betraying Bella's confidence, sorry for letting her down; but Bella reassured her in a soothing voice that it was all OK. Alfie was a scary guy, and she knew how persuasive he could be. It wasn't Sara's fault, and there was no way they were going to fall out over it. That would only be playing into Alfie's hands.

Dora snuggled down into the cushions, her energy levels depleted, and took my hand. I couldn't help but notice how old our hands were when compared to Bella's. The blue veins and papery skin of age were clear to see as I held my sister's hand gently in my own. A memory flooded back to me of holding this very hand when we were young, dragging her along behind me to fetch groceries for our mother from the local Safeway – tins of fruit salad and Smash potato and packets of fig rolls, seeing how many Green Shield stamps we could accumulate. My teenage hand was slim and graceful as I pulled Dora along impatiently by hers, the soft podgy five-year-old hand, always a bit sticky from jam sandwiches and never-ending aniseed balls. I had felt her a nuisance back then, but now over fifty years later I never wanted to let her hand go, ever again.

Dora, her face pale, her eyes shadowy, still tried her best to keep the conversation away from talk of her health. "I don't reckon young Alfie will be back here in a hurry. He didn't figure that a couple of old broads like us would be any match for him, but he was sorely mistaken. He thinks he's such a hard man, but he couldn't fight his way out of the fog."

I squeezed my sister's hand again, feeling it cool against my own. The business with Alfie Dodds no longer seemed so important. "We can talk about all that later, Dora; we want to talk about you now."

Bella nodded in agreement, her blue eyes watery and full of emotion. "Yes, we just want to be here for you, for whatever you need."

I thought I knew my sister inside out, but it turned out there was so much in her life I didn't have a clue about. But things were beginning to seem clearer now, as if a cloud had lifted.

"So that's why you were so gung-ho with Alfie just now, walloping him with your bag, saying you'd got nothing to lose; it was because of the cancer, wasn't it? That's why you hit that man in the pub too, wasn't it?"

Dora looked down at her lap, her bottom lip wobbling. It broke my heart a little. She had always seemed so strong, so formidable, like a force of nature; but to see her vulnerable made me want to take care of my little sister all over again.

"And I guess that's why you went back to Bristol: not just to see Feline... or Keith."

She nodded her head. "Well yes, I wanted to check up on my lovely pussy cat, of course I did, but I had an appointment with my oncologist, for a CT scan and... stuff."

Bella's eyes were wide and worried; I figured mine would look much the same.

"I know I should have told you both, but I just didn't want to say it out loud." She sighed deeply, finally feeling the relief of unburdening herself. "If I admitted it to you, then it would make it all real and I didn't want that; I didn't want to feel like a sick, vulnerable old lady. That's not me, and that's not how I want the world to see me either."

"But how long have you known?" Bella's voice was gentle, her hand also clutching Dora's.

"A while. I was back and forth to the doctor's for a bit, not feeling right, and they did all sorts of tests. I just thought it was rheumatism or something, but anyway it turned out I had this tumour. So I needed to have surgery, they hoped that would sort it out, but it didn't."

She dropped my hand for a second to rummage up the sleeve of her cardigan for a crumpled tissue to dab her eyes with. "It turned out they had found it too late and it had spread; typical of me really, you know how I Iike to be everywhere at once."

She let out a hollow, humourless laugh. For the first time I noticed how frail she looked beneath her bravado and inch-thick shield of make-up.

"I'm not saying it was easy when I got the diagnosis, it really wasn't. I couldn't believe it at first, felt like I was stuck in a bad dream. After I got the news, I just sat in my chair at home for days staring out of the window at the world passing by outside, just carrying on like normal. But I saw nothing. It was as if I had given up, didn't see the point of anything any more, like I had already lost the battle, like I was soundlessly screaming into the void. I was blaming myself, my life decisions, railing at God. Believe me, I would have muttered incantations to the Devil if I had thought he would help, I was just that desperate. It all seemed so unfair. But then, what is fair? I've had a good life, been luckier than most, so that's when I gave my head a little wobble. I was still alive, still had a fair bit of life left in me. I reasoned that the best thing I could do was just make the most of the time I had left, and that's what I intend to do; and you're either with me now or against me, girls."

I hugged my sister, as did Bella; a clear sign of our solidarity. Of course we would be with her, support her in whatever way she needed.

"So last autumn when you went on that Mediterranean cruise with Pamela from Pilates, was that really where you were?"

She looked sheepish for a second and then shrugged. "That's when I had my operation. I just didn't want to worry everyone, so I said I had gone away. I was in hospital for a few days and then I recuperated at home. Keith was an absolute godsend; he's been the best friend to me, he really has. He nursed his wife for a long time before she passed away, and he's the most patient man. I owe him a debt of gratitude, I really do. The Macmillan nurses were angels too; I couldn't have got through it all without them, and I'm sure I'll need them more in time."

My heart ached. I felt completely wretched. I should have been there for her too. I *would* have wanted to be there: supporting her, sharing the pain the best I could, helping her heal, but I had never had the opportunity. My own sister diagnosed with The Big C, and I had never known. But I couldn't blame Dora for not telling me; I knew we hadn't been as close as we should have. I really believed we were now, but so much time had been wasted. Thank God we still had some time, and it wasn't too late. It's true what they say about hindsight: how I would change things if I could.

"I wondered why I never saw any pictures of your cruise; you're normally the selfie queen. I should have known that something was wrong."

Tears were flowing freely down my cheeks now. Dora reached up her sleeve to locate another tissue and tenderly dabbed at my face.

"This...this is what I didn't want; to see this look on your face. I wanted to save you the pain. Please don't blame yourself, this is how I wanted it."

I sniffed unattractively and forced myself to stem the flow of tears. I nodded at my sister. Whatever she wanted she could have. It was her rules now.

"I just want to be me. I don't want people treating me like I'm already dead; there's plenty of life left in this old bow-wow, so nobody's going to write me off just yet."

Bella had been as quiet as a mouse up to that point. "But you said it had spread."

"It has; unfortunately there's not a lot they can do for me. I'm OK now, but it will get worse in time. I take painkillers, and I have those tablets." Her head nodded towards her handbag. "But I'm fine at the moment, not quite ready for the knacker's yard just yet."

Bella gave her a small watery smile. She was being brave, but not nearly as brave as Dora. My sister, always the poster child for positivity, gave my arm a little poke with her finger.

"Cheer the fuck up, Evie, or I might just have to give you a wallop with my handbag too. I won't go down without a fight. I'm so much more than this disease, and it certainly doesn't define me. Yes, unfortunately, like the Tory party, inevitably the cancer's going to win; but until then we will carry on as normal. If I'm honest, as someone who's burned brightly her entire life, I know I'm fading now; I can feel it. But while there's breath in my body, I'm going to kick up my heels and dance. Believe me, when the Grim Reaper comes for me, I'll be going down swinging, and I don't just mean my handbag."

"So that's why you came to stay out of the blue?"

"Of course it is; I had to come home, and home to me will always be by your side. You're my older sister and I love you, there's nowhere I would rather be. And haven't we had a laugh, my darling?"

I nodded my head in agreement. I couldn't argue with that. There had been a fair few laughs alright.

"And the icing on the top of the cake was to get to know Bella too. Who'd have thought at my age, with no bairns of my own, I would get the opportunity to become so close to a little darling like our Bell."

Bella was openly crying now and hugging tightly into Dora, her blonde head against my sister's ample bosom.

"Having her here has been like having the daughter and granddaughter I was never lucky enough to get in life. I feel truly blessed. I'm exactly where I should be now, and despite everything I'm happy...so happy."

She wiped the tears gently from Bella's cheeks. "And to help you with Alfie just made that icing a little bit sweeter."

Bella lifted her head from Dora's shoulder, her wide blue eyes full of concern. "But what if he goes to the police and says you attacked him with your handbag, knocked him down? We could all be in trouble. I didn't want to bring bother to you both; you've been so good to me, and I don't want to cause you grief, especially not now."

"Don't you worry about that, my darling. Alfie might only have two brain cells, and both of them are fighting for third place, but even he's not that stupid."

I had to agree with my sister on this one.

"What, us get into trouble? Two little old ladies acting in self-defence against a bully like him? No chance, his street cred wouldn't take it for a start, and even if he did report us, I doubt the police would believe it for a second. Believe me, sometimes there's something to be said for living in such an ageist society: us oldies are invisible and irrelevant. They couldn't possibly believe we'd been up to no good. We'll just say we were watching *Countdown* with our knitting."

Bella grinned a smile that made her appear even younger than her twenty years. There were light brown freckles sprinkled over the bridge of her nose, and she had a beautiful angelic aura about her that came more from a good soul than any beauty counter. "I'm so happy I've met you too, both of you, you're my family now and I love you."

We all embraced again. She was right. We were family.

"You're just so brave, Dora."

"Rubbish, girl, there ain't no one braver than you. Look beneath the surface and we're all raw and exposed, fighting our own demons, whether they be health, financial, relationships, whatever; it's how we decide to fight these demons that's the important thing. And all three of us *are* fighters, all in our own way, even if we're so very different. But that's what makes us all unique, and that's what makes us such a fabulous family.

Chapter 27

· ♥ · ♥ · ♥ · ♥ · ♥ ·

I was back out on the town again at Olive Affair. Honestly, I should have had shares in the place the amount of business I had given them. But not on a date this time. After the Edward debacle, I was pausing my pursuit of love; well, just for a bit anyway. After him, I'd thought that would be the end of me dating forever. But now I wasn't so sure. I might return to the dating scene in time. Or I might not. I hadn't decided.

What I had decided was that I was going to make my sister my top priority. And that started with her ticking off everything on her bucket list. It turned out there wasn't actually that much that she still wanted to do in her time left. Dora had never shied away from adventure during her six decades on this earth. She had already ridden a camel in Africa, scuba dived in the Red Sea and bungee jumped off the Lloyds Amphitheatre in Bristol.

She had never been a shrinking violet when it came to white knuckle adventures: if you weren't living on the edge, she felt you were taking up too much room. Unfortunately, she wasn't fit enough to hike the Inca Trail to Machu Picchu any more, or visit the Taj Mahal – not in this lifetime anyway. And cage diving with great white sharks really didn't seem appropriate for someone who was already on borrowed time.

The night after she'd broken the news of her diagnosis to us, she told Lottie. I was so proud of my girl that night: she adored her auntie, and I knew she was devastated, but she never cried; just the tiniest wobble of her bottom lip as she hugged Dora and declared, "We're going to paint the town every colour of the rainbow, just like your wardrobe. My Auntie Isadora forever!"

We had all sat together that night in my little lounge – me, Lottie, Bella, even Jacob who was Facetiming from his uni halls. Now his was a face we all liked to spend time with. And we compiled "Dora's doing it" list. We marked the occasion with her favourite takeaway – doner kebab pizza and garlic mayo. I even had a couple of slices myself, confident in the knowledge that there was a full bottle of Gaviscon in the bathroom cabinet. I was much more laid back in my attitude to food now. I wasn't so militant in my counting of the calories. Let's face it, life was too bloody short. I would no longer wrap up half a Kit-kat for later. I was a changed woman.

Jacob enjoyed his own pizza during the call – vegan. It wasn't from a local takeaway either; he'd apparently made it himself. For the boy who had existed for burgers and fried chicken, this was a turn-up for the books. It seemed he had just finished with his latest girlfriend, but she had left him with a couple of things – half a tin of her organic deodorant and an urge to boycott the meat industry. He now had real ethical concerns about animal welfare and the environmental impact of eating meat. There was a time I would have scoffed at this, as I scoffed my bacon sandwich. But not any more; he was a principled man, and I was proud of him.

We talked and talked that night: about Dora's life with Oscar, us as kids, her hopes and dreams, some that she had achieved, others that now she never would. Finally, we had her list complete: all the things she still realistically wanted to achieve before she dropped off her perch and retired to the giant pizzeria in the sky. After all, Dora was convinced that calories didn't count on the celestial plane.

Most of her wants were small, the most important being to spend time with me. That was no problem – that was the easiest thing in the world to achieve. I would be stuck to my sister like her shadow on a sunny day. We all made a pact that night that we would ensure she managed to cross off every single item on the list. There were ten of them in in total, and in no particular order:

To have a good old knees-up with all my girl friends

To enjoy a four seasons pizza while listening to Vivaldi

To kiss a man with a lip ring to see if it tickled

For my friends and family to "be more Dora"

To go on a gastronomic tour of India

To attend a masquerade ball

To drink absinthe

To learn a new musical instrument

To go skinny dipping

To eat a Cadbury Curly Wurly and to hell with the dentures

The list stayed where it had been written – on the coffee table in the lounge. She wrote it several months ago now, and so far we had managed to cross off a couple. My sister had enjoyed her Curly Wurly very much, Bella and I not so much as we had to witness her pick caramel out of her teeth for the rest of the evening. She had also pretty much mastered her musical instrument – the ukulele. Jacob had bought it for her, as he figured it might be an easier option for Dora to master than his favourite guitar.

We had the delight of hearing *You are my sunshine* and *Twinkle Twinkle Little Star* on a screechy loop for several weeks as she practised. Apparently these were the easiest songs to learn; though they were certainly not easy on the ear drums. But true to her wish, she had learned a new musical instrument. It was quite an accomplishment, considering everything she was going through.

As much as I would have liked to, I couldn't ignore the fact that my sister was steadily going downhill. The hospital appointments were becoming more frequent. And although the essence of Dora was still very much there – the quick wit and the outrageous sense of style, the exuberant love of life – she just seemed diluted somehow, as if her battery was only charging to ten percent rather than the Duracell Dora we had all been accustomed to.

My stomach would anxiously knot, knowing that at some point I was going to have to say goodbye to my sister forever. But not yet. Please God, not yet.

So that was why we were out at Olive Affair. It had been top of her list to have a good old knees-up: drinks, dinner and dancing after. We were even planning to go to Eduardo's nightclub, which I hadn't frequented since the 1980s when it had then been known as The Limelight Lounge – all sticky carpets and stickier cocktail glasses. From what I'd heard, its modern-day reincarnation was no better. But I was happy to go; anything to make my sister smile.

Dora had wanted us to all to "be more Dora" and dress like her. That was seriously out of my comfort zone, so I dug out my birthday outfit. After all it was gorgeous, cost an absolute bomb and I hadn't had the chance to wear it since the disastrous date with Edward. I was no longer saving anything for best. If my sister's diagnosis had taught me anything, it was that it really was later than you think – wear the dress, take the trip. I'd even changed to buying double chocolate biscuits for my afternoon brew instead of the cardboard ones of old. Life was just too damn short.

As always, I was left waiting for Dora, worried that the taxi would arrive while she was still half-dressed and unable to find her other earring. I kept glancing at my watch, conscious of the time and the very real possibility we would be arriving at the restaurant late. But Dora flounced into the lounge with minutes to spare – a glorious cornucopia of colour. She was wearing a silken low-cut maxi dress, all swirls and psychedelic print, with sequins and jewels twinkling prettily under the ceiling light.

She was the very antithesis of understated, and I loved her for it. It was a showstopping little number all right, and a confident choice for a woman in her sixties; but I felt fiercely proud of her. Her generous bosom was on display, just as she liked it, but it was clear to see she had lost weight; the fabric hung from her frame more than I knew she would have liked. But she looked beautiful, really beautiful.

From the look on her face, I didn't think she thought the same of me. "Oh no, Evie, that simply won't do. Everyone has to "be more Dora", and that means dressing like me too. I'm not saying your dress isn't nice, it's beautiful, but it's not right for tonight; far too traditional, much too safe. You're the fashion equivalent of a grey sprinkle on a rainbow cupcake."

She held out her hand for me to take. "Come on, there's still time before the taxi arrives. I'll find you something perfect from my wardrobe."

Chapter 28

So there I was, now dressed in the "perfect" outfit. Perfect may have been stretching it somewhat, as I felt like I could easily scoop first place at a bad taste Dolly Parton look-alike party. In truth, my outfit would make dear Dolly run for the Smoky Mountains as if her shapely derrière was ablaze.

It was a flamingo pink number, cut on the bias to flatter, and believe me there was little to flatter in this get-up. My décolletage was on display and I was dripping in diamanté. Even my earlobes were feeling over-dressed, weighted down with drop earrings that could easily have moonlighted as stately home chandeliers.

Dora had even given my make-up a bit of a "freshen up" too, and I now had shrimpy pink lips and matching cheekbones. My hair had been fluffed up like an Old English Sheepdog at Crufts. Take the sheep out of the equation, and it was spot on. And she had brought tears to my eyes with the amount of backcombing I had to endure, but she just shook her head at my protestations and informed me that it would all be worth it when I saw the finished product. After all, the higher the hair, the closer you were to heaven. When she eventually finished torturing me, she looked me over with definite pride. So I, Evelyn Weaver was a vision in shocking pink (and boy, was it shocking): a later life diva dressed to impress, or possibly distress. Only time would tell.

It was a short taxi ride to the restaurant, and Dora proudly shot me a "see, I told you so" look when the middle-aged driver referred to us a couple of "bobby dazzlers". She was so looking forward to her night out, and I just kept my fingers crossed that it would turn out to be everything she hoped.

We were just about to enter the restaurant when Dora turned to me and tugged nervously on my sleeve. A look of concern twisted her features, her previous confident countenance clearly gone.

"Do you think this is too much, even for me? I know I like to show my boobs, but tell me honestly, Evie, do they look like a plate of undressed tripe? This dress was reduced in the sales, so I had to have it, but now I'm not so sure. Is it just too much cleavage? Plus, I really want to order pizza tonight, and my boobs are terrible crumb collectors at the best of times."

My poor sister. After everything she had been through, her confidence had taken an almighty knock. She had never been one to give a flying fart about anyone's opinion of how she looked. She dressed for herself, and if you didn't like it, you needn't look. But now her self-esteem was dropping faster than Alfie had after she'd bashed him in the balls.

I placed my hands firmly on her shoulders and looked into her beautiful green eyes that still shone more brightly than any sequin on her dress. I answered her with complete honesty.

"Your dress was reduced, was it? Well, I'll tell you this for nothing, you'll reduce every man in that bar to a quivering wreck once they see you in it. You look beautiful, my darling – radiant and ravishing. Never mind Lottie and Lila and the young ones out tonight; I'll need to keep all the fellas away from you." I nodded towards her bust. "They'll all be ogling your fine china."

She laughed, and I could see her nerves melting away. But I wasn't fibbing; it was all true. She really was so pretty. She may have felt tired and more than a little defeated, but standing there together it was as if we were young girls once more, the years simply stripped away. I hugged her and held her close. And we both knew in that moment that no more words needed to be exchanged. We loved each other. Nothing more, nothing less. Sisters.

There were a select group of us venturing out on the town that night. Aside from Dora and me, there would be Bella, Lottie and Lila too. All lovely girls, so it should be fabulous. Dora had resisted inviting any of her Bristol friends; she said she just wanted her closest gals there. I feared that meant she still hadn't told her other friends about her diagnosis. I realised how reticent Dora felt about telling anyone. It was all cause and effect: if she told her friends how ill she was, she would no longer just be Dora, a force to be reckoned with, the brightest light in any room. No, she would become Dora, the cancer victim. And she wasn't ready for that, not yet anyway. But tonight wasn't the night to grill her on the topic. The only thing on the grill this evening should be the langoustines for the tapas.

I had my arm linked through Dora's as we made our way into the dimly lit restaurant. It was warm and inviting and customarily busy for a Saturday night, all soft lighting and easy jazz adding to the ambiance, just as it had been on my various dates there (the less said about them the better). It didn't take long to spot the girls. They might as well have had a flashing neon sign above their heads. Never had I seen so much faux fur and glitter in my seventy years on earth.

"Mum, over here." Lottie was enthusiastically waving at us. She was dressed in a figure-hugging striped maxi dress with a cropped denim jacket on top. The dress was multi-coloured, like one of those Fruit Pastille ice lollies Jacob used to devour in the summer when he was little. I suddenly had a fond memory of my grandson – all multi-coloured tongue and grubby knees.

Lottie had never previously been one to favour wearing horizontal stripes, reckoning them the epitome of unflattering fashion. I felt a little tug of regret – for it would have been me that had convinced her of that. I really had been a sanctimonious old so-and-so at times. But despite the stripes, her flamboyant make-up and the fact she had, like me, had her blonde locks backcombed till she looked like she'd suffered an electric shock, she looked magnificent. We were tasked with channelling Dora's style that evening, and boy, had my girl done her auntie proud.

Dora let out a little whoop of delight and raced over to her niece, swooping her into a massive bear hug. "Lottie, you look positively darling. I'm sure I've got that dress at home too; I'd accuse you of nicking it from me except mine is at least three sizes bigger." She laughed, her face simply radiant.

"Thanks, Auntie Dor, I got it from the charity shop. I just went in and demanded they show me all their most flamboyant stuff, and it was the first thing they brought out. To be honest, it's a little out of my comfort zone, but I finally get what you've been saying all along – dress cheerful and bright and you feel cheerful and bright. And all the people who keep smiling at me has been amazing. Even on the way here, some old chap told me I had made his day. He called me 'Josephina in her technicolour dream dress'."

Bella was nodding her head. "Well, he was right; you do look dreamy. You're crushing it, Lottie, you look completely snatched. In fact, you should have the emergency services on speed dial because you're on fire, girl."

Never mind Joseph from the Old Testament and his colourful cloak; once again I was left feeling like Methuselah listening to the younger generations talk. When I was a girl, everything was "groovy" and "far out"; but "crushing it", "snatched" and "on fire" – that sounded more like something straight out of a Netflix crime documentary than a compliment in my book.

Lila moved in for her turn to hug Dora. Her blonde hair, which was so often slicked back in a stylish chignon, had been gently curled and hung prettily on her slim shoulders, which just happened to be encased in a crinkly silver bomber jacket that could have doubled as a suitable receptacle to wrap her executive lunch in or store her leftovers. "Well, just as long as some fella doesn't try and snatch our Lottie tonight; she's too bloody loved up with her Leo for any of that."

Despite the thick layer of rouge, it was clear to see that Lottie was blushing. I was delighted that things were going from strength to strength with her beau. They had just

officially moved in together, and rather than getting under each other's feet, they were loving every second. She
had even confided in me over a telephone call a couple of
days before that they had discussed the possibility of even
having a baby together.

Though Lottie was now 45, she was seriously considering it; and with Leo being that bit younger, it didn't seem
completely impractical. Leo would love to be a father, and
he was determined to be a hands-on dad. He had even
talked about retiring at the ripe old age of 36. But I suppose
he had made enough money to last them several lifetimes,
so why the hell not? They had been to see a doctor; there
had been talk of temperature and ovulation and such stuff,
and the plan was to see if things could happen naturally. It
might not happen overnight, what with Lottie's age, but
as she joked, they could have a lot of fun trying.

I wasn't sure at first how I felt about it. After all, there
would be one hell of an age gap between the baby and
Jacob, but apparently my grandson was all for it. He loved
his mother and got on like a house ablaze with Leo, so
he was "high key" excited about the prospect of having
a little brother or sister. And apparently him pushing a
baby around the local park would make him irresistible to
the opposite sex, as if the pram wheels magically squirted
pheromones. I didn't quite understand his logic here, but
who was I to argue? So, if my grandson was happy, and
my daughter was happy, then I was simply over the moon.
Perhaps another grandchild on the way: what could be
better?

I did know one thing for sure though: Jacob might be
delighted at the prospect of having a little brother of sister,
but there would be one person who wouldn't be quite
so happy – Daniel. Lottie's ex-husband was still smarting

over Lottie's relationship with Leo. A bit rich really, considering it was he who had destroyed their marriage in the first place, the conniving swivel-eyed rat, literally blown it to smithereens with a brazen bombshell named Roxy.

Of course, Roxy and Daniel hadn't stayed the course, due in part to the fact that she was an out- and-out gold digger and she viewed Daniel as her own personal goldmine. And when she had mined him dry, she had simply moved on to his mate. She was one of those "influencer" types I kept hearing people banging on about. You know the ones? They make a couple of videos on social media about blemish cream, and then suddenly imagine they're a celebrity. Let's put it this way, she was no Meryl Streep; but she would apparently go to the opening of a tuna can given half a chance, and behaved like she was showbiz royalty.

But she was long gone now, and Daniel was alone. He had dated a few women since Roxy, and apparently they had all wiped him out financially too. He favoured a certain type of woman these days: young, blonde and with the IQ of a blunt pencil. They would be far keener to strip him of his assets than his underpants, and when they'd taken all they could, they would scamper off into the night as fast as their twenty-something legs could manage.

He was now living in a bedsit in a less salubrious part of town, but no doubt still as pompous as ever. Some things never change. However, it wasn't so easy to look down your nose at all and sundry when you were sharing a toilet with three other men, all of whom were builders and existed mostly on a diet of meat pies, energy drinks and takeaway curries. Poor Daniel, that judgemental old conk of his must have its work cut out in that bathroom all right. I could only imagine the pong, and it wouldn't be Estée Lauder, that was for sure.

Dora gave Lila an appreciative once-over, taking in her shiny jacket and skin-tight Shania Twain-style tight leather pants and sky-high heels. Her expression was one of absolute approval.

"Well, you always look beautiful, Lila, but sometimes in your stuffy suits and shirts you're a bit of a bland bombshell. But we can't say that tonight: no, tonight you're a bona fide top of the range blonde bombshell if ever there was one."

Lila looked a little miffed. Her stuffy suits and shirts were top-end designer numbers, and no doubt cost much more than Dora's pension; but she chose to take no offence at her words. Always the lawyer, she would weigh things up strategically before deciding whether it was prudent to argue; and clearly this time it wasn't. "Well, thank you, kind lady." She gave a little bow, the satin pants creaking alarmingly.

Bella was looking beautiful too; but then again, she always did. However, whereas we all looked spectacular in our sartorial nod to Dora, we could easily have been mistaken for a glamorous drag act. Bella, on the other hand, in her fluffy neon green shrug, crimped hair and baggy harem pants managed somehow to remain achingly hip and not appear in the slightest "cabaret". That was the luxury of being young, I supposed.

We settled ourselves comfortably at a large circular table in the restaurant area (far better than a long table for talking). I couldn't help but notice the amused glances we were receiving from other diners. I was certainly dressed differently than on my previous visits. Their stares didn't feel judgemental though. The fact we had all chosen to dress in a rather outlandish fashion made none of us feel too conspicuous. Like we were a team – Team Dora. I looked towards my sister, sitting in pride of place at the centre of the table. She had always chosen to dress like this, every day of her life; a chance to take centre stage and bugger the looks. She would float through life bright and vibrant and brush off any judgement that came across her path. I had always felt that while I lived in the "real world", my sister chose to live in "Dora Land". But now I realised that my sister had had the right idea all along. Dora Land was the best place to be.

The waiter appeared at our table: brisk and efficient, once again the same waiter I always seemed to have. We were going to be exchanging Christmas cards at this rate.

"Can I get you ladies some drinks?"

Dora's eyes lit up at the prospect of incoming booze. "Oooh, yes please, darling, can we get a round of your finest Baby Daddies please?"

He nodded before departing to the bar, not before giving me a little wave of acknowledgement.

Baby Daddies? The mind simply boggled. I hadn't the faintest idea what went into a beverage of that name. Something quite potent, I would imagine, and possibly not to my taste. But it was Dora's night, so I kept my opinions strictly to myself.

My sister was rubbing her hands together in glee. "Fabulous, so we're all the designated drinkers tonight...buckle up, ladies, this could get messy."

Chapter 29

The dinner was excellent, as always; you really couldn't fault this place. Most of our group plumped for the tapas, but Dora was true to her word and ordered a pizza, as did I.

She had studied the menu for several minutes before shutting it with a resounding snap. "I'll have the Vivaldi pizza, please."

The waiter looked completely lost. "The Vivaldi pizza, madam? Er, I don't think we have that on the menu." A smile slowly spread across his face. "Oh...I see, you mean *Le Quattro Stagioni – The Four Seasons*."

Dora nodded her head. "Precisely, with extra cheese please."

This was another item ticked off her bucket list. As soon as she was presented with her food, which looked amazing, the resounding violin concerto was played throughout the dining room. Soft jazz no more, making way for the more rousing "Winter", my sister's favourite. Her eyes filled with tears as she listened, taking occasional bites of her pizza. I wondered if it was Lottie who had asked the venue to play Vivaldi in honour of Dora. That would explain the situation, and how important it was to her. Whoever had made the request I was glad, and thankful that the restaurant had been so accommodating.

The music was poignant and fitting. After all, my sister was now in the winter of her life. Time was short and we had no way of knowing whether she would even see another year or have the chance to experience the beauty and majesty of the changing seasons for herself. It took all my strength not to cry too.

I looked down at my plate as I willed the tears away. I had ordered pizza too, to hell with the calories. It looked delicious – goat's cheese and rocket. I had ignored my sister's wrinkled nose and look of disgust at my menu choice. She tried to persuade me to order the same as hers. Apparently, her Four Seasons was perfection: light and crisp and the perfect meat to cheese ratio. Dora had always taken her carbs very seriously.

Lottie cleared her throat and nodded to us all. "A toast, ladies: to Dora, like our outfits tonight, may her sparkle never dim."

We held our sticky glasses of Baby Daddies aloft and toasted my sister. "To Dora."

But sadly, her sparkle was already on the wane. Dora didn't have all the time in the world. None of us did.

But for tonight we were going to have fun, make the best of things, and that included drinking like our livers depended on it.

Lila was by far the worst for wear. She admitted that she'd indulged in a cheeky liquid lunch with some colleagues from her solicitors' practice, so tonight she was merely topping up her levels. She said she'd spent the day not so much working hard as hardly working. Her shimmery violet lipstick was all askew, much of it on her teeth, and there were blue mascara shadows under her eyes. She was certainly not her usual impeccable self, but despite all this she still managed to look gorgeous; if slightly less poised.

Lila recounted the tale of a former work colleague, one Jocasta Jennings, who had made a play for her boyfriend Seb. She had been quite the little madam, even making eyes (and a fair bit more) at the big boss to try and further her career. It appeared that the young woman had played more games than a finalist at Wimbledon. But Lila had managed to bring her down a peg or two before her inevitable departure from the firm.

"She soon saw the error of her ways." Lila let out a little gassy hiccup. "The trouble is that some women ruin it for the rest of us who want to be taken seriously in the workplace; they think it's still the 1970s and they can fuck their way to the top."

Goodness gracious. The conversation was really going downhill fast. Dora took the opportunity to put in her two pennyworth.

"Fuck their way to the top? Darling, I worked in a cake shop for most of my life, and I couldn't even have fucked my way to the middle. Anyone coming into Bun Jovi was strictly after a bit on the side, the side of their dessert plate that is. More apple turnover than leg over in that place, if you catch my drift. Mind you, there was this one sleazy guy who used to come in every other day just for one single ring doughnut. I did often wonder if he bought that cake for the intended purpose."

She shuddered slightly; clearly the memory of the dodgy guy and the doughnut hole was none too pleasant. She took a long swig of her drink before continuing. "To be honest, since Oscar died, I've not wanted to have a serious relationship; I'd much rather make a guest appearance in men's lives every now and then and then sashay away when it starts to get serious. Rather like my mobile phone contract: I don't like to be tied down, but prefer to have plenty of free roaming."

I bit my tongue not to mention Keith. I still wasn't convinced that things weren't serious with him.

Dora pushed her pizza away, clearly done with it. She had barely eaten half. Her legendary appetite had waned of late.

"The trouble is that nothing was ever as good as it was with Ossie. My love for him was everything; no other man could even come close. Yes, it was nice having the odd bit of slap and tickle with a fella, but it was never as satisfying as being with someone you really loved and who really loved you. Someone you could be completely exposed with – body and soul. But I fancied him too, boy, did I fancy him. I tell you girls he was a right looker, my Ossie. As fit as a butcher's dog, and his trouser department was top notch. It was girthy like a tube of sour cream Pringles, and he knew exactly how to use it too. Oh yes, he knew his way around a double divan all right."

There was a faraway look on her face now. She was remembering her husband and all his charms. I had to quell the impulse to admonish my sister, warn her to keep the conversation less gutter-based. But this was her night, and nothing was off limits; even talk of my late brother-in-law's meat and two veg.

But she hadn't finished, and still had some wisdom left to impart. "Yes, sex with someone you love is so much better. Casual sex, or "smash and dash" as I think it's called, is good in a junk food sort of way – cheap, hot and tasty, but overall unsatisfying. Ossie, on the other hand, was like the finest *filet mignon*, and quality like that only comes along once in a girl's life."

My sister turned her attention to me. "How are about you, Evie? I know you've had a bit of bad luck in the love department lately, but don't you want to encounter passion again, even now you've turned the big seven 0?"

"I think I'd rather encounter a bit more goat's cheese on this pizza at this point in time."

She nodded sagely. "Fair enough, your Andrew was the love of your life, like Ossie was to me. And let's face it, your luck with men since then has been exceptionally bad." Her face suddenly brightened up; it was as if someone had shone a light directly at her. "Hey, what about dipping your toe in the lady pool? Apparently, a lot of us older ladies are changing it up and going lesbian."

I shot my sister a wary look before reaching forward to gently brush some pizza crumbs from her décolletage. She was right, her breast shelf was a terrible crumb collector. And she hadn't even eaten that much.

"Despite just touching your boobs, I can confirm that I am not in the slightest swayed towards anything sapphic, thank you very much."

"Fair enough, it was just a thought."

Bella, who was sitting across from us, gave an audible sigh. It was clear she was thinking about Alfie. "I really hope I meet my Oscar or Andrew one day."

Dora reached over the table, nearly knocking over the pepper grinder in the process. "You will, my darling, you will. You never know, the man of your dreams may even be here tonight, or if not then on his way very soon."

We all took the opportunity to check out the talent at the bar, in case Bella's ideal man was indeed in attendance. The elegant bar area was raised and set back from the restaurant. It was a relaxed space where one could enjoy an aperitif before dinner or a digestif afterwards. There were a few men relaxing on the high bar stools, but unfortunately for Bella they were strictly more Z list than A. There wasn't one of them worthy of our girl's affection.

That didn't stop them looking though. Bella was oblivious, but a few of them were surreptitiously giving her the glad eye, one making it more than obvious what his intentions were as he blew a kiss in her direction. He was much older than her, possibly mid-forties, an oily-looking lothario type with overly tight trousers and garish pink shirt. The horror on Bella's face on clocking him was quite something.

Dora's voice was soothing as she reached over the table and once again squeezed the girl's hand. "Don't you worry about him, not one of us would be interested in that creepy little shit. But it's just typical he thinks he can pull the youngest in the group. The state of him? He's got a chin as weak as these cocktails, and his trousers are so tight he's got a mammal toe."

I didn't know what a mammal toe was, but I could hazard a guess. And I had to agree with my sister that he was enough to put any woman off her bedtime Horlicks.

Lottie had been a little quiet all evening: smiling often, but not really participating in the conversations. I knew she was finding things tough. She was putting on such a brave face, but I understood the news about Dora had really hit her hard. She reached out and touched her auntie's arm briefly. "You're looking so lovely tonight, Auntie Dor, really happy."

"That's because I am, Lottie."

"But…" The tears she had clearly been suppressing all night began to leak from her eyes, her bottom lip trembling. "I just think you're ever so brave."

My sister laughed, but there was little humour in it. "I have to be; there's not much else I can do, and really I can't complain, my darling. Well, I could, but where would that get me? I'd rather have a large white wine than a right whine. Talking of which, let's have another round."

She glanced back towards the bar area, keen to get some attention from the staff. She comically did a double take when she spotted the new barman, who was just starting his shift for the night. He was knotting a black apron around his slim waist before taking position centre stage behind the bar. He was classically handsome, with olive skin and thick wavy black hair, and clearly a hit with the ladies from the amount of appreciative looks he was receiving. My sister was one of them. She was eyeing him up the way she used to appraise a particularly creamy chocolate éclair.

"Bloody hell, would you just take a look at the bum on that barman? Ooh, he's a little smasher."

I furnished my sister with my most withering glare. "Behave yourself, Dora, he's about thirty."

"And? What can I say? I'm a deeply flawed individual." She let out a raucous laugh that attracted the attention of several other diners and caused one passing waiter to drop a plate. "OK, so I get a little naughty when I'm on happy hour measures; but I think you'll agree he's what's commonly known as a triple threat: tall, gorgeous and can shake a mean martini too."

She could see I was still unimpressed, so she raised her hands in a gesture of mock contrition. "OK, so I'm being a bit inappropriate."

"A bit?"

Lottie had just returned from the ladies' loo where she'd been fixing her make-up, and caught the end of our conversation. She made it her mission to check out the barman too.

"I have to agree with Auntie Dor, he's as hot as steak pie in the Sahara. In fact, I would go so far as to give him a standing ovulation."

Chapter 30

•❤•❤•❤•❤•❤•

This was Lottie's way of segueing all conversation to her baby plans with Leo. Of course, I already knew, but this was the first time that Dora, Lila or Bella had heard of their important life plans. Everyone was thrilled, no one more so than Dora, who was simply over the moon.

"I couldn't be happier for you, my girl. That's the one regret of my life, that I never gave my Ossie a baby. It took you a while, but you've finally found the man of your dreams; now what could be more perfect than having a baby? Part of him and part of you and completely wonderful. We really need to toast this...if I can ever get a bit of attention."

Before I could stop her, two fingers were firmly in her mouth and that famous whistle of hers was bouncing off the walls. All eyes swivelled towards us, including those of the buff bartender. My sister gave an innocent twinkly smile as if butter wouldn't melt. "A bottle of champagne please, and five glasses."

Over the bottle of bubbly, we chatted and reminisced. We put the world to rights, and the night simply flew by.

There was talk about the dark times of lockdown, when we were all isolated and couldn't be with our loved ones. Missed precious milestones, moments we would never get back. And how happy we had been once we were finally released blinking into the wide world again and could all be together once more.

Bella hooted with laughter at hearing Lottie recall the instance when she and I had gone for dinner together at a local pub restaurant (at an appropriate distance from other diners of course). We had to order our meals directly from the table rather than at the bar, as we had on previous occasions. Me being completely clueless, I'd thought the whole menu was printed on that little square box that was called a QR code. I had wondered if it was April Fools' Day as surely it must be a joke. How could all the dishes be printed on that funny little square? I didn't have my glasses with me, but even so. Lottie had scanned the menu with her phone and showed me how the "modern world" worked. At least I was much more "with it" now. Well, I hoped so anyway.

Bella gave me an affectionate smile, which I translated as "ahhh, bless". It was so easy for the young – they had grown up with technology, so it was just commonplace. That said, I am so thankful I was young when I was. I don't envy the youth of today, I really don't. Boy, do they have it tough.

I hit back at Lottie's tale with a bit of reminiscing of my own. When Daniel left her (to be with the repugnant Roxy), money had been in scarce supply. My daughter had discovered the delights of alternative retail therapy in the many local charity shops. She had bagged herself a good few bargains, though not the fitted leather trench which had gone straight in the bin when she got it home, after discovering the previous occupant's used G-string and butt plug in the pocket. I really thought the staff were supposed to check all items thoroughly before sale.

It wasn't just the charity shops that my daughter patronised. She got on nodding terms with all the staff down her local Asda too, and quite often shadowed the yellow sticker man around like his personal stalker. Jacob and she discovered some interesting food combinations those days. Near-date avocados and corned beef made an interesting dinner, kippers and hummus another. She once had a dozen packs of turkey nuggets in her freezer, as they had been marked down to 50 pence apiece. Even though she was against ultra processed food in principle, desperate times called for desperate measures.

How things had changed. Now she had Leo, and her business was thriving, money worries were a thing of the past. It was good to be reminded where you had been in life though. It keeps you grounded. We are all just a few bad decisions away from being on that breadline. And on that line, the bread is anything but fresh; it is out of date and mouldy.

Lila waved her hand at us as if to say, "Enough with all this vanilla talk of shopping and such like." She was clearly champing at the bit to recount a tale or two from her colourful dating past. Now that she was happily loved up with Seb, remembering her hedonistic days long gone was her only way of living dangerously.

There was the tale about one chap who could only maintain an erection if Lila barked at him like a dog. She wasn't sure whether she found this amusing or incredibly insulting. But after a few minutes of yapping like a

Yorkshire terrier her throat was as dry as a bowl of dog kibble and the fella in question was still as floppy as an undercooked Yorkshire pudding. You could never call our girl a quitter though, and she had rubbed that weary willy as if she was expecting a genie to appear and grant her three wishes.

She laughed at her own memories. "I had to give up at that point; I was worried about repetitive strain injury in my wrist, and the poor chap was beginning to chafe. The truth was that no matter how hard I rubbed that rod, there was no way it was ever turning into a diamond."

We all laughed at this. Lila certainly had a way with words; not one that was strictly fit for polite society, of course, but she was certainly amusing. She took a delicate sip of her champagne before continuing.

"Mind you, he was still an improvement on that guy I had a couple of dates with a few years back. He was in his late thirties and still lived at home with his mother. That should have been a red flag straight away; well, to be fair it was, but he had a look of James Franco about him, so I could forgive a lot. They lived in a beautiful terraced house in Ilkey, you know the ones, all period features with attics and basements and gorgeous old fireplaces."

We all nodded, impressed. Those properties went for a pretty penny.

"Well, we'd been out for a lovely dinner, and he'd been the perfect gent up to that point, but when we returned to his place, he had barely served me a cup of weak tea when he was desperate to show me the basement. He said the renovation was incredibly high spec and he felt a woman such as me would really appreciate the attention to detail. Oh, there were plenty of details all right – ball gags, ankle restraints, even a feather tickler. It only turned out to be a fully equipped sex dungeon. I didn't know where to look. Well, actually I did; there was a spanking bench and a sex swing and enough dildos and assorted toys for the whole of Bradford to rock up for an impromptu orgy. I turned around at this point to tell him I was not impressed that he thought I would "appreciate" such a room when I saw what he was wearing."

Bella interrupted, her eyes as wide as saucers. "Why...what was he wearing?"

Lila gave a sly smile and took a sip of her champagne, clearly enjoying making us wait. "Well, he'd only dropped his trousers, and he was standing there in all his glory, and his glory was only caged."

I was seriously confused now. Caged? What was she going on about.

Lottie looked confused too, shaking her head, her blonde curls bouncing. "What do you mean, like a chastity device?"

Lila nodded vigorously. "Precisely, his old chap was in a cage. It was quite impressive really, good workmanship had gone into that device; it must have cost him a pretty penny."

I still wasn't sure I was understanding properly. "You mean he had his bits and pieces in a cage? What, like a hamster?"

Lila nearly choked on her champagne. "Not exactly, he was wearing it so he couldn't fiddle with himself down there. He said it would be an honour if I would be his mistress and could be the only holder of the key."

Dora's eyes were shining. She was loving the story. "And what did you say? Do we have to address you as Mistress Lila now?"

"Nah, it wasn't my thing at all. I mean, each to their own, and I'm not one to judge, but it just doesn't float my dinghy. And when it came to it, that wasn't even the most disturbing thing about that dungeon."

There was a collective intake of breath. What could be worse than a man with his meat and two veg locked up in a cage?

"What was worse was the whiff down there. It was a dark room, obviously, all black leather, rubber and red furnishings; but there was a musty smell of damp and decay, like when you've forgotten some wet clothes in the bottom of the washing machine. He might have spent a fortune on his decadent dungeon, but he had obviously failed to get it damp-proofed. It was enough to make your stomach turn, and that was without a go on the rusty fuck swing. And in the middle of the room, amongst enough apparatus and pulleys to make a Tory MP wince, was a circular bed dressed in satin sheets with his mother's knitting on top of it. Apparently, they had use of the basement on alternate nights. They had a rota stuck to the fridge so they wouldn't get mixed up. Believe me, girls, I consider myself broad-minded, but that night my mind was well and truly blown. Fancy sharing a sex dungeon with your eighty-year-old mother."

We were all shocked. Perhaps Dora less so than the rest of us; she simply munched on an olive and nodded her head slowly. There was still not much in this world that could shock my sister.

I sometimes wondered if all Lila's tales were strictly true. Surely no one could have been that unlucky in love and had so many scandalous encounters. But Lottie would always assure me that Lila was an open book, and that book was a hundred percent factual and most definitely

X- rated. She had indeed led a colourful life, that's all there was to it.

Bella was quite clearly in awe of Lila. Being young and a little shy, she still had a lot to learn in life. "You should write a book, Lila. I reckon it would be a bestseller; I know all my mates would buy it too."

I jumped in at this point. "I'm sure it would make a very...err, interesting read and perhaps you should write it, Lila. I don't want to sound like a killjoy, but please don't any of you buy it for me for Christmas. I would much prefer a nice scented candle, thank you very much."

The atmosphere at the table was open and relaxed. I hoped the night was everything Dora had wished it to be. In truth she looked delighted, so fingers crossed. I had noticed in the last few days that she would often wince, as if a sharp spasm had shot through her entire body. Maybe this had been going on for a while and I hadn't realised. But now, knowing how things were, I was more tuned in to my sister's condition.

Tonight, Dora seemed completely unburdened by any pain. Perhaps she shouldn't have been mixing her medication with alcohol, or perhaps that was exactly what she needed. What I did know was that I needed to keep my sister in my life for as long as possible. Maybe that was selfish of me, but I couldn't let her go; and I hoped I wouldn't have to for a long time to come.

The last few months she had been with me had certainly been a rollercoaster, but I wasn't ready for the ride to end. I didn't want to swap the fun of the fair that was life with Dora to the bland existence I had become used to. I just couldn't.

I realised how much I had changed: perhaps become a more authentic Evelyn; showing my feelings and being comfortable to do so; less of the buttoned-up stiff-upper-lipped lady of old. And where had that ever got me? Apart from chronic indigestion and a perpetual look of having a bad smell under my nose. I felt the new improved version of me was so much better.

I didn't want to ruin our good moods, or bring down the temperature of the room, but there was something I needed to say while we were all together. "Can I talk for a moment, Dora?"

Dora's happy smile instantly died on her lips. "Oh no, am I getting a telling off? You sound so serious. I feel I'm in big trouble, like you're a sniper with the red dot fixed firmly on my forehead."

"We're just concerned about you; you're always so positive and cheerful, but you don't have to be, you know, you don't have to 'Mary Poppins' everything. I...I mean we..." I cast my hand around everyone at the table, "we love you and we're here for you, for anything you need, we just wanted you to know."

"I *do* know, my darlings, and I love you all too. And I know that not one of you would want to be in my shoes." She laughed briefly. "But then again, none of you are stylish enough to pull them off anyway."

She wriggled her toes in her jewel-encrusted psychedelic *Crocs*. Touché. Dora was letting us know that she appreciated us, but that was the end of the matter. Tonight was not for talk of the future; tonight was for the here and now. She drained the end of her champagne flute with a little burp. "Delicious...now then, are we having another round of drinks?"

Lottie was out of her chair in one graceful move, which was good considering the amount she had had to drink. She grabbed her denim jacket from the back of her chair and shunted the cocktail menu further down the table, away from Dora. "Maybe we should move onto Eduardo's now; happy hour is over here, and these prices are going to get eye-wateringly steep."

Dora reached for her coat to indicate she agreed. "My beautiful niece, still thrifty as ever, I see, as anyone who's seen you attack the reduced aisle in Asda can attest to, no doubt. Come on then, let's go clubbing."

Bella was bounding off her chair like an excited puppy. "Ooh, great, and I've got my ID just in case I get carded."

Dora sighed deeply and shook her head with wistful regret. "To be carded again, imagine that. Unfortunately, that's no longer likely for us, eh, Evie? Anyway, one look at my neck is a dead giveaway. But you enjoy your youth, Bella, my love, it doesn't last for ever. What I wouldn't give to have my time again. But nothing lasts for ever, nothing ever does."

A rather attractive man chose that very moment to saunter past us. He was probably in his late thirties with shoulder-length wavy brown hair that gave him the air of a sexy pirate, if there was such a thing. He was dressed in a tight band T-shirt (one of the ones Jacob enjoyed), doing little to hide his bulging abs and tight-fitting jeans, showcasing a nicely pert derrière. All in all, quite the package. But the one thing that obviously impressed my sister the most was that his lower lip, just above his lustrous beard, bore a shining silver lip ring. Fate had decreed that another thing could be ticked off Dora's list this night. She tapped him on his shoulder as he made his way casually by.

"Excuse me sir, could I just be asking a favour off you."

We all exchanged amused glances. The poor chap didn't stand a chance.

Chapter 32

•♥•♥•♥•♥•♥•

The next few months passed in a bit of a blur. Dora's hospital appointments increased as her strength declined. She was still the same Dora, however; just a little faded, like a less vibrant version of herself. It made sense, I guessed: this horrible disease was erasing the colourful creation that she always was and replacing it with a shadowy image of herself. But there was one thing this illness couldn't rob from her, and that was her humour.

Bella, bless her heart, was still living with us. In truth she was an absolute godsend, endlessly cheerful and such a help to have around the house. When she wasn't working at the shop or busy helping me, she was right by Dora's side. They were the "terrible twins", as they liked to joke. It just went to show that age was no barrier to true friendship, and they were indeed the best of friends. Once I had been a little envious of their deep connection; now I was so thankful for it.

My sister refused point black to talk about her future. We knew that at some point she would need to go into palliative care at her local hospice in Bristol – St Agatha's. There was a sad inevitability to it. But not quite yet.

I had changed in the time my sister and Bella had been with me. I'd become less stuffy, not so much of a starchy old fusspot, but I had found myself sometimes now returning to type. I was stressing over the smallest of things and grumbling in a way that didn't befit the new me. Did I have enough teabags in for when visitors stopped by? Would I be able to finish my library book before it was due to be returned? Was the postman only pushing the mail halfway into the letterbox in order to piss me off? I knew why I was behaving this way. It was just to stop me from concentrating on what was really important and what I couldn't bear to think about – what I would do after my sister was gone.

There was also the matter of her bucket list. I was gutted that there were still things remaining on it. Many of them had been crossed off with a thick fuchsia felt tip pen (Dora's favourite colour), but some we hadn't managed to achieve. Dora reassured me that it didn't matter; most of the things she had thought up on a whim, and if she didn't get a chance to do them, then so be it. I appreciated her words, but wasn't sure if I believed her. And if there was a chance that the list was as important to her as I felt it might well be, then I had to find a way to make those things happen.

I looked over to my sister: on the settee under her favourite fluffy throw watching a repeat of *Midsummer Murders* and muttering that John Nettles was still a bit of a dish and she "wouldn't kick him out of bed for farting on the fitted sheet".

She was wearing one of her more colourful creations – a lime green tracksuit studded with diamanté that spelled out "born to misbehave" across the chest. Even though she had no plans to leave the house, she had her full face on; she'd even donned a pair of fluttery fake eyelashes. She wasn't giving up on herself any time soon, even though everything was taking that much longer. For instance, getting dressed took a monumental effort, and I would sometimes find her slumped on her bed with one leg through her knickers, half asleep and exhausted with it all. But just now she was smiling, dipping her Curly Wurly into her steaming mug of tea and noisily sucking the chocolate off it. We'd been able to cross that off her list twice now.

And I knew with certainty we would be knocking a few more off it tonight. I was hosting a dinner party for the first time in years. Jacob was coming down from university to attend, and I couldn't wait to see him. Lottie and Lila were coming too. Leo would be with my daughter, but Lila's boyfriend Seb had a sci-fi quiz commitment with his roommate Alan that he simply couldn't cancel. Probably for the best, since Lila had told us he was about as fond of curry as he was a punch to the gut, which was coincidentally the way he felt the day after a lamb Rogan Josh.

Bella had made plans to go to the cinema with a friend, but cancelled when I told her I was hosting the dinner. She wasn't missing the opportunity to spend time with us all – especially Dora. Memories needed to be made.

It would have been lovely if we'd all gone out to a nice Indian restaurant rather than stay in, as we hadn't left the house in ages. But Dora just wasn't up to it; she tired quickly, and for someone who had spent her life dazzling at dinner parties and loving to be the centre of attention, she preferred now to sit back in the wings rather than take centre stage.

So, we were staying in my cosy abode and having a dinner party, and I was to be head chef and bottle washer – God help us all. But I'd had the idea that if I could pull off a culinary feast of Indian cuisine, then Dora would get her wish (sort of). I was bringing the gastronomic tour of India to my sedate little semi in West Yorkshire.

I wasn't the fanciest of chefs by any stretch of the imagination; normally the most exotic I got with my recipes would be adding an extra splash of Worcestershire sauce to my shepherd's pie, or sprinkling a little cinnamon into my apple crumble. But for my sister I was willing to pull out all the stops. I had Lottie firmly on speed dial to assist with some of the trickier recipes, and was cheating with a few dishes from the local takeaway that I knew were definitely outside my comfort zone. But all in all, I considered the bases covered, including a vegan option of each dish for Jacob. Dora would need to uncap her fuchsia felt tip again soon, as we were going on a gastronomic tour around India on a wet Friday night and it was (fingers crossed) going to be fabulous.

I planned the menu meticulously myself, with the help of the internet and a dusty old Madhur Jaffrey cookbook I'd discovered in the back of the larder behind the seldom-used pressure cooker and out-of-date spice jars. We would kick off in north-western India, in the Punjab, with aromatic butter chicken and vodka-laced lassi to drink; then moved swiftly on to southern India, namely Kerala, for lamb Biryani and coconut rice; and finished in west India, in Goa, with a chicken Vindaloo. I personally had no intention of trying this last dish, but Jacob assured me it was right up his street. Apparently, he and his uni mates ate a lot of spicy food, even having "hottest curry" eating competitions with the boys from the rugby club. This would inevitably involve many cans of lager and a blocked toilet, no doubt.

The meal was being rounded off with sticky Gulab Jamun balls with vanilla ice cream for dessert. They were Dora's favourites, which she likened to doughnuts, insisting they were "gooier than Greggs". High praise indeed. Plus, there would be fudgy little squares of milk barfi to enjoy with our coffee.

I left Dora content and watching television while I made magic in the kitchen. Bella was due back from work around 5:30 pm, and the rest of the guests were due shortly afterwards at six. I had Radio 4 and *Gardeners' Question Time* for company and distraction while concentrating on the intricacies of the recipes. I didn't even notice the hours pass until Bella was by my side at the steaming hob, offering her help. I shooed her away with a tea towel, telling her to have a shower and get herself ready for our guests. I reassured her that I had everything well under control, which I did. Mostly.

Lottie arrived first – prompt as always, with the tall figure of Leo following slightly behind. She swept into the room in a cloud of perfume and kisses, turning her attention to Dora, who had been snoozing on the settee. Lottie leaned down to plant a kiss on her cheek, waking her like Sleeping Beauty from a dream. My daughter knew it was getting harder for Dora to find the energy to get up from her seat, so insisted she stay put. I knew my sister loathed having no energy. She had always been the one first out of her seat to greet visitors with all the exuberance of an excitable puppy. But those times were gone.

"Hello, Lottie, love... and hello, Leo." She cast an approving eye over Lottie's man, taking in the fine-looking specimen he certainly was. She hadn't had the opportunity to meet him before, and was obviously impressed. "Well, aren't you dishy. I might just leave the curry and have a portion of you instead."

A little colour appeared high on his cheekbones. He was blushing, which made him even more attractive.

"Lovely to meet you, Dora. I've heard so much about you from Lottie."

Dora laughed and wagged a finger in his direction. "Don't you believe a word of it, my boy." She patted the seat next to her. "Come and sit beside me and tell me all about you. I already know you're not short of a bob or two, which is a good thing, but I want to know all the important stuff: what music you like, what's your favourite pudding, and will you make sure you look after my niece in the way she deserves; she's worth more than all the riches in the world, you know."

Leo sat down beside Dora as instructed and smiled at her warmly. "You've no worries on that score; she's the most precious thing I've ever had in my life, and I will treasure her always."

"That's good enough for me, cocker." She turned her head to address Lottie. "Your mum's been cooking since early this morning, and the amount of effing and jeffing going on in that kitchen, I don't know if we might not end up ordering in fish and chips."

I gave my sister a stern look. "That's nonsense; I just said fiddlesticks when I dropped the tub of ghee on the lino."

"Well, it was definitely an 'f' word. But I told Evie not to go to so much trouble for me."

I shook my head firmly. "Nonsense, Dora, I want to do this for you, and the truth is that I've really enjoyed myself; I've had so much fun getting all the different herbs and spices for the dishes. The colours and the aromas – it's so much more exciting than making a dull old Lancashire hot pot. My shopping used to be all Marmite, marmalade and thick-sliced white; and now look at me, buying fennel seeds and saffron and the like. Rakesh from the Asian grocers is the most interesting chap, you know; his grandson is going to Cambridge to study law. He's incredibly proud, and was showing me photos of him."

Leo had brought in a blue plastic bag which he passed over to Lottie; she rummaged around in it, a look of concentration on her face. With a "ta-da" she pulled the contents out and held it up for us all to see.

"I know this isn't quite what you hoped for, Dora, but I thought we could wear these and maybe play a bit of Baroque music on Alexa. I think they're suitable for our own intimate masquerade ball."

She was holding a stack of Venetian-style masks: elegant white faces decorated with gold lacquer, in carnival style, and swirly silver eye masks on sticks. There was something for every taste and each was unique. She'd no doubt purchased them from eBay or the like, but they were elegant enough for our needs. My sister's eyes were brimming with tears.

"Thank you," I mouthed to my daughter.

Lottie handed me one and Leo passed another to Dora. "I've got one for all of us; aren't they fun?"

Bella suddenly appeared in the doorway, fresh-faced from her shower, her blonde curls still damp on her shoulders. She looked lovely in her low-slung jeans and baby pink polo neck jumper.

"Here, catch." Lottie tossed a white-faced mask in her direction.

Bella's face was a picture as she scrabbled to catch it, her panic giving way to relief when she caught it, realising then it was light and plastic and not likely to shatter into a billion pieces.

"Cool." She secured it to her face with the ties. It suited her perfectly. She looked the picture of elegance, fit for the finest party, save for the fact she wasn't wearing a flowing gown but her ripped jeans.

"Hey, you must be Leo." Bella reached over and politely shook his hand. "It's great to meet you."

Leo returned the gesture with the widest smile. He really was the most handsome young man. I appreciated the fact that he had dressed up for the evening – elegant linen shirt and smart well-cut slacks. His preferred uniform was casual T-shirts and jeans or shorts, but even in his usual style he still cut a dashing figure. Lottie's ex used to be so fussy about his clothes: they had to be high-end and perfectly pressed, but Leo had more style in his little finger than that man had possessed in his entire wretched body.

I was so thankful that Lottie had had the foresight to procure these masks. I knew she must have been of the same mindset as me, knowing there was a very real possibility that unless we did a little creative thinking, Dora wouldn't ever have the chance to complete her list.

Bella sniffed the air comically like a hungry bloodhound. "Ooh, something smells yummy."

Lottie followed suit. "Yes, Mum, it really does, you clever thing."

I smiled delightedly, but I couldn't take the credit for everything. "It's not all me, I'm afraid. I've had to get a few dishes from the Korma Sutra Café on the High Street, but

I've still done a lot from scratch, and the desserts are from Barfi Barn."

Lottie looked amused. "Honestly, Mum, there was a time when you would only ever shop in Waitrose, or Tesco at an absolute push; and now look at you, shopping local in all these exotic stores. I'm so proud of you."

In fact I was pretty proud of myself too. There was a whole world of culinary experiences to be had out there in the big wide world, and I had limited myself. I'd been limiting my life in so many ways.

The doorbell rang and Lottie let out a little whoop of glee before racing to answer it. She was hoping it was Jacob; his train was due into Leeds station over an hour ago and he had declined a lift home, saying he was happy to get the number 12 bus. Upon hearing an even louder whoop, it was clear that it was indeed my grandson at the door.

Lottie bounced into the lounge with the tall slim figure of Jacob in her wake. He was looking so grown up, I felt a huge pride swell in my chest. Such a gentleman and so very handsome, even in his scruffy jeans and raggedy old jumper. It didn't matter though; he was perfect to me.

He was smiling broadly, his twin dimples making him appear momentarily like a cheeky little boy again. "Hi, Gran; hi, Auntie Dora." He planted a kiss on both our cheeks before waving over at Leo. "Sorry I'm a bit late, but I was busy getting this."

He dropped his rucksack on the floor and unzipped it to reveal a brown paper bag. He pulled the contents out with an extravagant flourish. It was a bottle of green liquid about the size of a small liquor bottle. Dora clapped her hands together clearly delighted.

"Absinthe!"

His cheeky smile was back. I had really missed it. "Yep – it's not hard to get hold of, but if we want to serve it like the French do, we really need to drip iced water through a sugar cube into the glass of Absin..." He fell abruptly silent, the word dying in his mouth. He was stopped in his tracks on seeing Bella.

She stepped out of the shadows, still wearing her mask, which she slowly lowered. "Hello...I'm Bella."

Chapter 33

I could hear the sharp intake of breath from my grandson. It was as if time had stopped in that very moment. It was just like a film, when the connection between two leading characters is almost palpable, like electricity fizzing in the air between them.

I shot Lottie an amused look. My daughter loved her old romantic movies, and from her raised eyebrows I knew she was thinking much the same as me. Our Jacob and Bella had just had "a moment".

In fact the mask, although beautiful, was not a patch on the perfection that was Bella. My grandson, who had come on in leaps and bounds of confidence since starting university, now regressed into a tongue-tied young boy again. He shuffled from one foot to the other, his cheeks flushing pink.

I jumped in to save him from any further embarrassment. "Jacob, would you be a love and help me bring some things in from the kitchen."

Jacob managed to drag his gaze away from Bella, as if he had suddenly broken free from a trance. "Ye...yeah, of course, Gran."

Alone in the kitchen, the questions started thick and fast. "So that's Bella."

"Yes, that's our girl."

"Gran, you never told me she was *so* pretty."

"You never asked." I handed him a large bowl of rice. "Take that out to the dining table, please."

We were going to be eating in the dining room, which was normally preserved for special occasions – Christmas and parties, so it barely got used. But that was going to change, like everything else. I was done saving things for best.

It was beginning to get late now, and I just hoped Lila would arrive soon. Although I was happy with my cooking, I wasn't confident how good it would be if left waiting too long. I was more than a little worried my curries would congeal, and nobody liked a skin on their dinner, unless they were having a jacket potato of course. I handed Jacob a stack of my best linen napkins to lay beside each place setting.

"So, Gran...about Bella, Mum said she had a boyfriend that was a bit of a dick and was giving her some trouble."

"She did, but that's all ancient history now. He's been off the scene for months."

Poor Jacob, he was trying so hard to appear nonchalant, but I saw straight through him; the way his eyes lit up on hearing Bella was single again was a dead giveaway. He should never play poker, as he'd lose his shirt, that was for certain.

With regard to Alfie, Bella had been very lucky. After the altercation on my front step, he had limped off home and decided what side his bread was buttered on. Getting into war with a couple of old codgers was not worth the aggro. So that was the last we heard of Mr Dodds; he had thankfully left Bella well alone and would continue to do so if Dora and I had anything to do with it. It was like Dora had said: bullies were cowards, plain and simple.

I polished one of the forks quickly on my apron. "If you like her, you should ask her out. She's a lovely girl and you're my favourite boy; it would be wonderful to see you on a date together…now stop distracting me and go and get the rest of the dishes."

Jacob smiled, his dimples evident once more and making him simply the cutest. "Thanks, Gran." With that he slunk off to the kitchen with his hands in the pockets of his baggy jeans. His body language was brooding and cool as a cucumber, but from his happy whistling I would wager he was excited as a kitten on discovering a fresh ball of wool.

The doorbell rang out again. Thank goodness. Lila at last.

We had the loveliest night. The food, well most of it at least, was delicious. The items from the takeaway were a triumph, my own dishes proving a little more hit and miss. That said, it didn't put me off. I was certainly going to prepare them again; after all, practice makes perfect and I had enjoyed my hours in the kitchen making culinary alchemy. So much better than piercing the film on my bland old ready meal and waiting for the microwave to ping. But we dispensed with the Baroque music midway through the meal.

Jacob and Bella barely left each other's side all evening. Eventually they left us "oldies" to it and headed to her room to listen to some of their favourite tracks. I looked to my daughter for guidance when Jacob and Bella suggested sloping off. I didn't know what was appropriate in this day and age.

When I had been a girl the chance of having a boy in my room would have been as likely as a sunroof on a submarine. My father would have had an absolute fit. In fact, he had insisted all likely suitors had to be vetted by mother and him before Dora or me were even allowed to go out to the local dance. There had been plenty of uncomfortable evenings spent sipping tea and nibbling on cheese toasties while some young man or other had been grilled more than the sandwiches.

But now Lottie just smiled at me, saying it was fine; they were both adults and sensible too. Plus, they were as sober as a judge on a juice cleanse; fortunately they hadn't been imbibing any of the green stuff. Unlike Dora, who had been having the time of her life – drunk as a skunk and singing Tom Jones' *Sex Bomb* at the top of her lungs whilst juggling onion bhajis.

It was after 11 pm before everyone had left. Lila headed to Seb's to hear all about the quiz; Lottie, Leo and Jacob went back to theirs. They dashed to their respective cars, keen to avoid getting drenched. The rain had been pelting down all evening, not pausing for a single moment. Bella returned to her room, no doubt to dream of Jacob. There was a soppy smile on her face a mile wide, like she'd been binge-watching puppy videos on TikTok. I had always been sceptical about love at first sight; even with Andrew and me, it had taken many months before I felt the ping of Cupid's arrow. But after tonight, I wasn't so sure. It really appeared that Jacob and Bella had been smitten at first glance. Dora had always believed it was a real thing, and maybe, as I was beginning to discover, my sister was often right.

And then there were two. Dora and me.

"So just me and thee then, sister dearest." Dora let out a little gassy hiccup. "Ooh, too much of the old giggle juice for me, I think."

She looked tired, thoroughly exhausted in fact, but when she spoke, her voice was light and her face radiant. "Thank you, Evie, for the best time. I even managed a little dance to Celine Dion. It's been perfect...just perfect."

I patted her on the shoulder before getting up to take the remaining plates into the kitchen. On second thoughts, I sank back into my seat. To hell with them, they could wait until the morning.

We sat in silence for a few moments, listening to the rain pattering against the double glazing. It was soothing somehow.

My sister sighed deeply. "It's been raining cats and dogs all night; aww, I miss my Feline."

"But Keith's been looking after her so well." My eyebrow rose quizzically.

"I know what you're getting at, but you're completely wrong. There's never been anything between me and Keith; we're just great friends. He's one of my favourite people in the world, but with his beard, kissing him would be like kissing Feline: nice in a fluffy brotherly sort of way, but about as stimulating to the senses as a piece of dry toast."

I stared out of the lounge window. The curtains hadn't been closed well, and I could clearly see the torrential rain hammering against the windows. It was getting heavier. But it was a warm night. We were into September now and summer was hanging on for dear life, not yet ready to surrender to the winter chill. The rain drummed against the windowpane like a drum roll, building up to finale of some sort. But what? I felt a germ of an idea growing in my mind.

I held my hand out to Dora. "Come on, let's go out to the back garden."

My sister looked visibly shocked, but slowly rose to her feet. Maybe it was the effect of the alcohol, but she didn't question me, just took my outstretched hand.

I led her through the house and then gingerly out of the patio doors into the neat, secluded garden beyond. I resisted the impulse to turn on the garden light, probably for the best considering what I had in mind for us. The rain continued to pelt down, the night sky heavy with cloud. The air smelled earthy – of damp soil, but with subtle background notes of lavender and sweet pea. I breathed it all in deeply. I wanted to remember every moment. The rain, as I had imagined, was warm and soothing on the skin, like stepping into a cosy bath.

"Come on, sis, let's strip."

I didn't often shock my sister, but this time I did. The look on her face was absolutely priceless. I was glad that, despite my reputation for being the sensible one, I still had the ability to shock. She didn't argue and began to unbutton her spotty blouse. I did the same, stripping off my jumper and skirt until I was standing in just my Marks & Spencer undies. And then, quick as a flash, they were off too. Dora laughed out loud as she removed her undergarments too, and we both stood shoulder to shoulder as naked as the day we were born.

And we danced, the rain hitting our skin, streaming down like a thousand little rivers. It felt wonderful.

There we were – two old ladies dancing in the buff on an unseasonably warm September night. And we laughed, laughed like we didn't have a worry in the world. The years rolled away until we were teenagers once again. Thankfully there were no onlookers to witness it all, as I was confident we didn't actually appear like teenagers; more likely a couple of escapees from some institution or other. But I didn't care.

It might not have been skinny dipping; but it was the next best thing.

Chapter 34

S ix months later

I couldn't believe that this day had come. How could it be that I was standing in the grounds of Willow Stream crematorium greeting my family before we made our way inside to say our final goodbye to my sister? It just wasn't fair. Goodbye? It felt like we'd barely said hello again since spending all those years apart.

I squeezed Lottie's hand. Despite the day and all it entailed, she looked positively glowing. She was in her final trimester now, only a couple of months until the baby was due. Leo was beside her with a comforting arm draped around her shoulders. They had just recently wed – a small intimate ceremony not far from home, just the two of them plus me, Jacob and Leo's Auntie Ivy in attendance. Leo had cut quite the stylish figure in his sharp suit, and Lottie had worn an elegantly simple cream dress cut on the bias, but she had never looked more beautiful. That was what happiness could do for you.

As weddings go, it hadn't been the most elaborate affair; and certainly not the showy circus that her marriage to Daniel had been. But unlike that marriage, this one was perfect in its simplicity. No angry Daniel complaining about the canapés being dry or the fizz being cava rather than champagne, and how his work colleagues would not be impressed. This wedding was about what was actually important – love.

My daughter smiled at me, tears shining in her bright blue eyes. I knew I was on the verge of crying too. I dabbed at her face with a tissue I had pulled out of my bag. I had been wise to bring a plentiful supply. Even with the tears, Lottie looked simply beautiful. But then again, my girl was always a looker, despite the outfit she was wearing. She wasn't alone – we were all in the same boat sartorially speaking. There had been a particular dress code decreed by Dora for her funeral, and woe betide anyone who didn't participate. She had warned us that she would return from the grave to haunt anyone who didn't join in.

We had first expected she would insist that we all "dressed more Dora" again; marked her passing in our most outlandish colourful creations, ticking off every colour combination in the book and piling enough clanky jewellery on top so that when we entered the chapel of rest it would sound like we were giving her a final round of applause.

But that wasn't to be the case. It turned out that Dora could still surprise. Her request was way more whacky than that. It was now March, a year virtually to the day since my sister had come to stay with me. And despite it being March, we were all dressed in our finest Christmas jumpers. Christmas had always been my sister's most favourite time of the year, so what better than to have us celebrate that at her funeral. She was always the comedian even to the end, and somehow managed beyond it too.

I linked Jacob's arm. He looked adorable in his snowman jumper with its pom pom fluffy snowballs dotted randomly across it. I linked my other arm through Bella's, who was dressed identically. Their relationship had been going from strength to strength. It made my heart happy to see young love flourishing. I stopped for a moment at the dark wooden door, wishing I didn't have to go through it and that none of this was real. But it was real, and we needed to do Dora proud, so with a deep breath to steady myself I made my way inside the chapel.

The room was packed. Dora had always been the popular one, and she still was even in death. It was a sea of Santa Clauses and Rudolph the Reindeers. I didn't recognise half the people here, but felt so proud of my sister. My wonderful Dora, that so many people loved her enough that they came to say their final goodbye. I saw Keith, his head bowed, his broad shoulders in his whimsical elf sweatshirt shaking slightly as he tried to contain his emotions. He was missing Dora very much, that was clear to see.

I spotted Lila and Seb halfway down and mouthed a greeting to them as I passed by, making our way to the front to take our seats. We huddled together on the front row: me, Lottie, Leo, Jacob and Bella. United in our grief.

The coffin was off to the side. I glanced at it for a second and then down at the order of service in my shaking hands. There was a beautiful black and white photo of Dora on the embossed cream card. I recognised the photo: it was from a holiday she had enjoyed in Greece when she was in her early forties. That's how I wanted to remember her – not dead in that box, her body ravaged by that cruel disease.

A few seconds passed and I was feeling brave enough to look towards the coffin without crying. It was traditional, polished oak; part of me had expected Dora to request a shocking pink one. She had still managed to stamp her mark on it though. On top was a lovely spray of yellow flowers – tulips and forsythia – and several framed photographs of my sister, ones that showcased her spirit, her energy, who she had been in life. A large framed wedding photo of a young Dora and Oscar was at the front, the pair smiling blissfully, so in love; another one showed an older Dora, dressed in one of her outrageous outfits and blowing a kiss towards the camera, looking vibrant and full of fun; in the final picture she was smiling and cuddling Feline in her arms. I wondered if the picture had been Photoshopped in some way as the cat appeared far less grouchy and feral than I remembered. Maybe she was only like that with me.

We started with a hymn: one of Dora's favourites, *Abide with Me*, for which the congregation were on their feet singing loud and clear and celebrating my sister at the top of their lungs. As the hymn came to a close, we took our seats as the minister, a quietly unassuming man in his late fifties, addressed us in his calm, soothing voice.

He spoke of Dora as if he had known her, which he had not. Everything he had learned about my sister had been provided to him by the family. Yet he spoke with authority, celebrating how many people had loved her.

He spoke of her younger life, her years with Oscar. I let his words wash over me. I couldn't complain, he had delivered the eulogy efficiently in a clear concise manner for someone who had never had the pleasure of meeting my sister. He had missed out on a treat, that was for sure. But I was glad he did a good job.

A few years back, I had attended the funeral of a friend from the bridge club, named Erica. The minister referred to her as "Eric" for the whole eulogy, waxing lyrical about Eric's many achievements in life. He hadn't even realised his faux pas when he spoke of Eric's love of needlecraft and cake decorating and was proudly the mother of three sons with husband Dave. We all watched in embarrassed silence, too mortified to correct him. It was excruciatingly awkward, to say the least.

A large screen at the front displayed a slideshow, recording many key moments of my sister's life. I was up there with her in many of them. How happy we had looked. I recognised one image instantly: we were at a local dance at The Twist and Shout club in the village where we grew up; me in my favourite patent knee-high boots and mini skirt, and Dora in a colourful pinafore dress. We had spent so many teenage nights there. Then there was Dora in dusty peach frills as bridesmaid on my wedding day, holding a towering plateful of vol au vents and sandwiches. She always did love a buffet. Then another of that fateful trip to Blackpool where Dora's curly hair had got stuck to her candyfloss. She could only have been about eight in that one.

The minister's voice was loud and clear again. "I would now like to invite Dora's beloved sister Evelyn to come forward and say a few words."

Chapter 35

•♥•♥•♥•♥•♥•

It seemed to take an eternity for me to reach the lectern – my legs were so wobbly and weak I feared they might fail me, and the envelope in my hand was getting increasingly soggy as my palms were sweating so much. Finally, I made it to the front and surveyed the crowd nervously. A sea of faces looked back expectantly, and I searched until I found Lottie's and fixed my gaze on her. She smiled encouragingly and mouthed "I love you, Mum." I looked down at the envelope in my hand and began to speak.

"Er...he...hello, I'm Evelyn, Dora's older sister. I didn't really know what I was going to say once I got up here. I suppose I thought I would tell you all what a wonderful woman my sister was; but no point in that, as you all know that already. Then I considered reading one of her favourite poems, *Do not go gentle into that good night* by Dylan Thomas; but I can almost hear her voice saying, "Don't read that, our Evie, it's been done to death...quite literally.""

Polite laughter rippled out and I held the envelope up aloft. "So what I'm going to do is let Dora have the final word, just as she always liked to."

The night after Dora passed away, the hospice staff had telephoned me. She had left a letter for me in the care of her favourite nurse, June, to be passed on to me once she was gone, with a message that I was to read it at her funeral. I was strictly not to open it before the day. Joan had reiterated this point, as my sister had warned the poor weary nurse that if I opened the envelope before the funeral, she would come back and haunt her. So, I had better follow orders. I wasn't going to break either my sister's or June's trust. Plus, June had told me, with an exceedingly worried tone, that a ghostly Dora singing the greatest hits of Celine Dion on a loop was the stuff of her worst nightmares, and no doubt worse than anything hell had to offer. Letting my sister rip open the veil that separates the two worlds to warble "It's all coming back to me now" was well above her paygrade.

With shaking hands, I prised open the envelope and extracted the single sheet of white writing paper. It was in Dora's distinctive swirly handwriting, which brought a lump to my throat just to see it again. The words blurred in front of my eyes as I blinked away tears. It was written in bright pink ink, probably the same felt tip pen she had used to cross out every one of her accomplishments on her bucket list.

I put my glasses on and with a deep breath began to read.

"Dearest Evie,

I am hoping that this is the first time you have read these words and have not taken a sneaky peek before. I want you to hear this at the same time as all my family, friends and adoring fans. If curiosity did get the better of you, then I am no doubt back at St Agatha's, my ghostly apparition on track 4 of Celine Dion's 'My Love Essential Collection' and driving poor old June to drink.

Anyhow, you'd better all be in your Chrimbo jumpers, and I mean ALL! I'm looking at you now, Lila, you're not too chic for a bit of Christmas tat, you know."

I paused at this point, my eyes seeking out Lila on the fourth row. She was dressed appropriately in a bright pink sweater with Santa on the front and a speech bubble bearing the immortal words "Santa's favourite ho ho ho" and was miming a heart to me. I smiled; Dora would have loved that. I returned to my reading, my eyes frantically scanning the page to find where I had left off.

"I'm not sad that I'm gone, not really. I'm just sad that I've had to leave you all. And I thought long and hard about what I wanted to say. Should it be a dirty limerick or a love letter to you all, letting you know how precious you all were to me? But you know my heart, I was never one to hold back. I said everything I needed to in life.

What I will say is don't cry for me. I'm back with my Oscar now, finally back home, and that's reason enough to celebrate. My pain is gone and I'm free again.

I lived a good life; boy, did I have some fun. So don't be sad, and if you must be sad, let it be because of the bitesize Brussels sprout quiches at the wake. Yes, that's right, the buffet is Christmas-themed too, and a room full of the after-effects of Brussels sprout quiche is not going to be pleasant, ha ha ha. Glad I'm not there to smell it.

I'm so thankful for the life I've lived: my family, my many friends. But what I'm most happy about was the opportunity to reconnect with you, Evie. We didn't always see eye to eye, but I can honestly say that apart from my Oscar, you were the love of my...my life."

My voice faltered. I was finding it hard to get the words out, so overcome with emotion. I dabbed at my eyes with the soggy tissue that was now nothing but a mushy lump. I took a long deep breath to steady myself before continuing.

"I bet she's crying now – the soppy old goose."

There was a gentle ripple of laughter, and I glanced over the sea of kindly faces once more. So many folk that all loved my sister.

"I know this should be all about me, but I don't want to do that. What I want to do is to talk more about my sister, someone who in the last few months has blossomed. And now I'm gone, I want that to continue. So here in front of all my family and friends and a few old boyfriends thrown in for good measure, I want her to make me a promise. Promise me you'll go to Venice, Evie. Take that trip that you've always wanted to, but never have. Go and grab yourself a bit of la dolce vita before it's too late. It really is later than you think. Goodbye, my sister, goodbye, my dearest family and friends, I love you all and goodnight.

Dora xxx"

I folded the letter and replaced it neatly in the envelope. And I made a silent promise to the heavens. One I had no intention of breaking.

I slowly made my way back to my seat. Lottie patted my knee affectionately, and I smiled back at her. I felt utterly exhausted.

Music suddenly filled the room. Celine Dion was to play during the final part of the ceremony, for those few moments before the coffin was rolled away. Her dulcet tones sprang out in the silence, singing *Ave Maria*, and the beautiful poignancy of it caused many a tear to flow.

I caught Jacob's eye. He had been in charge of providing the music to the funeral director, and I nodded my head proudly. He had done a champion job. Tasteful, respectful... Suddenly there was a change of pace; Celine was still singing, but the album had jumped to the next track.

It was hard to think of a more inappropriate song for a funeral service: but here it was, Celine Dion in all her warbling glory singing *I'm Alive*.

There was a hushed gasp that seemed to reverberate around the entire room. Jacob was out of his seat ready to silence the song, but I held my hand up and winked at him.

"Leave it be; Dora would have loved this."

And then I laughed, laughed like I would never stop. Goodbye, my darling sister. Gone but never forgotten.

Chapter 36

• ❤ • ❤ • ❤ • ❤ • ❤ •

As soon as I walked over the threshold, I felt Dora. Maybe it was the faint scent of her lingering perfume, or the many knickknacks jostling for space on the mantlepiece. Dora had never embraced the minimalist movement, and thought Feng Shui was something to be had with fried rice and prawn crackers. It felt as if she was still in the house, perhaps in the next room, and ready to flounce in at a moment's notice with an enormous grin and a witty wisecrack.

I had always criticised her home: said she wasn't keeping up with all the dusting. Well, to be fair, I don't think anyone could with a porcelain cat or Russian doll sitting cheek by jowl on every conceivable surface. All the clutter used to set my teeth on edge. But today I felt it oddly relaxing. Everywhere I looked, I could just feel my sister. And I really needed that, as I missed her so much.

Dora had left me her house in her will, along with her crystal collection and enough sachets of mayonnaise to dress every salad in Selby. She had firmly believed in the importance of having a spare supply of condiments in your clutch bag, just in case of emergencies. Those emergencies included surviving a too dry tuna jacket potato, or similar. I was seriously underwhelmed by the packets of mayo, but the house – I hadn't expected that at all.

I had been putting off travelling down to Bristol for a while, feeling it would be too upsetting to be here without her. But standing in the house she had owned for so many years, I wished I had come much sooner. Here I was now, and I needed to get busy. I was tasked with sorting out her belongings. A new tenant was moving in, coming this afternoon for a recce of the place, and I had to decide what to do with all my sister's stuff.

I planned to keep some sentimental items for myself: photographs, keepsakes from over the years, and I knew there was no way I could part with her prized teaspoon collection; that would be sacrilege. The local charity shop could then have most of everything else.

I made my way slowly into the narrow galley kitchen. It was tired: a little old-fashioned with its country-style wooden units and printed tiles, but it was warm and homely too. I couldn't help but think back over the years to all the gooey cakes that had been baked here, the many egg mayonnaise sandwiches that Dora had made for us, the thousands of cups of strong tea brewed up in that old brown pot.

It was all so evocative of times long gone, bringing back so many different memories. Part of me wanted to keep everything, for nothing to go to the charity shop. But I knew that wasn't sensible; for a start, I hadn't room for it all. I found a roll of black bin liners in the cupboard under the sink and ripped off a few. I could at least start clearing out all the old food items. That would be a start.

There was a loud rap at the front door. The new tenant must be early. I made my way out of the kitchen and down the long hall, with its psychedelic carpet, to open the heavy front door. Keith was standing there, shuffling nervously from one foot to the other. He was a refined, handsome-looking type of chap with thick, neatly trimmed hair and matching beard, perhaps a little stuffily dressed in his shirt, cardigan and tie, but still evidently liking to look smart though long retired.

He reminded me a little of my Andrew in some ways. I couldn't quite put a finger on it. They weren't similar in looks, but there was just something about the way Keith tilted his head that reminded me of my late husband. Their mannerisms and perhaps their very aura just seemed similar to me.

He was a tall man, so he looked down at me a little self-consciously, knowing this was the first time I'd been to my sister's house since her death and not wanting to overstep the mark at all. He was holding a pet carrier with an angry-looking Feline Dion inside. She was glaring out of her plastic prison, her fur on edge, and she looked near fuming when she spotted me staring in at her. Clearly my sister's death had done nothing to soften the animal's loathing of me.

"Hello, Keith, do come in."

"Thank you, Evelyn, I don't want to intrude. It's just that I've got Feline here, and I hope you don't mind, but I would like her to stay with me. I know I've had her while Dora stayed at yours, and then when she was in the hospice, but I didn't know long-term what your plans were for her. It's just not the same with Dora not being here; I really miss her, and at least the cat makes me feel I've still got a bit of her with me. I'd be so grateful if she could live with me permanently."

Mind? I was thoroughly delighted that he wanted to take the furry fiend. I had been dreading the thought of taking her back to Yorkshire with me, but knowing how much my sister loved the mangy moggy there was no way I could have dropped her off at a cat shelter (although admittedly the thought had crossed my mind more than once).

"Of course you should have her. Come in, Keith, and I'll make us a nice cuppa so we can chat for a while."

He entered the house slowly, wiping his feet on the coir door mat, and I directed him into the lounge while I went to make the tea. My sister had always kept a stock of UHT milk in the larder, so I opened one and a packet of her favourite triple chocolate biscuits.

I set a mug of steaming tea on the table beside Keith and offered him the plate of biscuits. He took one, thanking me before biting a huge chunk out of it.

"These were Dor's favourites; boy, I'm sure going to miss her. Her and Oscar were the two best friends I've ever had." He sighed and took a gulp of tea to wash down the biscuit. "Oscar was the calm, sensible one and Dora was the live wire; they were so perfectly suited and now...now they've both gone." His voice wobbled a little and he bowed his head so I wouldn't see the tears collecting in his eyes.

Maybe I had been wrong all along and Dora had been telling the truth that there was never anything romantic between her and Keith. He was clearly distraught at her passing, but seemingly at the fact of losing another dear friend, not a lover. Perhaps I was overstepping the mark, but I was still curious enough to ask.

"So, you and Dora...you weren't boyfriend and girl-friend then?"

From the look of shock on Keith's face, he really didn't need to answer.

"Heavens, no, we were friends, good friends, but there was never anything like that. When my wife and Oscar were alive, we used to go out a lot together, or have dinner parties at home, but then Ruth passed away and Oscar too. Dora and I were the ones left behind and we just rubbed along in our grief, playing board games and sharing meals every now and again, almost like family. It gets lonely, you know, being on your own."

He didn't need to tell me; I knew only too well.

"That's not to say she didn't have plenty of boyfriends over the years; she did, you know. Why, a few of them were there at the funeral. She broke a fair few hearts in her time did your sister, and no mistake."

I smiled at him with genuine warmth. It was lovely that they'd had such a good close friendship for so many years. It was a rare thing these days.

He took another gulp of tea. "You make a decent brew too; not as good as your sister's, but not bad either...So with the house, are you going to be putting it on the market? It will be strange to see new folk living in it. I've been here for nigh on forty years, and Dora was in hers for not much less; but I suppose time moves on, nothing stays the same forever...more's the pity."

"No, I'm not selling, I'm going to be renting it out. I've found the perfect tenant that I'm sure you'll get along with like a house on fire, so you've no need to worry."

As if on cue, the doorbell rang. "Speaking of which, that will be them now."

Keith sat up straighter in his chair, a slight frown tweaking his lips downwards. He was clearly a little wary of meeting his new next-door neighbour.

I rushed to greet the tenant, and after taking their coat showed them into the lounge to meet him.

"Keith, I'm delighted to introduce you to Bella, your new neighbour."

Keith rose slowly from his chair, his expression softening as a smile lit up his face. His eyes crinkled at the corners and his anxiety drained away, making him appear much younger.

"Bella! Oh my, Dora talked so much about you; she absolutely adored you. How wonderful." He was clapping his hands together now, like an excited little boy at Christmas.

Bella had also appeared nervous coming in but now smiled, a great beaming grin that was as bright and welcoming as the sun breaking through the clouds on a bleak dreary day.

"I'm so pleased to meet you, Keith." She peered into the cat carrier that was beside his feet. "And this must be the famous Feline." She reached through the bars of the cage and gently stroked the cat's nose. From where I was sitting, I could hear the animal purring. Charming; so it was just me she despised then.

To me it had been a complete no-brainer for Bella to move into the house; she was obviously the perfect tenant. I knew in my heart that Dora would have loved the idea of her friend settled in her home, the place where she had been so happy for so much of her life. My sister had truly loved this house: it was much more than a brick-built

1930s semi-detached house in a quiet sedate street; to her it was her heart, where she had been safe. And knowing how much my sister had loved Bella, she would want this to be her safe place too. They had only known each other for a short time, but during that time they had formed a friendship that was rare to find and as precious as any jewel.

There was also the fact that Dora had insisted some of her ashes be sprinkled around the base of the old oak tree in the garden, the same as she had done with Oscar's. It had been their favourite place to sit together. They would always be together now in the place where they had been truly happy.

How could I sell their home? To have a stranger living in it just seemed jarring to me. But I knew Bella would look after the place, stamp her own mark on it, but keep the essence of Dora alive throughout it too. I couldn't ask for any more.

And after everything that had happened to Bella, when I had suggested her moving to Bristol, she had jumped at the chance. It was the opportunity for her to start a new life: a fresh start – the life she really wanted to live. Forget Alfie and all the drama that entailed, she would be finally able to breathe again. Yes, she would miss her family, but they could visit, and she would come back to Yorkshire plenty too. She had had to give notice at her shop job, but she already had some interviews lined up in Bristol, and was even thinking about returning to education part-time too. I hoped this would become her reality; I had seen how much Lottie had loved returning to education, and I believed Bella would too.

And there was no chance of her being lonely either. Bella and Jacob were devoted to each other, together any opportunity they could get. My grandson was hoping to do his MA at Bristol, so they wouldn't need to travel up and down the country any more to be together. Would things work out for them long-term? Who could say. They were so very young. But Bella really was the loveliest girl, so I had everything crossed for them. And I knew that wherever Dora was, she did too.

Chapter 37

The following year

It was just as beautiful as I had imagined in my dreams. I had longed for this day, but never truly believed it would happen. Here I was in Venice, and it was all thanks to my little sister.

I took a long sip of my Aperol Spritz and sighed. I had never felt so content. The blue of the Grand Canal twinkled under the hot sun like a million diamonds glittering. It was bliss, just to be whiling away the afternoon at a waterside bar, watching folk in the distance strolling over the Rialto Bridge; it felt just like being in a movie.

For many years I had watched the rush-hour traffic pass my front window, wondering about those busy people and their lives; all those people returning to their respective homes after a day at work. I had been lonely then. Now I watched the traffic too, but this time boats and gondolas floating down the canal. The traditional gondoliers in their stripey jumpers occasionally waved as they passed by. But now I wasn't lonely.

"You look so relaxed and happy, my love."

I turned to my companion and smiled. I was happy. Happier than I had been in a very long time.

Keith looked relaxed too. Dressed in his elegant linen shirt, he could easily have been mistaken for a dashing local rather than a Brit abroad. His skin was slightly tanned, the little hairs on the back of his arms shining golden under the hot sun.

We had been in Venice for a few days now; and it had been perfect, so far removed from life back home. Everything just felt magical: the architecture, the food, the beauty of it all simply took my breath away.

We had enjoyed spaghetti carbonara the previous night, and I had thought fondly of Andrew; how he would have loved it here, and how he would have loved that pasta. But I knew in my heart that he would be happy for me; happy that I was finally realising our dream, and happy that I had found Keith. He would have really liked Keith. Everyone did.

It had just been a friendship to start with, but as time passed, it had seemed the most natural thing in the world for us to be together; so we became a couple. He was a good man. Had I found the love of my life? Who could say. I certainly loved Keith, but whether it could ever burn as brightly as the love I held in my heart for my late husband, only time would tell. But never say never. As Dora would often say, "Love is not just reserved for the young."

But being here made me feel young. Not in my bones, they ached like crazy walking over the many bridges, but in my soul. We had been to concerts, I had danced, we had laughed. There really were no limits but the ones you put on yourself.

"We've certainly put a fair old dent in the holiday budget," Keith joked, nodding his head towards the many shopping bags on the floor between us.

I had admittedly had a bit of a splurge. The leather handbags had been impossible to resist, the leather so soft and buttery, and I had treated myself to several in various colours. Of course, there were gifts for Lottie and Bella too, beautiful leather-bound stationery for Bella, which would be perfect for her art course at university, and a silk scarf for Lottie, which would show off the blue of her eyes to perfection.

I had to get something lovely for Dora too: Isadora Avira Knight, my granddaughter. She was just over a year old now, and the most precious little girl; all giggles and dimples and a bundle of spirited energy, so like my sister, her namesake. My granddaughter's middle name was just perfect too – Avira, which meant bright, courageous and resilient. What could be more perfect? It was just how my sister had been, and it was how I knew my granddaughter would be in life too. Her cheeky little smile and her bright twinkly green eyes convinced me of it. I only had to look at her to be reminded of Dora.

We had bought her a beautiful gift: a Murano angel for her dressing table. It was gorgeous multicoloured glass, and so reminiscent of Dora in one of her most flamboyant outfits. When little Dora grew up, we would tell her all about her Great Aunt. We would keep my sister's memory alive.

Keith attracted the attention of a passing waiter and ordered another cocktail for me and a beer for himself. "Just another couple of days, and it will be back to Bristol."

I removed my sunglasses for a second and addressed him with a bright smile. "I've had the time of my life, but I'm ready to go home, to our home."

It was true. Venice had been everything I had hoped it would be, but Bristol felt even more special to me. Keith and I had moved in together. After all the years in Yorkshire, I had returned to the city where I was born. We were living in his house, and it was now my happy place. Bella was still living next door. She had made it such a lovely home, but as I had hoped, Dora was very much there too. There were plenty of photos around the place of my sister smiling happily, that moment in time preserved forever.

Bella had even erected a little wooden seat around the base of the oak tree where Oscar and Dora's ashes had been scattered. She loved to sit there and sketch. She said it was where she felt most happy. She had also used some of my sister's favourite clothes to make cushion covers, and a little blanket for Feline Dion to sit on. Feline was now happily residing with Bella full-time. That had made perfect sense too. The cat adored Bella as much as it abhorred me. And Keith could still see her whenever he wanted. In fact, Feline often brought him little presents which she would leave outside our patio doors – a random sparrow wing here, a mouse head there. She really was delightful.

At first Lottie had a few reservations about me moving to Bristol. It was a big step, but once she could see how happy Keith and I were together, she had given us her blessing. Plus, she had plenty of reason to visit, as Jacob had managed to secure his place at Bristol to further his studies. It was as if all the pieces were fitting perfectly into place, even down to the fact that Lila and Seb were going to come and stay soon. Apparently, Lila was getting bored of the bars and clubs in Leeds, and Bristol nightlife was right up her street. And as in most things in life, Seb would be along for the ride.

So, I sold my house in Leeds. It was hard, but not nearly as hard as I had expected it to be. At the ripe old age of seventy, I was grabbing life by the scruff of the neck and giving it a damn good shake. And I was making new memories: memories that didn't include daytime television, microwave meals for one or dust-covered library books. Time stayed still for no one, and whatever time I had left, I was going to bloody well enjoy it.

Keith reached over the table, took my hand in his and tenderly kissed it. "Thank you for coming into my life, Evelyn Weaver. I love you."

I squeezed his hand. "And I love you too."

The waiter returned with our drinks and a small plate of stuffed olives. As Keith paid, I reached down and trailed my fingers through the water. The canal was cooler than I had imagined, the water refreshing to my fingers. A breeze suddenly picked up, ruffling my hair slightly. And that was when I heard it: my sister's voice.

"I'm proud of you, girl; Evie the diva, Evelyn the incredible."

My heart was in my throat. I glanced towards Keith. Had he heard it too? Clearly he hadn't, as he was still engrossed in reading the guidebook we had found in our hotel room.

Was I going mad? But no, I had heard it, as clear as day; and I'd only had two cocktails, so I certainly wasn't drunk. My sister's voice. And then I heard it again, clear and sweet, a voice I had missed so much.

"Everything is how it is meant to be."

I looked over to Keith again, but he was still oblivious. I felt a deep calm slide over me, the like of which I had never known before. My sister had been adamant I should come here, so I had. And now she was here with me too, if only for a moment.

She was right about other things too. Everything was turning out exactly as it was meant to be. I lifted my glass to the beautiful blue sky and toasted my sister.

"Good night, my darling Dora. And thank you for everything."

The End

About the author

 I always wanted to write. I remember as a child I would look forward to getting home from Middle School so that I could write my stories and get lost in my own little worlds. Sadly, as I grew older, I lost my courage to write, put my notebook away and there it remained for many decades.

After being diagnosed with cancer for a second time I knew if I was going to make my childhood dreams a reality, I would really need to get my skates on! Not literally of course as I have two left feet and could trip over my own shadow.

After writing the successful "Playing with Fire – The True Story of Fireman Scam" with my twin sister, detailing a very difficult few years in our lives I knew writing was still what I really loved to do.

A children's book I wrote at ten years of age is being faithfully recreated (some 40 years later) and is due to be published soon. I'm so excited by this, it will be amazing for children everywhere to get to know "Humphrey" after all these years.

The first novel in my "Teapots and Tequila shots" series is "The Reinvention of Lottie Potts." This series will concentrate on strong female friendships. Women in their thirties, forties and older encountering all the ups and downs of modern-day life. With plenty of tears, tequila, and cheeky humour along the way.

Two thirds of profits from the sales of "The Reinvention of Lottie Potts" and a portion of profits from sales of all further books in the series will be donated to Great Ormond Street Hospital and Epilepsy Society.

https://www.klcrear.com

Also by K.L. Crear

The Rein-vention of Lottie Potts

Lottie Potts is happy enough - or so she thinks. Her life is slowly ticking away as she spends her days watching old films and day-dreaming about another, better, version of herself.

But Lottie isn't one for change. That is until a blonde bombshell blows into town and knocks her husband Daniel completely off his feet.

Lottie is forced to take a long hard look at herself. She is fat, in her forties and thoroughly fed up. Does she fight for her husband and the safe predictable life she knows? Or is revenge, like her favourite ice cream, a dish best served cold?

With her trusty circle of girlfriends and a surprising return from a charming face from her past, Lottie embarks on a transformative journey. Buckle up for the roller-coaster ride of laughter and tears as Lottie navigates the twists and turns of her reinvention, discovering the genuine essence of life along the way.

Lila Glover Wants a Lover

Lila loves to have fun. Free and in her late forties she enjoys the thrill of dating younger men, no strings attached just plenty of good times. So why then has the dating scene lost its sparkle? The thrill has gone, and she would much rather have a night out with her girlfriends or a night in alone enjoying a good film and an even better bottle of wine.

Enter Seb, her dependable workmate who's been patiently waiting in the wings, his affection for Lila evident to the world. To Lila, a relationship with Seb seems as likely as finding a calorie-free cream cake – his style is questionable, and he's just too safe and dependable, a genuinely nice guy but maybe just too nice for Lila.

But then Seb does the unthinkable – he starts dating Lila's sworn frenemy, who transforms him from a caterpillar into a butterfly. Suddenly Lila sees Seb in a whole new light. Has the window of opportunity now slammed shut, too late for Lila to make a move?

In this wickedly funny tale, love is a battlefield, and Lila is armed with determination, humour, and the willingness to break a few rules to find her happily ever after.

A Christmas Caroline

Caroline's got frugality down to a fine art. She can make a tin of soup stretch for days, considers "reduced to clear" her love language, and thinks Christmas is just a daft excuse for people to throw their money away on tinsel trimmed tat.

But Christmas Eve night takes a turn when her best mate, Marlene, drops in for a chat. Lovely, right? Except Marlene's been dead for seven years and she's got a message for Caroline, she will be visited by three spirits and if she doesn't pay attention, her future's looking bleaker than the contents of her fridge freezer.

Caroline's convinced she's having a hallucination. Ghosts? Surely not! But as the night goes on, she starts to wonder if she might just learn something worth more than her latest discount voucher. And for someone who knows the price of everything and the value of nothing, this might be the wake-up call she didn't see coming.

Move over Ebenezer – this modern, laugh-out-loud retelling of the Dickens classic has a new Scrooge in town. Perfect for fans of Sophie Kinsella.

Playing With Fire

"In my 23 years of policing, I have never encountered a man as manipulative as Greg Wilson... a compulsive liar who has shown absolutely no remorse... If somebody wrote this as a script for Coronation Street, it would be too outrageous."

– Detective Constable Chris Bentham

Coleen Greenwood was overjoyed to meet James Scott, a heroic firefighter and man of her dreams. Little would she know her dreams would soon become a nightmare as his web of lies started to unravel.

The astonishing true story of one man's lies and a family's fight for justice.

This is the full untold story that was made into the BBC Sounds podcast series "Love-Bombed with Vicky Pattison" which reached No1 in the UK Apple podcasts playlist within the first week of its release. Features as an episode of "Red Flag" on UKTV Play.

A portion of profits from sales of this book will be donated to Women's Aid - www.womensaid.org

Healing From The Burns

"The background to this offending shows frankly jaw dropping arrogance and cruelty in the way that you so persistently and wickedly deceived your victims, particularly Coleen Greenwood."

- Judge James Adkins

Greg Wilson is now in prison. Finally, it is over for Coleen and Karen. They can now move on, take time and heal. But is it that easy? Or is there still much more of the story to come? The uplifting follow-up true story to "Playing with Fire." How after the darkest days have ended, light will always break through.

A portion of profits from sales of this book will be donated to Women's Aid - www.womensaid.org

www.ingramcontent.com/pod-product-compliance
Lightning Source LLC
Chambersburg PA
CBHW031255120726
47906CB00003B/746